A hunted community. A haunte[d] **spans centuries.**

Men are disappearing from Toronto's gay village. They're the marginalized, the vulnerable. One by one, stalked and vanished, they leave behind small circles of baffled, frightened friends. Against the shifting backdrop of homophobia throughout the decades, from the HIV/AIDS crisis and riots against raids to gentrification and police brutality, the survivors face inaction from the law and disinterest from society at large. But as the missing grow in number, those left behind begin to realize that whoever or whatever is taking these men has been doing so for longer than is humanly possible.

Woven into their stories is David Demchuk's own personal history, a life lived in fear and in thrall to horror, a passion that boils over into obsession. As he tries to make sense of the relationship between queerness and horror, what it means for gay men to disappear, and how the isolation of the LGBTQ+ community has left them profoundly exposed to monsters that move easily among them, fact and fiction collide and reality begins to unravel.

A bold, terrifying new novel from the award-winning author of *The Bone Mother*.

RED X *is a tale of terror. It includes graphic violence, implied sexual assault, animal violence, family violence, strong sexual themes, and discussions of racism, ableism, anxiety disorders, homophobia, and suicide. It is intended for mature readers.*

RED X

A NOVEL

BY DAVID DEMCHUK

Strange Light and colophon are registered trademarks of Penguin Random House Canada Limited.

Library and Archives Canada Cataloguing in Publication data is available upon request.
ISBN: 978-0-7710-2501-3
ebook ISBN: 978-0-7710-2502-0

Grateful acknowledgement is made for permission to reprint excerpts from the following copyrighted material:

"I Feel Love" Words and Music by Giorgio Moroder, Pete Bellotte and Donna Summer. Copyright © 1977 (Renewed) WB Music Corp., Warner-Tamerlane Publishing Corp., Rick's Music, Inc. and Sweet Summer Night Music. All Rights on Behalf of Itself and Rick's Music, Inc. Administered by Warner-Tamerlane Publishing Corp.Inc. All Rights Reserved. Used by Permission of Alfred Music and Sweet Summer Night Music.

"It's My Life" Words and Music by Jon Bon Jovi, Martin Sandberg and Richie Sambora. Copyright © 2000 Universal Music Publishing International Ltd., Bon Jovi Publishing, GV-MXM, Sony/ATV Music Publishing LLC and Aggressive Music. All Rights for Universal Music Publishing International Ltd. and Bon Jovi Publishing Administered by Universal Music Works. All Rights for GV-MXM Administered Worldwide by Kobalt Songs Music Publishing. All Rights for Sony/ATV Music Publishing LLC and Aggressive Music Administered by Sony/ATV Music Publishing LLC, 424 Church Street, Suite 1200, Nashville, TN 37219. All Rights Reserved. Used by Permission. Reprinted by Permission of Hal Leonard LLC.

"Bela Lugosi's Dead" Words and Music by Bauhaus. Copyright © 1979 Bauhaus 1919 Music. All rights reserved. Used by permission.

Book design by Matthew Flute
Cover image: acilo / Getty Images
Interior art: Jared Pechacek; (Ink spot) larisa_zorina / Getty Images;
(map) *Plan of the Town of York. Corrected.* By J. G. Chewett

Printed in the United States of America
Published by Strange Light,
an imprint of Penguin Random House Canada Limited,
a Penguin Random House Company
www.penguinrandomhouse.ca

10 9 8 7 6 5 4 3

Penguin
Random House
Canada

caraidean gu sìorraidh

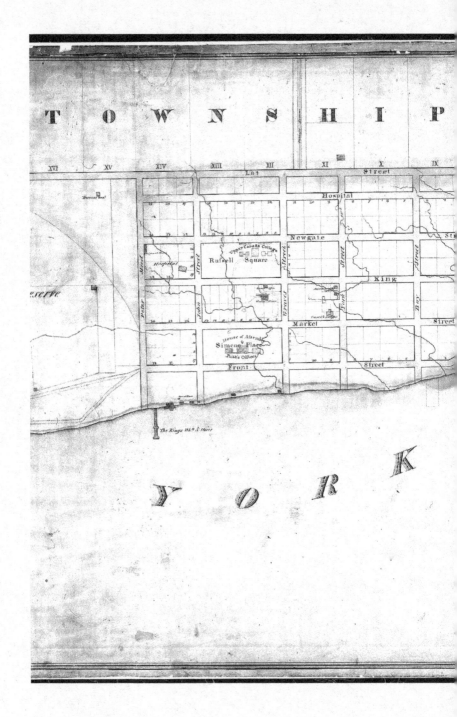

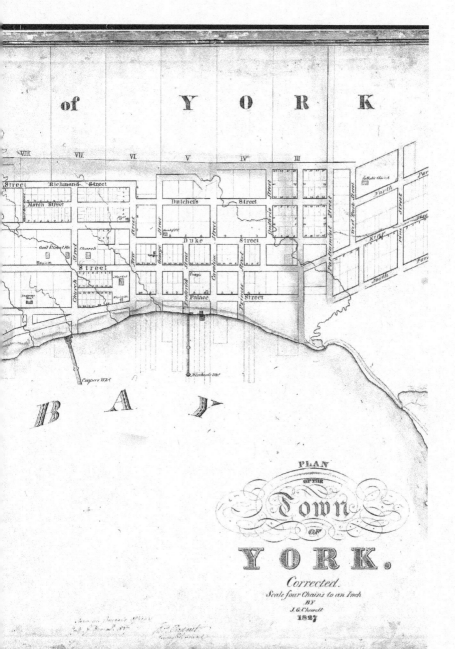

PLAN
OF THE
Town
OF
YORK.
Corrected.
Scale four Chains to an Inch
BY
J.G.Chewett
1827

The City of Toronto, once the Town of York, is nestled against the Great Lake Ontario, ensnared in an intricate web of rivers, creeks and streams, valleys and ravines—a wildness woven into its heart that the burgeoning metropolis has struggled to suppress, reshape, contain, and control over the last two hundred years.

Established in 1793 as a British colonial outpost under King George III, York was built on the traditional lands of the Mississaugas of the Credit First Nation, the Haudenosaunee, the Anishinaabe, and the Huron-Wendat, and was then known as Tkaronto, "Where the Trees Stand in the Water," "The Gathering Place."

Now Canada's largest city, Toronto has survived battles and rebellions and riots, two great fires, two massive blackouts, earthquakes, a hurricane, and outbreaks of cholera, typhus, Spanish flu, HIV/AIDS, SARS, and more. Even so, thousands arrive each year from across the country in pursuit of education, employment, community, and belonging. Waves of immigrants and refugees from around the world have made its neighbourhoods their home.

At the southern edge of the city are the waterfront and the Port Lands, including **Cherry Beach**, built on land reclaimed from the lake and the marshland and from the delta of the Don River.

To the north is Old Toronto, which includes the quaintly cobblestoned Distillery District, **Corktown**, and the St. Lawrence Market.

To the west of Old Toronto is the downtown core, the old and new city halls, and the financial district, built over what had been the poorest area of the city, formerly known as **The Ward**.

North of Corktown is the Garden District, which includes the inner-city neighbourhoods of **Regent Park** and **Cabbagetown**—their crumbling rooming houses, squat brick tenements, and squalid high-rises now falling prey to developers and speculators. The Garden District is home to **Allan Gardens**, a central park whose principal feature is an ornate Edwardian conservatory. (Its predecessor, an Orientalist pavilion that notably hosted a lecture by a young Oscar Wilde, burned to the ground in 1902.) Like Corktown, Cabbagetown was once inhabited by poor Irish immigrants who worked in the distilleries, and is so named for the cabbages they reputedly grew in the front yards of their rowhouses and cottages.

North of the Garden District and west of Allan Gardens is **Toronto's gay village**, a hodgepodge of bars, clubs, bathhouses and pubs, small shops and restaurants clustered around the intersection of Church and Wellesley. "All the churches are on Queen Street and all the queens are on Church Street," as the old saying goes. From there, the city stretches out in all directions.

Impressed by its tidiness, efficiency, elegance, and modernity, the late Sir Peter Ustinov famously referred to the Toronto of 1987 as "New York run by the Swiss." Much of that has changed in recent years, and sadly not for the better. The city was once a bastion of nineteenth-century Victorian morality, celebrated for imposing Christian values on its laws, citizens, and marketplace. Now, its brittle veneer of propriety and conformity is belied by its treatment of its most vulnerable residents. The quaintly refined facade is eroding; the mask of civility slips and falls, littering the ground.

Frequently derided as Toronto the Good—the Centre of the Universe—the city resented by the rest of the nation for its hubris, arrogance, and vulgar ambition now strives to reconcile its prim provincial attitudes with its world-class aspirations, and to accommodate the conflicting political, economic, and cultural values held by its substantial and disparate populace. Fearful of meaningful change and the demands it might place upon them, civic leaders routinely sabotage every improvement they propose—from increasing property taxes to expanding public transit to building affordable housing.

Preening, soulless, authoritarian, insecure, its singular achievement remains its many cinematic impersonations of other, greater cities. A chasm yawns between the wealthy and the disadvantaged, the privileged and the marginalized; one can see past its teeth to the back of its throat—more teeth, still more teeth, teeth all the way down.

Public services have eroded. The infrastructure is crumbling. Violence and hate are on the rise. A trans woman killed, her body found in a ravine and left unidentified for months. A murdered young woman found in a stairwell, not by the police but days later by her mother. Ten pedestrians killed and a dozen more injured by a van driver targeting women with his vehicle. Two people killed and thirteen others wounded by a mass shooter one summer Sunday. Cellars are seeping, foundations are cracking. Rivers are overrunning their banks. What was once buried, pushed underground, is now erupting, bursting up and through.

All around the city, past and present entwine like lazy lovers as the last light fades. Along streets and alleys, behind buildings and under bridges, the shadows deepen and darken. Whatever hungers within them cannot be contained.

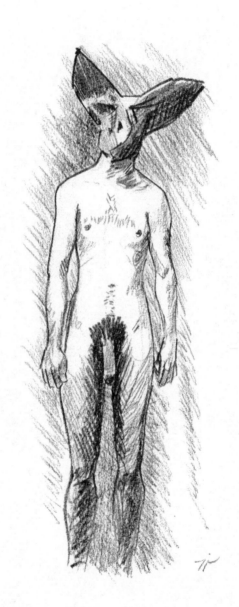

1984

Sometime that August, a young man named Ryan Wilkes vanished without so much as a whisper. The city was radiant and shimmering in the late summer heat. A thin film of humidity adhered to the skin, attracting smog and grit and inviting midges and mosquitoes to a sticky demise on one's forearms. *Ghostbusters* dominated the movie screens, a transit strike was looming, the Pope was coming to visit, and Bananarama's "Cruel Summer" was climbing the dance charts.

Ryan was in his mid-twenties, sandy blond, lightly freckled, not quite tall enough or old enough or beefy enough to escape the dreaded twink label. Newly in town from Windsor, Detroit's automotive sister city, with just a few months of metropolitan life under his belt, he mostly bused tables at a few of the bars, hoping to save some money to enter the design program at the Ontario College of Art. He worked as a barback at Boots, and also covered off a few times next door at Bud's, stepping in for someone sick or picking up a stray shift or two.

He didn't have a steady boyfriend, didn't really date, didn't go to the baths or parks, and rarely to other bars. He was a loner, mostly, estranged from his family, with a flight attendant for a roommate and not many friends. Sometimes, he'd have four or five days off between shifts, while his roommate held two- and three-day layovers; as a result, it took until Tuesday the 28th for anyone to realize he hadn't been seen since the Friday before.

Even then, people assumed he'd just gone back south or gotten another job—at a straight bar maybe, where he could make more money—or shacked up with somebody somewhere, or left for another city, Montreal or Vancouver, or even the States. His roommate wasn't necessarily surprised to see him go: the city may welcome you, but it might not invite you to stay. Still, it was confusing. His room, filled with all his belongings, offered no obvious clue. He wasn't a known drug user, and no illicit substances were found in his room, apart from a few mild sleeping pills he had "borrowed" from a friend. Suicide was a possibility, though he "didn't seem the type." It was only when a garbage collector found a neatly folded stack of clothes in an alley behind a stretch of weary old sex shops and strip clubs and porn theatres, the clothes that Ryan was last seen wearing, only then was his disappearance called in to the police. But with no sign of struggle, no significant leads, and no mother or wife or girlfriend or family to place pressure on them, the investigation was half-hearted at best. Missing gay men weren't what you'd call a priority. The flight attendant roommate and some friends and co-workers printed up flyers and posted them around the Village. Those lasted a few days before being torn down by street cleaners or papered over with photos of lost cats and dogs. The missing persons file languished, then dropped out of sight after just a few weeks. Late that autumn, on November 9, *A Nightmare on Elm Street* was released and made, as they say, a killing. The winter winds began to blow. The snow began to fall.

White T-shirt, white jockstrap, Levi button-fly cutoffs—wallet and cash and ID and keys tucked in the pockets. Dirty sport socks, beaten-down Chucks, and a navy-blue hanky neatly tucked into the left shoe. Ryan Wilkes, twenty-four, of 85 Isabella Street, was never found.

In the golden warmth of that August afternoon, in his sun-dappled den of a bedroom in his fourth-floor shared apartment, Ryan slept. As he slept, he dreamed. And in those minutes that felt like hours, he stood once more at the edge of the green-lit grove—the backdrop of all his dreams of late—and peered across to find the young man who made these woods his home. He always reminded Ryan of the itinerant workers who had lived in the woods in Windsor, in tents and trailers, working on nearby farms from spring to fall. His mother had called them vagrants, layabouts, hooligans. They frightened her a little, which must be why he liked them. There he was, the young drifter, on the far side of the clearing, at the foot of the towering ash-white sycamore where Ryan often found him sitting and smoking his slender waterstone pipe, the tobacco haze around him laced with licorice and sweet rum.

As the young man stood and shook himself off and ambled across the clearing, Ryan marvelled at the unspoiled beauty of the glade around them: the soft western breeze caressing the leaves, raising a gentle rush; the robins and sparrows calling out to each other, in greeting or in warning; the fox, a few yards beyond, chasing after a bounding hare till it hopped down into its hole and out of sight; and of course, the ancient tree itself, which presided over everything, the largest in the clearing and, seemingly, the entire forest. Ryan and the young wanderer had spent many dream-hours in each other's arms in the shade of that tree, talking and laughing and lazily fucking, startling the wildlife into silence. *A dirty fairy tale*, he had thought to himself. It was sad but somehow unsurprising that this was the person who knew him best, who listened most, who held him close despite his flaws. Ryan wondered, not for the first time, if this impossible fantasy was imperilling his connection to the waking world.

Then the young man was upon him, smiling widely, his arms open for an embrace. He was shirtless, his suspenders down around his hips, his pale naked chest blackly furred to match his thick shock of hair and his bold black brows. He pulled Ryan close, smelled the air all around him, then pressed his mouth onto Ryan's and kissed him as if to taste him. *You came back*, he said, his Scottish lilt teasing at Ryan's ear.

"It's only been a day," he replied.

A day too long! Come, sit. Keep me company. He gestured to the great white sycamore looming before them. Ryan pulled back, looked up at its waving, whirling branches, its shimmering silvery leaves. There was a new menace about it, some shift in the light, some uncanny movement that made him hesitate.

"I can't stay," he said nervously. "I have to work." He had been late a few times and couldn't afford to lose the job over his messed-up sleeping schedule. But he was afraid of disappointing his friend, who was painfully lonely in his world and counted the hours and minutes until Ryan's nightly return.

He's not real. The thought intruded, and the balmy breeze embracing them chilled. He drew himself back, looked into the other man's eyes. An icy flame flickered behind them and abruptly vanished. The drifter smiled again, as genial as ever.

That's a shame, he replied, his voice like honey from the hive. *But not to worry. We can spend more time tomorrow.* Then added: *I see you brought it.* Ryan looked down to find the tattered old red book the drifter had given him on the grass at his feet. He couldn't remember bringing it, dropping it. And yet here it was. *Did you write something in it for me?*

Ryan picked up the book, turned it in his hands, front to back to front again. Ran his finger along the deckled edge of the pages, raised his finger to his nose. It felt so real, smelled so real. "A poem," he answered uneasily. "Just something my mother taught me when I was home sick from school." He opened it, began to turn the pages, but the feral young man snatched it from him, held it close to his chest.

I'm sure it's wonderful. I'll read it whenever I need to feel you near. He tugged on Ryan's hand playfully, leading him to the ashen tree. *Sit with me, just for a moment. Don't leave me here just yet.* The sky darkened and the wind rose and the branches shuddered, flailed. They seemed to be reaching for him, ready to lash themselves around his arms, his body, and lift him off the ground.

He hadn't expected to fall in love with a dream. But now the dream was turning, as they so often do, and he would have to end it. He shook his head. "I can't come back."

The wanderer smiled. *You're afraid.* The sky grew darker still. *That's good.* He leaned in and whispered wetly, *Fear salts the meat.*

Blackness. He reached out instinctively. Had he gone blind? His hand pressed against a wall of metal, then another. Surrounded. A forged box, not much larger than a coffin. *I have to wake up.* He felt for a latch or a hinge or a knob. Maybe he could dream one into existence. A sudden sharp burning sensation—he jerked his hand away. The walls glowed a dim deep red.

This is what it's like, the drifter's voice everywhere and nowhere. *This is what it's like to be hated, and hunted, abandoned and left to die. You claim to love me, Ryan. Tell me so, and I will let you go.*

The box was a furnace now, and Ryan was roasting alive inside it. Blisters bubbling and bursting on his face, his fingers, his hair burning, his eyes swelling, poaching in their blackening sockets. "I love you!" he was shouting. "All right? I love you, I love you!"

The walls tore away with a screech, and he hurtled backwards into a limitless darkness. He pulled himself into a ball, eyes and teeth and fists clenched. A high, keening wail sounded in the distance, like a huntsman's horn, charging ever closer. *You see?* The voice in his mind. *We do belong together. And if you won't come to me, I will find my way to you.*

Ryan woke with a start, saturated and shivering, his arms clutched tight around his legs. Was he hurt? Was he sick? *Some kind of terrible nightmare.* His alarm clock shrieked. He grabbed it from the bedside table and pulled it close to his face, blinking through sleep. His shift started in an hour. He tried to remember the dream, what had been so awful, but nothing would come, not a word, not a sound, just a sick, dreadful feeling he couldn't shake. He got up, peeled off his sweat-drenched T-shirt and boxers, and stepped into the shower, a faint, sweet burning lingering at the back of his throat.

As Ryan was getting ready for his shift, Victor Lee, short and burly in a fresh white T-shirt, well-worn leather vest, and strategically faded five-button Levi's, sat in the back office at Boots, counting out cash and drink tickets for that night's emergency DJ, Miss Robin Reid. Boots was the vaguely butch men's bar nestled in the lower level of the Hotel Selby, and Robin, vaguely butch herself, would be stepping in with almost no notice after their Friday night regular, Jerry, called in claiming food poisoning—maybe true, Victor thought, if you considered alcohol a food.

He had waited till the last possible moment before calling her, which unfortunately was 11 a.m. He knew the rule: never call a working DJ before noon. He swivelled back and forth on one of the stools behind the bar, cringing as he counted one, two, three, four rings. Just as he expected to click over to a machine, the receiver picked up, followed by a fumbling rustle of sheets.

"Victor," she sighed. "Somebody better be dead."

"Not dead enough," Victor answered, "but there's always hope. Are you free tonight? I know it's short notice, you can always say no, but I could really use you here."

"Damn right I can always say no," Robin said, then sighed again. "Fine, fine, forget my laundry. I can get there for eleven. Sixty bucks, two sets, done at one. I hate playing after last call."

Sixty bucks. He was going to kick Jerry's ass. "Sounds great. Make sure you bring me your cab receipt."

"I'll bring you two. It's not like I'll be walking home. Is the AC working? Don't answer that. See you in a bit." The receiver clattered back onto its cradle. Dial tone.

Truth be told, Victor thought Robin was a far better DJ than Jerry, and would have hired her full-time if he could. She played longer sets, took fewer breaks, and knew how to pack a dance floor better than most of her male counterparts without resorting to "It's Raining Men" or "I Will Survive," and for that she deserved some kind of a medal. She had a way of moving from old-school disco to moody new wave to bouncy dance pop to brassy funk, riding the crowd's energy and emotions like a wave off the shore of Tofino. She gave a nod to the bar's masculine vibe with her black tights, leather jacket, white RELAX T-shirt, and biker cap perched on her short black afro. Still, there were always one or two complaints that a gay men's bar should have a guy in the booth, preferably one who was tanned and shirtless, trim and toned. And white. A treat for the eyes as well as for the ears. "I didn't come here to watch some black chick dance around with herself," a regular told him once. "If I wanted that, I'd be down at the Zanzibar."

Another had gone up to her in the middle of a set and drunkenly asked, "Are you supposed to be a man?" and she had turned and answered, "Are you?" The drunk stormed over to the bar and went off on Victor like a car alarm till he introduced the drunk to Nate the bouncer and Nate introduced the drunk to the door. He hadn't been back since, and neither had his shitty drunken friends. Victor didn't care. Toronto's clubs were always playing catch-up with New York and San Francisco, ignoring the talent that was right in front of their face. He knew that Robin was something special, and the people who came for the music knew that too.

He sealed the envelope, wrote her name on the front, pulled out his keys, and unlocked the cash register. He tucked the envelope near the back of the till and locked it again. One thing done. He ducked out from behind the bar and started back towards the office when a strange sound made him slow down, then stop. He listened, and listened. It was a low, heavy hum, and it was coming from the storage room next to the back door.

Slowly, softly, he inched his way forward, the hum growing louder with every step. Was somebody in there? He stopped again. Something small and light, with tiny legs, landed on the back of his neck. He reached his hand back to brush it off and it flew up onto the tip of his middle finger, bit down into it, and stung him deep in the crease behind his knuckle. He let out a yelp and snapped his hand down, flinging the insect onto the floor. He stomped on it, then lifted his shoe to look.

A yellow jacket.

He looked at his finger, livid and swelling, then back up at the old oak door. The hum was now nearly a roar. "No fucking way," he whispered. He looked around the edges of the frame, at the gap between the bottom of the door and the sill, at the elaborate Victorian brass backplate that held the discoloured glass knob and the wasp-sized keyhole beneath it. Victor could picture the swarm on the other side, dense and seething with heat and rage, looking for a way to escape.

"Hey, what's going on?" the new kid, Ryan, said behind him. "I've been knocking and knocking."

Victor jumped back with a jolt, his heart pounding. "You just scared the shit out of me," he hissed. "Do you hear that?"

"What? No. What happened to your hand? It looks like you punched a refrigerator."

"Yeah, something like that." He stopped and listened. The kid was right. The loud, droning buzz from behind the door was now dead silent. Ryan reached for the knob—and Victor reached over to stop him—but he shrugged Victor off and gave it a twist, pulled it open, and revealed . . . nothing. An old ladder, some paint cans, boxes of old files, cases of brown stubby empties. A ten-year-old bottle of drain cleaner. Nothing.

Ryan waved his hand in front of his face. "Something smells terrible."

"How did you get in?" Victor asked as he peered inside the little room then swung the door shut. *Screw it, I'm calling pest control, I heard what I heard.*

Ryan pulled Victor's keys out of his pocket, handed them over. "The door was open. These were in the lock."

Victor reached into his pocket. Empty. He was sure he'd had them just a few minutes ago.

"Hello?" someone called from the front. "Is anybody here?"

Victor checked his watch. Five thirty-four. Shit. "Yeah, we're coming," he called back. He turned to Ryan, handed the keys back to him. "You take the bar till the DJ gets here. The clover-shaped key is the cash drawer. I'm going to go stick this in some ice."

Robin made sure she was dressed and ready by nine so she had plenty of time to choose her music for the night. Two sets, eight to ten songs per, another six to eight she could swap in to either set depending on the mood and flow of the crowd, plus three or four likely requests and a few of her own personal favourites as backups. And a couple of ten-minute mega-mixes in case she had to run to the washroom.

She was sitting cross-legged on her living room rug, holding one headphone up to her ear when she heard a light tap-tap at the door. She lifted the needle off the record, stood up with a groan, and opened it. Mrs. Lau from three doors down, an older woman who came from Hong Kong years ago with her now-late husband, was standing in her floral terry cloth robe and curlers, wringing her hands with worry.

"Look at you, all dressed up! I'm sorry to bother you, it's a silly thing. I was just coming back from downstairs, I was getting my mail, and my cat ran out of the apartment—and now I can't find her. Have you seen her or heard her at all?" She forced a brief, tense smile.

Robin smiled back to try to put her at ease. "Oh, that's not silly at all. But no, I haven't. This is the first time I've opened my door all day." She looked over the woman's shoulder down the hall to the building's front stairwell. The cat could have run downstairs to the lobby, or the alcove with the mailboxes, or towards the rear door and down the back stairs to the laundry room. Or upstairs to another floor. "I'll tell you what," she offered. "I'll check downstairs if you go up and see if she's on three or four. I'm sure we'll find her."

Robin slipped her shoes on, grabbed her keys, checked both sides of the hall as she walked over to the stairs, then started down towards the main floor. She realized she had forgotten to ask its name or what it looked like, but it wasn't like she was going to find more than one cat loose in the building.

She made her way down slowly, looking right and left over the forlorn furniture scattered around the front entrance, careful not to startle anything that might be nearby. "Here puss puss puss puss," she called softly, realizing how absurd she sounded. She walked to the two mismatched tweed couches and knelt down to look under them, checked around and behind the plastic potted plant display. Nothing. She headed down the little corridor to the mailroom. "Here puss puss puss." Felt around inside the box they used for discarded flyers. Nothing here either. She checked the back door—solidly shut—then reached into the darkness for the light switch for the back stairs. The bulb flashed and snapped off with a pop, filaments ringing in smoke-stained glass, but not before revealing someone curled up on the landing of the stairs below her.

"Hello?" she asked cautiously. "Who's there?"

A moment passed and then a voice very softly said, "Hi."

Robin peered into the darkness, unsure of who or what she had seen. "Are you hurt? Do you need some help?"

"I'm just cold," the voice said. "It's okay, I won't stay long." A young man, she guessed, early twenties, maybe younger. Street people came in from time to time. Some were homeless, some had mental health issues, but they were generally harmless. Even the junkies in the area mostly just wanted somewhere to shoot up and rest and then move on.

"I don't suppose you've seen a cat down there?" she asked.

"She's right here," he replied. And sure enough, the sound of purring floated up to tickle Robin's ears.

"She's run away from someone's apartment," Robin said. A cat wouldn't purr if it felt it was in danger, would it? "I'd like to bring her back if I could."

Another silence. "Lily, go see mummy."

After a moment, a wiry tortoiseshell cat bounded up the stairs towards her and began rubbing itself against her legs. Robin bent down and picked her up, and the cat immediately began licking her hand. She had a little spray of grey hairs around her nose and chin—she was older than she looked.

"Good night," Robin called back. "Take care of yourself." No response. She turned and carried the cat back up through the lobby and up the stairs to the second floor, meeting Mrs. Lau as she was coming down.

"Lily, there you are! Come see mummy." She reached out to take the cat from Robin and it started purring like a lawn mower. "Where did you find her?"

How did that boy know the cat's name was Lily? "Just on the back stairs heading down to the laundry room," Robin answered. She discreetly peeked at her watch. It was time for her to get moving.

"She was my son's cat," the woman said, stroking Lily under her chin. "She is very old now. She still misses him, I think."

An unease crept over Robin, spreading out from the pit of her stomach. "Your son is . . .?"

"I don't know, nobody knows," the old woman replied with a shrug. Robin saw her eyes were starting to glisten. "The police never found him. He's been missing for more than ten years." A loud, sharp ringing came from Robin's apartment, startling them both. "Oh my. Is that your phone?"

"My alarm," Robin replied. Her pulse was thrashing in her ears. "I have to get ready for work."

"Oh, well then. You have a good night. Don't work too late! Thank you for helping me find Lily." The older woman gave a little wave and made her way back up the hall. "You are such a naughty girl, scaring mummy."

Robin closed her door behind her, turned off the alarm, picked up the phone, and dialed the cab company. *Great,* she sighed. *Never sleeping again. Never going down to the laundry room again.*

Victor dried off his sore and swollen hand with a bar rag and held it under the brass banker's lamp near the cash register. After twenty minutes in an ice bucket he kept in the back, he had been able to bring the swelling down and wrap his finger in some gauze and tape he found in the recesses of his desk drawer. It still wasn't great, but at least he could bend his fingers. Despite the evening's dramatic beginning, it had been unusually quiet for a Friday, one of many slow nights since a steady trickle of regulars had begun to migrate to Chaps, which still had its "new bar" glow since opening over on Isabella the year before—plus a younger crowd, newer lighting and sound system, and functioning AC. Meanwhile, Boots had the same old spots and floods, the same old dance floors, the same old clientele, and the same four-day-old hot, swampy air. By ten, it was cooler on the patio than it was inside.

Victor was just getting the DJ booth set up when Frank, his favourite asshole cop from 52 Division, stepped in the door—out of uniform this time, and with someone young enough to be his grandson. It wasn't even ten thirty. The patio had a few people on it, but the room itself was empty. Victor glanced over at Ryan, who was prepping a trayful of drinks for Phil to take outside. Good—he wouldn't have to explain what was about to happen. He hopped down onto the dance floor and hurried towards the door before Frank and his friend could get very far.

"Good evening, officer. Is this gentleman old enough to be in here?" The younger man was clearly uncomfortable—he looked like he could flee at any moment.

"This," Frank said, as if leading a bus tour, "is yet another faggot bar." He turned to Victor. "This is my new partner, Hank. Frank and Hank, great names for a great team. Hank here is going to do all my pickups from now on, as the doc has told me I have to watch my back."

"Nice to meet you, Officer Hank," Victor said. "I'm still going to need to see some ID." For all he knew, this was some kind of setup.

"You're funny," Frank said in the least amused way possible. "Go on, Hank, whip it out."

Flushed with embarrassment, Hank pulled his wallet from the back of his pants, showed Victor his driver's licence. He had just turned twenty-two a few weeks ago.

"Thanks," Victor said. "So, what can I do for you?"

"I'm training my boy here," Frank said. "Hank, tell him what I taught you to say."

Hank's eyes darted around the room. "By our estimation, the number of persons on this premises has exceeded its posted capacity," he recited nervously. "We are required to close the establishment immediately and charge you with a violation of the Liquor Licence Act."

Victor looked over to the sign posted by the door, which stated that the maximum capacity, employees and patrons, was 195 people. As usual, this all was bullshit.

"See? He's a bright boy, he'll go far." Frank gave him a few pats on the shoulder. "So, why don't you be a good little turdpusher and go get what we came for."

Victor glanced over at the bar and saw that Ryan was trying to sort out a particularly complicated order. He lifted up the bar flap, manoeuvred down to the far end, pulled up a six of J&B and another of Canadian Club, and set them down on the bar top.

Frank motioned for Hank to go over and get the boxes. Hank grabbed the J&B box and Victor set the Canadian Club on top of it. "I'm Victor," he said. Hank jumped as if he'd been struck, then scurried back to Frank.

They turned and pushed their way out the front door just as Robin arrived, nearly knocking her over and then brushing past her as if she didn't exist. She stood there for a moment, incredulous, then shook her head and made her way up to the bar.

"You're early," Victor said as she set her crate of music on one of the stools.

"What was all that about?" she asked.

"My monthly donation to the Policemen's Ball," he replied. "Come on, let's get these up to the booth. Ryan, I'm going to ask Phil to take over behind the bar so I can get you out on the floor."

Ryan looked up from the tray he'd assembled, nodded, then set it out on the bar top for Phil to pick up. Victor checked the time. Ten forty-five. Three hours to go and the kid already looked wiped. Thankfully, the orders got easier the closer they got to last call. No one would be ordering Long Island iced tea after midnight.

Robin pulled a handful of patch cables and her Walkman Pro out of her black leather backpack and poked them into the soundboard, while Victor set the plastic crate of music down onto a wooden stepstool next to her. Even though Victor had fans running on either side, her T-shirt was already soaked through. *Free show for the boys in the front.* Her taxi had been a ramshackle sweatbox, with a driver who had sung along to a wobbly eight-track of Kenny Rogers hits, and now in the bar the air was hot and close like someone's breath on the back of her neck. Victor apologized that the AC still wasn't fixed from the previous weekend—no doubt because it was "a faggot bar" and at the bottom of every tradesman's list.

"You should have told them I'd be here," she teased. "I'm very demanding when I want service."

Victor blushed—actually blushed—and asked if she wanted a drink to cool herself down. Anything with alcohol would just go straight to her head, so she asked for a soda with lime, heavy on the ice.

As she made some adjustments on the mixing board, she looked around and saw a few familiar faces wander in from the patio—as well as the new kid, Ryan, who was picking up glasses from the corner tables and over near the men's room. One whole side of the room was empty. It was early, but still, she counted, what, fifty people? And the air around her was already blue with cigarette smoke. She glanced over and saw that about two dozen others were outside, where it was cooler, and for a moment she wished that she was out there with them.

She looked back towards the bar and saw Ryan standing alongside the row of stools, watching her. He smiled sheepishly and took a ten-dollar bill out of his pocket, came up to the booth, and asked almost too quietly if she could record her set for him. "Of course," she answered. "Any special requests?"

He shook his head shyly, then asked if she had any Prince, "like from before 'Purple Rain.'" She smiled and said that it was his lucky night, pulled a blank cassette out of her bag, skimmed the plastic off, and tucked it into the Pro.

As he turned to go, she saw that he had left something on her console, an old beat-up red notebook. "Hey, you forgot this," she said, holding it out to him. "You don't want any of us peeking into your private thoughts."

He looked at her, unsure of what she was talking about, then saw the book in her hand. You'd think she had pulled it out of a hat; he couldn't have been more shocked. "I, um, yeah," he stammered. "I—don't know how that got there. Thanks." He grabbed the book from her like it was on fire, then sped off across the room to hide it behind the bar.

Seems like everyone's having a day. She checked her watch, reached into the crate, slid out her first song of the night, and set it down on the turntable: a heavily funkified version of "In the Midnight Hour" by Roger of the Zapp brothers. She looked out to catch a couple of heads nodding along, and then saw a few of the boys on the patio stand up and bring their beers in. Promising. Victor danced his way over with her drink and placed it on a cruiser table well away from the sound equipment. Each gave the other a thumbs-up, and with that the night was under way.

It was just after midnight, when Victor was checking in on the last few tables on the patio, that some guy up from Rochester waved him over and tried to pay for a round of drinks with American money, then got angry when he found out the exchange rate was lower than at the gas station around the corner. "We're a bar, not a bank," Victor said. One of the friends offered to pay instead, and this made the American even angrier. They all sat in quiet embarrassment, eyes everywhere, as the American went on his little tirade and called Victor a racist slur he hadn't heard for three whole weeks, then asked to speak to the manager. "You're talking to him," Victor snapped, which of course just made things worse.

"We should move inside anyway," someone slurred from the far end of the table—a tall, freckled ginger, drunk and fidgety and uncomfortable. "Something stinks out here." He was looking nervously down the side laneway. One of the lights near the garbage cans had burned out, and that often drew rats and sometimes a skunk or a raccoon. The odour was wet and rotten—and somehow familiar.

"You've been talking shit for an hour," the American barked back at the redhead. "We're not going anywhere." But three of the others stood up and pointedly started looking through their wallets. Taking his cue from them, Victor gathered up their empties then went inside and waited for them to leave. When he came back a few minutes later, he expected to find he'd been shortchanged or stiffed entirely, but the pile of money under the ashtray included an extra twenty, which almost made up for their bullshit.

Victor was at the register cashing out their table when he saw Ryan stumbling out of the men's room looking pale and upset. "What's going on? Are you okay?" Victor asked. "Did something happen in there?" His first thought was the angry American. Victor knew from experience that you could walk into anything in a gay bar washroom, from a blow job to an overdose to vandalism to a full-on assault. He had heard some shouting in there late one afternoon and walked in to find two thugs kicking an older patron who had probably propositioned one of them. They stopped and stormed out, and Victor was forced to leave the bar mid-shift to take the old guy to the ER. He was fine after some stitches, but Victor had been haunted by it for days. Sometimes, you just had no idea what was going on around you.

Ryan shook his head and tried to push past, but Victor reached out and stopped him.

"It's okay," Ryan said. "I just . . . I had a bad night, I guess, and now it's catching up with me."

Victor started to tell him that he could take a break and rest in the back office, but Ryan was halfway across the room before he could even open his mouth.

Victor turned, carefully opened the washroom door, peered inside. Nothing and no one. It was empty and still, except for a light flickering over the farthest sink and mirror. The place could use a proper cleaning, though, that much was obvious. That same weird smell, too. Maybe something was wrong with the pipes.

Robin caught the moment between Victor and Ryan out of the corner of her eye, didn't think too much of it. But a few minutes later, as "Somebody's Watching Me" by Rockwell bounced out of the speakers and across the now-packed dance floor, she looked over the crowd and found her gaze fell upon a waifish young man in a loosely woven white shirt, suspenders, grey trousers, and weathered black boots, looking like somebody's stablehand. He was standing over by the restroom doors, right where Ryan and Victor had been—not leaning against the wall, as you might expect, but just standing and openly staring at her. There was something about him, something so striking, she couldn't help but stare back.

You see me, his eyes seemed to say. Sharp black eyes under thick black brows, wiry jet-black hair springing out from the top of his head. Did she know him? Had they met somewhere? *You see me.* A sly smile curled the corner of his lip. *Well, fancy that.*

A sharp crackle from one of the speakers snapped her back to reality. She had forgotten for a moment where she was in the song, and was startled to find she had just a few seconds left to mix into "Lucky Star." She quickly caught the beat and faded from one track into the next—then looked up again to find he was no longer there. Instead, a darkness lingered where he had stood, an intensity that shadowed and thickened the air until it surrendered to the light and music and movement of the room.

The rest of the night went by quickly as she played what turned out to be one of her better sets. While the bar never quite filled up, the dance floor remained busy right through to the end. She sprang a few surprises, including a rare live bootleg of Prince's "Lady Cab Driver" just for young Ryan, and an urgent, throbbing remix of Shannon's "Give Me Tonight" that her ex-girlfriend Jo had brought back from New York a few days before. Victor ran up to help with the lights, first plunging the room into blackness and then punching through with bursts of purple, green, and ruby red. Robin dropped sharp bursts of "Let the Music Play" into the mix while shafts of white darted around the edge of the floor with increasing intensity, inscribing a cage of light around the mass of shirtless men within. As the song reached its climax, Robin looked out over the crowd— and past them—and saw the black-haired boy once more, this time against the far wall. It was odd, he was somehow less distinct now, as if he was on the other side of a mist-covered window. He gave her a strange little wave as the PAR cans above her bloomed bright and faded with the song's final notes. When the house lights came up, he was nowhere to be seen.

"DJ Robin Reid everyone!" Victor shouted into the mic, then added those two fateful words: "Last call." A half-dozen patrons near the front clapped for her, which was unexpected, and four others ran up with five-dollar tips. Victor made his way back to the bar as she slid her records into their sleeves and then into the crate. She turned, unplugged the tape player. Ryan's cassette was inside, but she couldn't spot him, nor even remember how long it had been since she'd last seen him. When Victor returned, she asked if he was out cleaning up the patio.

"No, he left a little while ago, sorry," Victor said. "Did he get his tape from you?"

"Yeah," she fibbed, not really knowing why. "I just wanted to say good night. It's nice to have a fan." She tucked the player into the front of the crate, wound up the patch cord, and tossed it in.

Victor pulled the envelope out from the till, counted out her night's wages plus an extra twenty for her trouble. "Want me to call a cab?"

She shook her head, hoisted the crate, and squeezed past him. "It's faster to flag one down." She gave him a smooch on the cheek and headed out the door, slowing as she passed the spot where the boy had been standing. The air smelled faintly of ozone, like the wake of a summer storm. And something else: something earthy, sweaty—musk and salt and clay. A wave of dizziness washed over her—*it's still so hot in here*—and she stepped outside into the cool evening air to find a taxi already parked and waiting. It was thankfully not the sweaty old Kennymobile she had been trapped in earlier.

She slid the crate in and herself alongside it, gave the driver her address, then glanced past him to her left, into the clutch of shadows across the street. "What's that over there?" she asked. It looked like an animal, sick or frightened, circling and panting and looking back at her.

"Over where?" he said, and then it bounded towards them, ran right across their headlights. The driver slammed the brakes and they both flew forward. "Holy shit!" he shouted, then turned back towards her. "Are you okay?"

"Yeah, yeah," she said, peering into the darkness where it had run. "I'm fine, I—I guess it was a dog. Or maybe a coyote, up from the ravine? Big, though." She shook her head. "Great way to get killed."

"Probably a coyote. Nights like this, they smell the garbage, they come up and root through it, maybe nab a few cats," the driver said, pulling away from the curb. "They're more scared of us than we are of them."

Robin nodded, wondering if that was true.

She looked back over her shoulder, though they were blocks away by now and the street behind them was empty. It could have been a coyote. Whatever it was, it did seem to be afraid.

Victor broke for a few hits off a joint, just to take the edge off. His finger still ached from the sting; he would have to check it and change the dressing when he got home. He looked over towards the darkened laneway alongside the patio, saw nothing, heard nothing except the dull thumping of the speakers down by the dance floor and the wail of sirens tearing through the downtown core. He turned and looked up at the building behind him, glimpsed some movement behind a few of the small curtained windows. The Selby was a gay hotel that had once been the mansion of the Gooderham family, well-known distillers from the century prior. Some of the overnight guests on the third floor had complained of odd drafts, whispers, strange shadows and sounds. Perhaps the ghosts of the Gooderhams didn't much care for their libidinous house guests. Or maybe someone just didn't like the smell of pot drifting in through their window.

He thought back to Ryan coming out of the men's room and wondered what had distressed him so. Victor recalled seeing him at the booth at one point, chatting with Robin and flipping through the box of twelve-inch singles and dance mixes she had brought in with her, then handing her ten bucks for a dub. It was one of the most flattering things you could do for a DJ, asking for a tape of their set. He was a nice kid, smart, kind of good-looking, if a bit shy and self-conscious. He'd be good for the place, if he could lighten up a little. It was odd that he'd leave without saying good night. Maybe he didn't leave alone?

Victor looked up and out at the city's glittering skyline. His father had been on the engineering team behind several of the tallest buildings in view. His parents brought him from Singapore to Agincourt, an Asian-populated neighbourhood in the northeastern part of the city, when he was ten years old. His father had worked in a small but successful consulting firm, while his mother had hosted luncheons and afternoons of bible study for other displaced wives from families that could provide friendship, status, and advantage in a difficult new land. Victor had attended some of these luncheons and was repeatedly told what a fine husband he would be when he was older, and that he should pursue engineering like his father, or possibly medicine. His parents had nudged him towards a few potential girlfriends during his school years, but he feigned a greater interest in his studies and, fleetingly, the church.

Then, as he turned twenty, his yé ye died, his grandfather on his father's side, and his parents moved back home to help deal with the family business and estate, while Victor stayed behind to finish school. He never did finish, which was the cause of one fight, and then, when his grandmother died as well, he did not return home as ordered. In her phone call about the funeral, his mother stated that she had found a suitable young woman for him, single and eligible, eager to marry. This provoked their final fight and led to their estrangement. He had been close to his mother, so he was shocked at how coldly and cruelly she had broken with him. With his allowance abruptly cut off, he took on a few serving jobs at restaurants and pulled together enough money to train as a bartender. From there, he was able to work his way up to where he was today, for well or for ill. He rarely acknowledged it, even to himself, but he enjoyed his job. He understood the business, he understood his customers. He was proud to be part of a place where friends and strangers could come and be themselves. He doubted he'd ever see any money from his family, even in an inheritance. But he did hope one day to have a bar or a restaurant of his own.

He looked down at his feet and saw a red *X* on the pavement—city crews marking gas or water lines buried beneath where he stood, presumably. He felt like a character in a Bugs Bunny cartoon, unaware that they were in the spot where an anvil or a piano was about to be dropped from on high. As he stubbed the joint out on the wall and tucked it back in his shirt pocket, a chill came over him and a prickle of gooseflesh crept up his arm. For a moment he was sure that someone or something nearby was watching him. Was Ryan still there? An animal? He looked along the alley to his left, then to his right. *There's something out here.* He shivered a little, then shook it off, pulled open the door, and slammed it shut behind him.

Phil was still around, so together they ushered the last few stragglers out into the night, then cashed out and cleaned up and said their goodbyes. By the time Victor locked up and headed out onto Sherbourne, the street was still and dark and empty. Everyone else was long gone.

When Robin was six years old, her grandmother back in Jamaica died—died in her sleep, which the stream of neighbours and aunts and uncles and cousins that followed all said was a blessing. She hadn't been the most tactful child, so once the visitors were gone and they were alone in the house, she interrupted her mother crying in the kitchen to ask her if Grandmama would ever come back, if she would become a ghost. Duppy was the word she used. Older kids in the schoolyard had been scaring younger ones with stories about duppies roaming the earth, howling by roadsides, haunting houses, causing sickness and death, and she had lain awake in fear several nights because of them.

Her mother wiped away her tears with the heels of her hands, pulled Robin close, and told her: *The people who leave us, we still have their light. We can't see it, but it's with us. And that light shines on us anywhere we go.*

With that, her mother's tears started streaming again, and she gave Robin a swat on her behind and told her to get ready for bed.

Lights that shine on us even when we can't see them. She set the crate of records down inside her front hallway, switched on the lamp by the door. She missed her grandmama, and now her mother too. Mumma died shortly after she and Robin came to Toronto and Robin started university. Robin still had family and friends back home, but she had never visited them. She knew she had hurt them by fading from sight, but she couldn't bear the thought of having them treat her like a perpetually unanswered question, a stranger behind a familiar face, a changeling. A duppy. *No husband, no children, no life.* She turned and closed the front door behind her and locked the deadbolt with a snap.

She left the music where it sat but removed the Walkman, placed it on one of the stereo speakers, and popped the cassette out. She found a Sharpie on the shelf, wrote RYAN on the cardboard cassette liner in big, bold letters, followed by XOXO ROBIN, then tucked in one of her business cards: *Robin Reid—Queen of Clubs* it proclaimed on one side, and on the other was an image of an actual Queen of Clubs with her face superimposed. She snapped the case shut then propped it on top of the receiver, where she'd be sure to see it in the morning. Looking at it, she remembered the black-haired boy, pale and gaunt in his shirt sleeves and braces and grey dungarees, with his cold, hard, hungry stare. And then she thought of the boy in the stairwell, the one who was so cold. In the cab home, she wondered if he'd been in the building before, and whether he had overheard Robin's neighbour calling for her cat: "Lily, come to mummy." *That must be it*, she decided.

A flicker of movement caught her eye, something near the crate of music by the door. She looked over and saw that a card or a case or a box was jutting out, caught between the record sleeves. As she got up and came closer, she recognized it as the weathered red notebook that she had found on her console and had given back to Ryan. She had seen him squirrel it away behind the bar. So what was it doing here? Had he come back to the booth and tucked it inside when she wasn't looking?

She carefully lifted it out and examined it. It smelled like an unopened room in a musty house, equal parts lavender, vinegar, dust, and decay. It was easily more than a hundred years old. The cover was made from a fine crimson leather, now brittle and worn, exposing dried glue, yellowed muslin webbing, and tight, tiny stitches. The spine, embossed in gold leaf, was scuffed and flaking. The dust from it shimmered on her fingers. The marbled endpapers were faded and stained. She opened it to the first page, which held only one word in a language she'd never seen, surrounded by knots and swirls and curlicues. It might have been somebody's name.

The next few pages seemed to be in the same strange language, more plainly written but still unreadable. Other languages followed—French and German and others she didn't recognize. Some entries had just a few words, others appeared to be poems or stories, elegant and fanciful on one page, hastily or angrily scrawled on another, the pen having scraped and gouged through the paper.

The first English entry, about thirty pages in, was an old nursery rhyme written in a spidery hand.

> *Sing a Song of Sixpence,*
> *A bag full of Rye,*
> *Four and twenty*
> *Naughty boys,*
> *Bak'd in a Pye.*

Then came page after page of letters, wishes, diary entries, erotic fantasies; sometimes just a person's name and their occupation, sometimes a list of people in their family, and sometimes a string of curses. She flipped to the last entry and found a puzzling poem that read more like a song:

D'ye ken John Peel with his coat so gay?
D'ye ken John Peel at the break o' day?
D'ye ken John Peel when he's far far away?
With his hounds and his horn in the morning?

For the sound of his horn brought me from my bed
And the cry of his hounds which he ofttime led
Peel's "View, Halloo!" could awaken the dead
Or the fox from his lair in the morning.

D'ye ken that bitch whose tongue was death?
D'ye ken her sons of peerless faith?
D'ye ken that fox, with his last breath
Curs'd them all as he died in the morning?

Yes I ken John Peel and Ruby too
Ranter and Royal and Bellman so true
From a find to a check, from a check to a view
From a view to a kill in the morning.

A hunting song, or so it seemed, though much of it went over her head. She turned the page and found a drawing, a dog or a wolf walking on its hind legs. She thought once more of the coyote across from the Selby, pacing and panting. *They're more scared of us than we are of them.* She wondered what else they were scared of.

She looked around her apartment and for a moment felt like the shadows were creeping in on her from every corner. She brought the notebook into her little galley kitchen, set it on the counter, then got down onto her hands and knees and opened the doors that led under the sink, felt around in the back behind the plunger, and pulled out an unused candle in a tall, clear glass holder, the figure of a saint pasted on the front. She stood up, held it up to the light. *Lidwina of Schiedam—Patron*

Saint of Ice Skating. She remembered now, it had been a joke house-warming gift; she had moved in on an especially frigid New Year's Day and the friends who had helped her had all hated her for it, so this was her surprise in exchange for pizza and beer.

She set the candle on the counter next to the notebook, struck a match, and tucked the flame down towards the wick. It filled the room with its rich warm light. Already she felt comforted, somehow less alone. She went back into the living room, sat down on the couch, unfolded her mother's itchy old green plaid blanket, pulled her legs up under it, and watched the flickering light dance across the walls until she finally fell asleep.

D'ye ken that bitch whose tongue was death?

She couldn't breathe. She couldn't move. Something was kneeling on her chest, suffocating her, perched on top of her while she struggled to fill her lungs.

Then something warm and wet splashed her cheek, right beside her nose. She opened her eyes as another droplet fell, briefly blinding her. She blinked and blinked.

It was the cat, Lily, just inches away from her face, and in her teeth she held a twitching, bloody mouse.

Robin screamed. Startled, the cat dropped it on her face and ran.

She screamed again, sat bolt upright, flinging the dying creature onto the floor. In the shafts of morning sunlight, she could see her arms and chest were spattered with mouse blood, and smears of it criss-crossed the front hallway right up to the edge of the rug.

The front door was hanging open, creaking softly as it swayed. Mrs. Lau peeked around the edge of the door frame and cried out, looking terrified. "What happened? Are you hurt? I will call a doctor!"

"No, no, it's fine, I—" Robin brought her feet down onto the living room rug, right onto another puddle of blood. She fought an over-whelming urge to vomit. "Lily got into my apartment somehow, and I guess she went on a killing spree." She pointed at the little grey body on the floor, which at last appeared to be dead.

Watching where she stepped, the old woman came through to the living room, picked up the mouse by its tail, and took it back into the kitchen. "Oh no, Lily was in here too! I will help you clean up." Robin heard her kitchen trash can swing open and then shut with a bang.

"There's some peroxide in the bathroom," she called. She hobbled across, trying to avoid making more of a mess, when she stopped in the kitchen doorway and stared. The Arborite counter and checkerboard floor were covered in a frenzy of bloody paw prints. A wet grey foreleg lay on the tile nearest the door. The candle was still burning, its pale flame casting a creamy glow across her stack of herbal teas. And the tattered red notebook was gone.

§♦

"Who is Nicholas?" asked Trevor, Ryan's roommate. Eight days had passed since anyone had seen Ryan, and Trevor and Victor were in his room searching for his family's phone number in Windsor, looking through his coat and pants pockets, his desk, the boxes in his closet, and the various scraps of paper piled on the nightstand, the seat of the armchair, and around the portable TV perched on the dresser. Trevor was holding a yellow sticky note he had found next to the bed. *Nicholas* was scrawled on it, jumbled but legible, as if he'd written it down in a hurry, or right after waking up.

"Not a clue," Victor answered. "He never talked about guys. I thought maybe he'd taken the vow."

With AIDS infections on the rise in the city and conflicting information circulating about how it was transmitted, what the incubation period was, and even what all the symptoms were, some guys were limiting themselves to group massage or jack-off clubs, while others were abandoning sex entirely. A third group, maybe the largest, was having as much sex as before and possibly more—with varying levels of anonymity, precaution, defiance, and fatalism—followed by hours and days and weeks of anxiety about whether the virus was now spreading from cell to cell inside them.

"That's all there is. Just the name." Trevor stuck it onto the corner of the desk. He was already imagining how much work it would be to clean out the room and find someone new. Maybe he should just go it alone for a few months.

"He never mentioned it to me," Victor replied—and yet the name did ring a bell from somewhere, if not from Ryan. A customer at the bar, or a guest at the hotel? There was that moment at work, by the washroom, the last night he saw Ryan, when he seemed so frightened. But Victor hadn't seen anyone.

"What're all these?" Trevor moved the nightstand aside, revealing a pile of sketchbooks by the bed. He picked one up, flipped through it. Drawings in pencil and charcoal, most of them men, most of them nudes. One man came up again and again: black hair, black brows, piercing eyes, hairy chest, nice uncut cock. "Cute, he drew his own porn." He turned the book around so Victor could see. "Ring any bells?"

"Lots of them. But no, I've never seen him before."

Trevor turned the sketch back around and looked it over carefully. "Me neither. If I was going to run off with anyone, though, I'd want it to be him."

While Trevor looked through the sketchbooks, Victor sifted through a sheaf of snapshots and postcards he'd found in Ryan's bedside table. It was strange, poring over the personal items of someone who was both familiar and a stranger, looking for clues to a mystery that might not be a mystery. And it was strange being here with Trevor. When Ryan hadn't shown for work on Saturday night, Victor had called twice, left two messages, but got no response. He did the same the following afternoon, when Boots hosted its weekly tea dance. He was dismayed, but assumed that Ryan had "quit without quitting," a not-uncommon phenomenon in the service industry. So he was surprised when, the following Tuesday, he had answered the phone at the bar to find Ryan's roommate, Trevor Mullin, on the other end. He'd been away working all weekend and had come back to Victor's messages. Ryan was nowhere to be found. It seemed too soon to call the police over what might turn out to be nothing; Trevor suggested they wait till a full week had passed. He had a funeral to go to the following Saturday, but said Victor should come by for lunch so they could figure out next steps. As Victor was getting dressed to head over to Trevor's, though, the police called to say that Ryan's clothes and wallet and ID had been found, and that was never a good sign.

When Trevor opened the door, he realized that he and Victor had gotten together once a few years earlier, well before Ryan had come to the city. (Victor had figured it out about four minutes earlier, as he was looking at the buzzer board.) It was one of those coincidences typical of the gay community, like finding out that you share a dentist or that you used to live on the same street. They had eyed each other one Wednesday evening at a rally protesting the baths raids—Trevor tall and blond and boyishly handsome, Victor shorter and broader, with a stocky, muscular build—and then had seen each other again later on at Stages, the dance club above the Parkside Tavern. They made their way to each other, and then to the door, and then went back to Victor's place for some vigorous sex that prompted a next-door neighbour to pound on the wall and left them both giggling like schoolboys. They shushed each other, and Trevor rode Victor's cock slower and deeper, Victor jerking him until they both came in a rush of murmurs, gasps, and sighs, just seconds apart.

After, as they lay together, Victor became a bit teary and confided that a friend of his had just died in New York, from some kind of one-in-a-million skin cancer. *He went to the gym, he didn't smoke, he didn't use drugs, he was a fucking vegetarian.* If someone like that could up and die at the age of thirty, what did it mean for the rest of us? Trevor didn't know what to say—he just held Victor closer. But he too had heard of men getting suddenly ill, in New York and San Francisco and cities overseas. And then, a few weeks later, there it was in the *New York Times*—RARE CANCER SEEN IN 41 HOMOSEXUALS—though Trevor knew through the flight attendant grapevine that the number was considerably higher, and encompassed more than just gay men.

"I thought I heard him come home last night," Trevor sighed, sifting through a pile of cheque stubs and matchbooks and cab receipts and credit card bills. "I heard footsteps in the hallway, I actually lifted my head off the pillow, and I thought I heard him come into my room, all the way to the end of the bed."

"Okay, that's not creepy at all," Victor said, thumbing through a handful of old porn zines from New York that somehow made it across the border.

"Right? I sat up, I called his name. I came in here to look, and of course found nothing. Everything was the way he left it." Trevor sighed. "I guess this is what it's going to be like now—all these new silences, and you fill them with whatever you expect to hear." He pulled down a postcard pinned to the wall, held it under the light. It was a promotion for a screening of Kenneth Anger's Magick Lantern Cycle at an art gallery on Queen Street, a fundraiser for one of the bathhouses damaged in the raids. The cycle had screened over three nights at the beginning of August. Had Ryan actually gone? He didn't seem like the type to sit through an evening of experimental film, no matter how many dicks were on display. But maybe he was? The art books and sketchbooks and posters and postcards suggested a side of Ryan that Trevor hadn't seen before. Or maybe just hadn't noticed.

"I had a bad dream," Victor said abruptly—bashfully, as if he had done something wrong by having it, or maybe now by mentioning it. "I don't remember much of it, but Ryan was in it, at least at the end, and he was in the bed with me, and he was so cold, his hands were like ice, and he pulled me up onto my side so that I faced him. He said . . . something like: 'If he reaches for you, then he's already caught you.' Something like that. He sang it almost, like a children's rhyme."

"Jesus, and you think my shit is creepy." Trevor pinned the Anger postcard back on the wall, next to an Odorama card for the John Waters movie *Polyester*. "Who's supposed to be reaching for you, Ronald Reagan?"

Victor shrugged. "I don't know, it didn't make any sense. I mean, I don't even know why we were in bed together. I liked him and all, but I was never actually *into* him. What do you think it means?"

"Nothing, it doesn't mean anything," Trevor replied. "It's just garbage that your brain is trying to get rid of, to make room for new garbage. We're all having bad dreams. We all have a lot going on."

"Funny thing, though," Victor added. "I woke up and I was covered in cum. It shot up out of my boxers and under my T-shirt."

"Definitely not Reagan, then." Trevor was examining a plain white postcard with a hole punched in it, signed by Yoko Ono. *A hole to see the sky through.*

"It was my first wet dream in years," Victor continued. "I didn't even know what it was. In the dark, I thought it was blood. I threw myself out of bed and ran to the washroom, I was so scared."

Blood and semen. The precious bodily fluids. Maybe Ryan *had* been diagnosed—maybe he *had* run off. Nicholas could be an AIDS counsellor, or maybe the name of a doctor. Trevor knew there were bars and restaurants that would flat-out fire you, and others that wouldn't allow you in food prep areas or let you handle glassware or garnishes or ice, "for the comfort and safety of the customers." The service industry didn't have drug plans or medical plans. You were at the mercy of the health care system itself. So maybe Ryan had panicked and ran—but if so, where and for what?

"Oh, look." Trevor reached for an old Penguin paperback, worn, with creases in the spine. It was a high school copy of *The Hound of the Baskervilles*. He took it from the shelf, opened it up. Ryan's name, Windsor address, and phone number were on the inside front cover, carefully printed in blue ballpoint. "Bingo," he said, and handed it to Victor. "Let's give that a try."

"Do you really think he'd be back at his mother's?" Victor asked.

"No," Trevor answered. "But the police might have called her, maybe told her something they're not telling us. It's not that big a city, people don't just disappear. And if they do, they don't leave their clothes and shit behind."

And yet they did. Men had gone missing from the bars and clubs and baths, one or two every few years, for as far back as he could remember. There had been talk on and off of serial killers, gangs of thugs, cops who wanted to "teach the fags a lesson." He couldn't help but wonder if Ryan had walked down the wrong alley, asked the wrong guy for the time, and now was face down in the water somewhere along the shore, or tossed into a dumpster.

Victor stepped up behind him, put his arms around him, rested his head against Trevor's neck. "Hey," he said, "it's okay."

It was comforting, and oddly arousing too. Trevor could feel the bulge in Victor's jeans pressing against him. Something inside him stirred, surprising him—he almost never played with the same guy twice—but as he relaxed into Victor's embrace, he glanced over at Ryan's bed and felt a rush of revulsion. He had a sudden urge to look beneath it, certain that something was under there, listening and watching. "Not here," he whispered.

"I ain't afraid of no ghosts," Victor whispered back with an audible grin.

"Yeah," Trevor answered. "But I am." He turned and, taking Victor's hands in his own, led him out into the hallway, towards his own room and onto his own bed. As they began to undress, to kiss and touch each other, he was sure he heard Ryan's bedroom door click shut.

જી

Ryan's mother, Lucille, was upstairs putting laundry away when the phone began to ring. It was always the way. She set the basket down on the bed, turned, and made her way back down the stairs. The answering machine clicked on just as she reached the living room. In the moment before the outgoing message finished, she looked down at the phone and saw it was a Toronto number. She let out a sharp sigh—something to do with Ryan, obviously. She stood there as the loud beep sounded, and then steeled herself as the caller began to speak.

"Um—hello. It's Trevor, Ryan's roommate in Toronto. He's been . . . away for a few days, more than a week actually, and I was wondering if he was visiting you or if you had heard from him. If you haven't, then I guess we should figure out what to do next. You can call me back if you like, or I can try you on Monday. Maybe he'll turn up by then." He gave his name again and then his number, and then he hung up. And then the machine clicked off. The indicator light began to flash: *Danger. Danger. Danger.*

Lucille stood there staring at the phone. She wanted to reach for it, to pick up the receiver and dial, to ask about Ryan and to help think of where he might be. But she couldn't. She no longer knew her son, had barely known him even when he was growing up in her house, and she didn't want his number showing up on the phone bill for her husband to see. She couldn't bear the hours of shouting, the days of silent recrimination that would result. She pressed the button to erase the message and reset the machine, and made her way back upstairs.

As she approached the final steps, she slowed, surprised to find that the door to Ryan's old room was open. They used it mostly for storage now, so she kept the door closed, the blinds down, and the curtains drawn. She stood at the doorway, peered inside. Nothing seemed to be disturbed. "Hello?" she called out, and instantly felt foolish. As she reached into the room to grasp the doorknob, she stopped—almost stepped back—then scolded herself and pulled it shut. *Honestly.*

She returned to her bedroom, to the clothes on the bed and in the basket, and filled each of the dresser drawers in turn. In the top drawer on the right, closest to the window, she found Ryan's last school photo from when he was sixteen. Rick no longer wanted to see it, but she couldn't bring herself to throw it out, so she kept it where he'd never normally look.

She looked down at it for a while and wondered if he had ever been as carefree as he looked in the photo. All teenagers had moments of despair—she'd had them herself. Nobody knew, not her husband and certainly not her son, but she had tried to kill herself when she was the same age, at a time when she felt so painfully lonely and misunderstood that she couldn't imagine ever being happy again. She re-created what turned out to be a rather ineffective suicide scene she had read in a trashy drugstore novel—lying neck-deep in icy water, blood leaking out of her wrists like wisps of red smoke. She drifted into unconsciousness thinking these sights and sensations and thoughts would be her last. She woke to find her mother screaming and crying and slapping her face. She looked down at herself and, realizing what she had done, began trembling, almost convulsing. "Stop it!" Lucille shouted. "You're hurting me!"

Her mother's terror turned into a selfish, callous anger. She reached into the tub, pulled the plug from the drain. "Clean yourself up," she ordered, then stood up and left the bathroom with a slam. The blood from her wounds now slowed to a trickle, Lucille rinsed herself off under the shower, bandaged her wrists with some gauze and white tape from the back of the medicine cabinet, washed and wiped out the tub, draped the towel over the curtain rod to dry, then slipped back into her room and closed the door. She had wanted to slam it off its hinges but instead closed it quietly, moved her desk chair in front of it, sat down, and began to sob.

She could hear her mother crying too, heard her pick up the phone and call her older sister, June. About twenty minutes later, June arrived at the front door, and the two of them sat in the kitchen, their voices just out of reach, until Lucille couldn't stay awake any longer. She curled up on the coiled rag rug on the floor and fell asleep.

The next day, she moved in with Aunt June, who lived in a sharp little Victory Home in East Windsor near the Ford test track. The next time she saw her mother was at Christmas, and the next after that was when she died the following spring. She had taken a fistful of sleeping pills, a recent prescription, and had aspirated as her unconscious body tried to expel them. The image haunted Lucille throughout her teenage years. By the time she was in her twenties, the picture in her mind was so vivid, it was as if she had found the body herself, though of course that wasn't the case. It was her mother's neighbour to the south, nice old Mrs. Ivey, who just knew that day that something had happened and felt the need to check on her.

Lucille felt an odd chill—*goose walking over my grave*, she thought. Too much time spent kneading the past. Her mother gone, Aunt June gone, Mrs. Ivey no doubt gone as well. Her father long gone, of course. And now Ryan had run off somewhere. Had he killed himself? Was there a family sickness, a predisposition? A bend in the line, as her dad might have said? "Let the dead bury the dead," Jesus said, according to Matthew. Lucille was never really sure what that meant. She heard the wind rise outside, rattling the panes. She had brought the laundry in just in time.

She made her way downstairs with the empty clothes basket, turned down the hall towards the kitchen, then stopped. Someone at the dining room window? No, no one, the whole backyard was empty. She moved towards it as yet another gust blew up with a harsh, dark howl. She looked down at the paving stones on the other side of the glass, saw that one of the neighbour's cats had brought a bird as an offering. Poor mauled creature, a robin or an oriole. And then, the oddest thing: she saw that the bird's body was framed by the wet prints of two bare feet, as if someone *had* been standing there and *had* been staring through the window. Children hopping the fence, perhaps, cutting through the yard, but they looked too large for that.

Then, splash splash—the rain began. In moments the footprints were washed away.

What does it mean to disappear? It's not just that one of
us is suddenly gone--run away, banished, locked up, dead by
our own hand or that of another. It's the not-knowing. You
see it all the time, a family with haunted eyes standing
in front of a microphone, wincing into the camera, their
child missing for years and all they want is closure. "How
bad can it be not to know?" you wonder, but you can see
it in their pale, drawn faces, hear it in their trembling
voices. Someone must have seen something or heard something. Someone must know. People don't just vanish.

I grew up in the late sixties and seventies, when sexual
liberation was transforming Western culture, but aspects
of gay life were still illegal or heavily restricted in
large parts of North America. A common narrative trope
in gay fiction at the time was that of the small-town
boy who runs away, or is cast out, hops a bus to the Big
City, and then either is drawn into a seedy underworld
that consumes and destroys him or, through talent and
determination, enacts a remarkable transformation (poor
to wealthy, unknown to famous, homely to handsome, male
to female), only to prodigally return to confront his
childhood tormentors. In reality, young gay men like
me were far more likely to be drawn into exasperating
temp agencies and dead-end admin jobs, enduring pain-
ful weekly phone calls from anxious mothers and complaints from other relatives whose letters and messages
you never returned, on top of twice-yearly visits home,
where your family ruefully observed how much weight
you'd gained or lost and where did you get those clothes
and why do you know so much about Broadway musicals, Old
Hollywood, ethnic foods, the opera?

Growing up and coming out, I fought with my mother so
many times about who I was and how I wanted to live my
life. I can see now that she was afraid for me, and I
inherited those fears. The Stonewall riots happened just
a few weeks after I turned seven. The first cases of HIV/
AIDS emerged as I turned nineteen. To her generation and,
for a time, to mine, being gay meant secret lives, police
raids, sudden firings, family expulsion, tabloid head-
lines, bashings, drinking and drugs, and an early death.
If something had happened to me, if I had been jailed
or killed, if I had disappeared, I'm not sure she would
have acknowledged me, and I don't think she would have
fought for me. It's hard to say this, and she's not here
to defend herself, but I see her heaving a heavy sigh
and telling herself that these were the choices I'd made.
I'd dug my grave, with my own shovel, and now I would
lie in it. I had been lost from the start. She wasn't the
only person who thought this way; this was the prevalent
feeling. Gay people were pitiable at best and garbage at
worst and, like garbage, they were disposable.

I had a great interest in film as a teenager, and hoped
I'd be a screenwriter or director when I got older.
To that end, I would spend Saturday afternoons at the
library around the corner from my home in Winnipeg's
West End, reading books about filmmaking and reviews of
movies I wasn't old enough to see. I especially enjoyed
Pauline Kael's reviews in the *New Yorker*, Jay Scott in
the *Globe and Mail*, Janet Maslin in the *New York Times*
(I'm still fond of her irreverent review of Argento's
Suspiria: "A great many graphic tips on how to carve
one's fellows into rib roast"), and Andrew Sarris in

the *Village Voice*. It was in the *Voice* that I first read
about a series of gruesome killings in New York City,
murders of gay men over a period of years. Their bodies
had been dismembered, stuffed into plastic bags, and
thrown into the Hudson River. The "Fag in a Bag" murders, some called them. The journalist was Arthur Bell,
who otherwise specialized in amusingly acidic reviews
of off-Broadway shows. In this case, a friend of his had
been killed in his apartment and the police and media
were doing little to investigate the crimes, as they were
thought to have been the result of anonymous sexual
encounters. The killer made contact with Bell and was
captured and convicted, but he was never conclusively
tied to the other murders. There was some speculation
at the time that the killer might have been a policeman,
or another gay man, or maybe even several men--loosely
organized or entirely unconnected, but somehow inspired
by each other. These killings became the basis for the
novel and film *Cruising*, which came out several years
later. I remember reading these articles and being
fascinated, frightened, and resigned in equal measure.
This is what happens to boys--to men--like me.

As I write this, in early 2018, an older white male has
been charged in relation to several gay-related murders
in Toronto, shocking the city, and police are expected
to lay more charges in the coming weeks and months.
Investigators are looking back through decades of
missing persons reports involving gay and bisexual and
closeted men in multiple jurisdictions. Tellingly, the
accused was only identified and pursued after a well-
regarded white male vanished--someone I'd known--and his

family and friends, his community, our community, publicly mobilized around his disappearance. His remains, among others', were found in some planters at a home in one of the city's wealthier neighbourhoods, where the suspect worked as a gardener. We have since learned that a number of Middle Eastern and South Asian men who went missing in the downtown area over the last ten years have obvious visible connections to the accused that the police never adequately explored. There has been some speculation about other disappearances in Toronto's past, and about disappearances in other cities, other countries even, where the suspect may have travelled over the years. We all know this man's name, we all know his sunny, smiling face. We know what bars he went to, we know what kind of sex he liked, the websites and apps he used to find potential partners or victims. But you'd be hard pressed to find someone who could name even three of the men he's accused of killing.

I shouldn't be doing this. It's all because I can't sleep--I'm too afraid. It's so stupid. This has happened before--the grinding teeth, the headaches, the night-mares, the sounds. I sit up in bed, I call out, "Hello?" *Genius move*. I'm working too close to the bone, I can't close my eyes. You create a thing and you think you can control it, but sometimes it turns on you, it starts to control you, it knows your weaknesses because you made it, it's part of you. It can reach right into you.

When I was eleven or twelve, my neighbour from across the street, who was just a few months older than me, asked me to take care of his dog--a bright, eager Lab-shepherd mix at the end of a piece of clothesline, while he went with his mother to the doctor about something or other. No one else was home. I foolishly said yes, even though the dog was nearly as big as me and certainly stronger. And, sure enough, no sooner were my neighbour and his mother driving up the street than the dog caught a whiff of prey on the late summer breeze and he bounded away, up to the corner and through the alley and down the block behind. The clothesline pulled through my hand, leaving a red, blistering burn. I screamed out the dog's now-forgotten name and ran after it, terrified it would rush into traffic and be killed. I heard a horrible high-pitched shriek and my heart dropped in my chest and I ran even faster, ran to a house near the end of the block where the dog had jumped the chest-high fence and caught, and was shaking in his steely jaw, a tiny grey rabbit, barely more than a baby, the pet of some little girl who had brought it into the backyard to chew on some grass. The rabbit had screamed, a wrenching, unforgettable sound, and had now fallen silent as the dog shook it and shook it and flung it to the ground, the girl's mother stepping out the back door, her jaw hanging in horror, and then the dog turned and burst back over the fence, back through the flurry of traffic to the far side of the street, and I turned and ran after it, tires screeching and squealing as the mother and child screamed, screamed out at me, and I ran all the way back to my neighbour's house, where the dog had spun to a halt and had thrown itself panting onto the grass, an instrument of death sudden and shocking that now nuzzled my leg and wanted a dish of cool water.

This is to say: There are frightening things in the
world, things that hunt by instinct, that watch and
stalk and corner and seize and shake us to death, fling
our remains where they may never be found--and then in
the next breath rush to their masters for a gentle pat
on the head. In that one raw moment we can just un-
exist, as if the earth--or something inside the earth--
has opened its maw and devoured us whole.

I have seen these things. At least one, at least once,
has seen me.

I moved to this city shortly after the CDC in Atlanta,
Georgia, first used the term Acquired Immunodeficiency
Syndrome to describe the virus that was ravaging gay
men, among millions of others, throughout North America
and around the world. In these years before the
Internet and social media, circles of friendship were
tighter, and those of social and sexual acquaintance were
looser and more diffuse. If you met up with a man in a
bar or a backroom or a porn theatre or a bus station or
a washroom or a bathhouse, you didn't expect to see him
again, wouldn't really know if he moved across the city
or across the country or to the other side of the world.
But as the virus spread, many of us made a greater
effort to know our partners, to make note of our mutual
friends, to ask after and check on them and determine
if one or another had fallen ill or retreated from view
or disappeared altogether. So many were closeted in one
part of their lives or another, or had families who were
angry or ashamed; you wouldn't see an obituary, you
wouldn't hear of a funeral. It's still hard to know what

happened to some of the men I slept with, dated, loved.
I've searched online for a few of them by name, by city,
by age, by school, by occupation, often without success.
Those who died before they could be immortalized by search
engines and social networks--it's as if they never existed.

Yet even now, though our every footstep is tracked and
traced by a thousand unblinking eyes, our every stripe
is swiped and every chip is checked, as every search and
view and click is absorbed into our history, we still
can slip from sight, simply cease to be. Those who watch
over us can rewind and review, zoom and freeze, can lean
in, pressing their thousand faces to a thousand screens,
and observe the precise moment when light is swallowed
by shadow, when sound is deadened by silence, when someone curls like paper touched by a flame and reaches and
blackens and crumbles into ash, into dust. But if they
watch, what will they see? And what will they do?

This may not be the story you expected. These fears,
these horrors, may not be the ones you thought you'd face
as you began to turn these pages. For that I apologize,
though I hope you'll stay with me. You see, a friend of
mine is gone, and I'm afraid, and I'm not sure what else
I can do.

1992

That was the year that Julian Crooks went missing. Nirvana's album *Nevermind* was nearing the top of the charts with barely any radio play. Lisa Stansfield and CeCe Peniston were big in the clubs. Jason Priestley and Luke Perry were crushworthy on *Beverly Hills 90210*. *The Silence of the Lambs* was about to sweep the Oscars. Nearly 4,000 men, 250 women, and an unknown number of non-binary people were dead from HIV/AIDS in Canada. And after decades of being scattered throughout the downtown area, Toronto's LGBTQ businesses and residents were consolidating in the burgeoning gay village at the intersection of Church and Wellesley. Safety in numbers.

Julian Crooks. Tight curly hair, light-skinned, glasses, slight and unassuming. He was last seen on an unseasonably warm Sunday in January leaving P.J. Mellons, a homey brick and brass bistro that was popular with the weekend crowd, and hurrying south towards Carlton Street. The sidewalks were coated with a slick layer of ice scattered with crunchy nuggets of salt. Gay men in colourful quilted jackets slipped and slid from brunches and boutiques to drag shows and dirty bingo while an assortment of women in plaid shirts, tattered jeans, and an abundance of collars and chokers sat in the window of the Devon, ate cheap and greasy chop suey and eggrolls, and rolled their eyes.

Julian was just a mile away from his shared house on Pembroke Street over in South Cabbagetown, a fifteen-minute walk. But, for whatever reason, he never made it home. No one along the way would have remembered seeing him. He was the kind of pleasant but nondescript young man whom few people would have glanced at twice. Unlike his brother and cousins, who wore sideways ball caps and chunky chains and brightly coloured streetwear, Julian opted for clothes that engulfed him in sombre greys, dark blues and browns, a cocoon from which he would never emerge: baggy black jeans and oversized sweatshirts, and hoodies that shadowed his face. Sometimes, people vanish in other ways before they disappear completely.

As Monday passed, and then most of Tuesday, Julian's roommates noticed he wasn't around, but each assumed the others had seen him in passing. It wasn't until his backpack was found in the park, half-buried under some crisp fresh snow, that they realized he hadn't been home for days. They searched his room, called friends and co-workers, unsure of what to do next except go to the police.

But with no signs of struggle, no significant leads, and no politician or public figure to push for more resources, the investigation was perfunctory at best. The housemates and classmates spoke to student reporters, ran a few ads in the local alt-weeklies, put some flyers up along Church Street, in the bars, and around the perimeter of the park. A homeless man found Julian's clothes under a light standard alongside St. Lawrence Market, shoved them into a plastic grocery bag, emptied his wallet, and dropped it into a mailbox. The missing persons file slid to the bottom of the pile, then into the back of a drawer after less than a month.

Black bomber jacket, an olive-green flannel workshirt, loose-fit Calvin Kleins, grey work socks, and a pair of black leather Reeboks. Blue nylon Velcro wallet with cash and ID. Army-green nylon MEC backpack stuffed with a grey Gap hoodie, felt-tip pens, a few subway tokens, a pack of sugarless gum, a marked-up draft of the Fringe play *Contagious!*, and a ring of keys. Julian Crooks, twenty-five, of 64 Pembroke Street, was never found.

❧

"So now you're a writer," said a voice from behind, startling him. Julian looked up from the old red notebook he was scribbling in, slightly embarrassed, to see his sponsor, Carole, a spiky-haired scout mom in a fleece-lined jean jacket.

"What? No, I'm—just putting down a few notes before I forget. About this stupid play." He closed the book and tucked it into his backpack, but not before Carole caught sight of it.

"Good lord, where did you get that old relic? It's like it's been to hell and back."

He shook his head. "It's in better shape than it looks," he replied. "It's cool, though, you feel like you're committing something to history. Carving into a monument."

"A monument for termites. That thing would fall apart if I breathed on it."

The waiter loomed beside them, filled her glass with water, and hovered expectantly.

"Hi there," she said as she scanned the menu, then declared, "Eggs. Benedict. Poached medium. Half fries, half salad. And a coffee, cream and sugar."

"Same, but no salad," Julian said, and handed the menus to the waiter, who left without a word.

"You're welcome," she called after him, then shrugged. "So, what's happening with the stupid play?"

Julian was the liaison with a small group of theatre artists who were creating a "funny, provocative show about the changing face of AIDS." So far, it was neither funny nor provocative, and it was barely a show.

"Well, I went over the script with them on Tuesday, gave them a list of questions and suggestions . . . which, I don't know. They want me to help, but they don't want to hear anything that I have to say. It's like I'm not even there."

"Sounds about normal to me. Maybe you should just pull out?" Carole asked.

"Maybe. I don't want to leave them in the lurch, complaining that I'm some flaky AIDS guy."

"Is that a thing?" she asked. "The flaky AIDS guy?"

The waiter returned with a basket of buns, plain and pumpernickel, with little tubs of butter, dropped it on the table between them, then soared off again.

"Oh, you know." He sighed. "You feel like you have to be *out there* and *do things* and *educate people* and be a *positive face*, pardon the pun, and then you overcommit and do too much and end up exhausted and then, boom, the balls you've been carrying fall all over the floor and you're the flaky AIDS guy." His voice cracked just for a moment, he was close to crying. It really did feel like it was all too much sometimes.

Carole reached over and held his hand. "It's all right," she said soothingly. "I've dropped a few balls over the years, and a few have been dropped on me. Everyone gets over everything eventually. None of it is worth ruining yourself over."

He nodded. She gave his hand a squeeze and he squeezed it back. Carole was one of the few people he could tell almost anything. She knew more about him than probably anyone, though she still didn't know everything, and that was okay.

"So, in other news," she continued. "Your one-year is coming up. It'll be five or six of you getting chips, I think—Sherry has the list. Someone stole our meeting room for the end of the month, so we'll have to hold off for a few days and maybe do a combined thing with NA. Is there anyone you want to invite—a family member, a friend?"

He looked down, shaking his head. "My dad is the supportive one, which is funny when you think about it. But he won't come without my mom, and she and I are done with each other. It's not even a topic."

"That's a shame," Carole said as the waiter set their coffees down in front of them. "They should be very proud of you. Are you going to do something to celebrate?"

"Not much. I might go to the baths," Julian answered. "I do that sometimes—not really even for sex, I just go get a room and close the door and lie down on the crappy little bed and listen to the thump-thump dance music and the sounds of everyone getting off around me, and then after a while I fall asleep. I sleep better at the baths than I do at home. It's really the only place in my life where everyone is like me."

Carole cocked an eyebrow at him. "Aren't there a lot of drugs there?"

The question brought him out of his reverie. As much as she was his friend, she was still his sponsor, and she was right to be concerned. "There are drugs everywhere." He shrugged. "I don't know, it's weird. I feel safer there, and I've met more nice people there than I ever have at a bar. That was probably my number one reason for drinking—being stuck in a crowded room, with all the noise and the laughing, where everyone could see me. When I'm at the baths, in my room, in the dark, by myself, it's like I don't exist."

"I get that, the overwhelming effort it takes to exist when all you want to do is be," Carole replied. "And I don't mean to be such a mom about things. I trust you to do the right things for yourself. Even if that means dropping some balls." She flinched as she sipped her coffee. It was a little tough. "So," she said as she reached for the cream. "What's the rest of your day about?"

"I'm meeting up with a guy, at the greenhouse in Allan Gardens. I guess it's kind of a date. He's the guy who gave me the notebook. It's a real antique, I think."

"Kind of a date, that's nice." She nodded. "I hope he's not an antique too." She gave a one-sided smile and Julian couldn't help grinning.

Then came the plates, seemingly out of nowhere and swimming with hollandaise, and splashes more coffee for each. Carole examined her meal and sighed. "Ugh, they're runny again, they never get it right."

Julian cut into one of his eggs and recoiled—a spot of blood in the yolk. He scooped it out with the tip of his spoon and set it aside under the leaf-lettuce garnish. No point in sending it back. He wondered if it meant something, good or bad luck. *I should ask Nicholas*, he thought as he started eating. *He seems like the kind of guy who would know about these things.*

An hour later, Julian was trudging down through the park from the northwest corner. As he turned towards the front of the conservatory, he saw Nicholas standing in the shadows near the door, wrapped in a blue wool peacoat, his hands thrust into his pockets. Despite the warmth and brightness, the park was nearly empty. A young dad and his toddler daughter were rolling balls of snow at the south end.

As Julian reached the front stairs, he wavered for a moment, slowed himself, put his hand on the rail. It was like a flash of vertigo, the pit of his stomach fell open, and for a second it was summer, summer in the park but different, the park of a bygone era, more bushes, more trees, and it was the dead of night, the paths studded with old gas street lamps, and the shadows of men drifting in and out of the darkness, hands touching chests, touching cocks, reaching and fondling, mouths against mouths, the soft rustle of leaves.

A sharp shock of winter wind out of nowhere, a biting spray of snow. Nicholas hugged him briskly, leaving him breathless for a moment, then took him by the hand. "Come," he said. "I want to show you something. It's just in the back, over here, where they're doing some digging up." Then he flashed Julian that sly canine grin that had first captivated him. "Don't worry. No one will see us."

Julian hesitated, turned around, cast his eyes back across the park. Dad and daughter and their newborn snowman, dogs barking in the distance. *It's okay, nothing's changed, it's just another bright white winter afternoon.* He turned back to Nicholas, felt the warm, inviting glow of his smile like a bonfire on his cheeks. He gave a quick, shy nod. Nicholas grinned and dragged him gleefully across the building's slippery terrace, around the side and down and out of sight. *Strange how cold and black it is, just inches away from the sunlight.*

೫

As the first light of dawn faintly coloured the eastern sky, Trevor Mullin stepped out of the back gate of his valley-side apartment and began his morning jog towards Carlton Street. The weekend's warm spell was over and he shivered under his thermal tights, nylon training pants, merino turtleneck, down vest, and bright-blue windbreaker. Red reflective strips cuffed his wrists and ankles and crossed his back from shoulder to hip. He'd had near misses with drowsy morning drivers before and didn't want to take any more chances.

He was just across from Allan Gardens and considering a turn south onto Jarvis when he heard a high, harsh, terrified yelp, and then a woman's shattering scream. He stopped, placed his hand on a corner light standard, turned his head left and then right, straining to listen. And then again—straight south from where he was standing, another horrible shriek.

He ran without thinking across the empty street and then down into the park, racing towards the giant, ghostly sycamore that jutted like a lightning strike from the frozen ground at the park's south end. It had to be over a hundred years old, the largest such tree in sight. At its foot was an elderly woman, short white hair, heavy tweed coat. Had she fallen? Broken her ankle? She was on her knees in the snow, staring upward and shrieking.

"Smoczek! Oh my god, Smoczek!" At first, it didn't make sense—was something flying above them?—and then she shrieked again. "My dog! He is in the tree!"

She pointed into the branches above her head and Trevor turned around then looked up, higher and higher, and finally he saw what she saw.

A sable-coloured Italian greyhound was thrashing and flailing, wild-eyed, tongue lolling, at the end of its leash from one of the higher branches. It was impossible—the dog was at least thirty feet off the ground—but there he was, and he was going to die, there was no way around it. None of the branches were low enough to climb, a fire engine would never come fast enough. They could only watch and wait.

Trevor knelt next to the woman and she began sobbing into his chest. *What the fuck—how did this happen? Should we be here? Are we safe, should we run?* He tried to speak to her, tried to ask her, but she just clutched him and wailed as the animal swung overhead.

After a few minutes, the dog stopped twisting and struggling, and drooped limply from its collar, swaying slowly from the creaking branch. Then a thunderous crack, and the branch let go, and the dog plummeted down with a sickening slam onto the mound of snow and ice beside them, shocking them both. Wailing anew, the woman pulled away from Trevor and threw herself over the animal. "Smoczek," she cried over and over.

Trevor didn't know what to do. He shivered all over as he stood in the chilly shade of the giant sycamore and breathed some warmth into his cupped, mitten-covered hands. As he watched, a shadow passed over the woman and the dog and then turned away. He looked up to see a red-tailed hawk circling warily above them. Had something tried to pick up the dog and carry it away?

He backed away from the tree, his feet uncertain on the patches of ice underfoot, and turned to approach the woman and the dog. For the first time, he saw and smelled the patch of burnt fur and raw, blistered flesh up along the animal's right side. It was as if something had exploded and blown it up into the tree, but that didn't make sense. He looked back up at the sky. Could it have been a freak electrical discharge, though the morning was cloudless and clear? Or possibly a fallen power line, or a buildup of gas from the sewer? The pipes and mains running under the park were old and in need of repair.

After a moment, the woman grew quieter.

"What happened?" he asked gently. "How did he get up there?"

But she just waved him away.

He stayed very still and moved his eyes from snowbank to path to mud patch to bench, till his eyes caught the trail of the dog's paw prints in the snow, over and around to the park's southwest side leading up to the conservatory, the back of which was under construction. Some kind of fuel lines? He saw where the dog's tracks veered towards a thick smear of blackness on the path leading down to the street.

Gingerly, Trevor stepped forward, shuffling his feet against the ice, watching for any possible hazard. He had read once about how a hydro vault near a traffic intersection had filled with melted snow, and the metal cap above it had been covered in ice and salt; a prize-winning Pomeranian had been electrocuted walking over it, and the owners had threatened a lawsuit against the city. As he reached the blackened area, Trevor saw that the snow and ice were melted in rough patches leading away from it, up and over and behind the whitewashed glass structure. The spot itself was scorched, and the faint smell of burnt fur and ozone still hung in the air. No sign of a live wire or an electrically charged manhole cover—just frozen snow and grass and dirt.

Farther ahead, he saw something round and green poking out from the snow. He realized after a moment that it was the bottom edge of a coat or a backpack. He took a few steps over to it, gave it a poke with his toe. Some of the snow fell away, revealing it more fully—an army-green oval bag with various zipped pockets, padded shoulder straps, and a webbed nylon band at the top for a handle. Likely stolen, ransacked, and dumped. It had a scattering of buttons pinned to it, various activist slogans: *AIDS Action Now*, *Queer Nation*, *ACT UP*, *I Will Survive*, *Glad to Be Gay*. He picked it up, shook it off, checked the small side pocket. He found a tag in a clear plastic sleeve with a name—Julian

Crooks—and an address just a few blocks away. He was about to unzip it and look inside but thought better of it. Instead, he slung it over his shoulder, looked back at the old woman, and saw she was trying to lift the dog now, trying to carry it. The path ahead of her was black with ice. Watching carefully where he stepped, he hurried over towards her. "Wait, wait," he called. "Let me help you."

At first, she resisted, just shook her head and turned away from him. But once she had the dog in her arms, once she felt the weight of it, she nodded, tears streaming, and let Trevor take it from her. She led the way out of the park and he followed, winding their way east to a numberless house south on Berkeley Street, a tidy stone cottage at the end of a slate path like something out of the Brothers Grimm.

She unlocked the leaf-green door, hesitated, then said, "You must be very cold. Please stay. I can make tea. Unless you must go to work." She didn't want to show it, he could tell, but she was afraid. Afraid to be alone.

"I can be late," he answered, and as she held the door, he carried the dog across the threshold into the darkened hallway.

"One moment," she said, and then hurried ahead of him, down the hall and through the kitchen into what looked like a laundry room or a mud room. The house was surprisingly spacious and bright, with much of the original wood and stone on display. He slipped off his shoes while he waited, his arms starting to cramp. The smell of burnt hair and flesh was faintly nauseating; it permeated the air all around him. The woman came back out holding a large floral terry cloth towel, faded and fraying.

"What happened back there?" he asked softly. "What did you see?"

She shook her head, wrapped the towel around the dog, whispering, "Ssh shh shhhhh," to it, carefully pulling it from Trevor's arms as if not to wake it, and then gently rested it on the pale-blue living room rug. She lightly stroked its head, then stopped herself and pulled the towel up over its face.

"Come," she said. "Take off your coat. I will start the kettle." She didn't have an accent exactly, but her stilted way of speaking suggested she was from another country, Russia maybe, or Poland, somewhere in eastern Europe.

He pulled the knapsack from his shoulder, then took off his coat and placed them both on an old wooden chair near the door. A shiver ran through him. His hands were like ice. "Is your bathroom upstairs?"

"Yes, yes," she said, wiping the tears from her reddened cheeks. "Up the stairs. The door on the right."

The bathroom was a small floral box lined with little shelves holding vintage bottles of Chanel No. 5, Topaze, and Lily of the Valley, tiny soaps in the shape of rose baskets, a yellowing bottle of Skin So Soft, and various colours of pastel face cloths and towels that were gradually fading into the same beige grey. Trevor turned on the hot water and plunged his trembling hands into the stream, rubbing them together to warm them. The numbness was quickly replaced with stinging, fiery pain. He glanced up at himself in the medicine cabinet mirror and for the briefest moment thought that someone was standing behind him, but one blink and the sensation was gone. He turned off the water, dried his hands, and, suddenly curious, pulled aside the curtain to peek out the window. The panes were covered over with wax paper and sealed with beige masking tape, presumably for privacy. *What about the other windows?* He stepped back, looked across the hall into the bedroom. That window too was covered over. *Has someone been watching her house, harassing her? Did someone murder her dog?*

He arrived back downstairs as the whistle from the kettle reached its peak and slowly died. She poured the water into a cabbage rose china teapot with a tiny chip in the spout, took two teabags from a nearby tin canister and tossed them in, then gestured for him to sit on one of the vinyl-covered kitchen chairs. She had the same old avocado-and-gold appliances that he had grown up with back in Scarborough. The cupboards were made of thin plywood, but they were stained a comforting amber colour that made him think of late summer light. He noticed what looked to be the starts of several collections: spoons from cities and landmarks over here; an assortment of mugs with faces over there; a cluster of dancing porcelain figurines on the shelves above the black-and-white TV in the corner.

"I must call to have him taken," she said, and for a second Trevor had to think about who she was talking about. "The animal clinic, will they know someone? Do they have a service?"

"I'm sure they do," Trevor replied, though he wasn't at all sure—his last pet was a cat when he was twelve, and he came home from school one day to find that it had been taken away and put down. He hadn't even known the cat was sick. "If they don't do it themselves, they'll arrange for someone, I'm sure of it."

"They will want money. I will have to find the credit card." She looked up at him. "How much does such a thing cost?" Maybe this was her way of coping, losing herself in the details to push away the enormity of what had happened.

"I can pay if you like," Trevor offered.

"No, no, it is fine, I can pay," she answered brusquely. "You have already been very kind. He was a fine dog, very smart, but too full of mischief."

"I still don't know what happened, exactly."

She flinched, turned away slightly. He immediately wished he hadn't said it.

"You don't have to tell me, I know it was terrible. I just want to be sure you're not in danger. Or whether I should call the police."

"No police, no," she said emphatically. Then softer, sadder: "I did not see, not really. He would chase anything, these dogs are like that. Off like the wind. We were in the park, we were at the tree, it's where he likes to visit and do his business. A squirrel, I thought it was." She was looking at the wall now, not at him, trying to remember. "I was not paying attention and then he jumped up, growling, he pulled the leash out of my hand. A squirrel. Something to chase. I was so angry. I turned and called out for him, he was down behind the greenhouse. Then a noise, like a gun, I tried to run to him. The ground shook, the horrible smell, I don't know what, and he was up in the tree. And then you came."

A noise like a gun. Did someone shoot the dog? But that didn't make sense either; a gunshot wouldn't have propelled the dog into the air. It would have taken a land mine to do that.

She poured the tea into two matching cups, set one in front of him with a spoon from the dish rack, gestured at the sugar in a clear glass bowl on the table. She took a small carton of milk out of the fridge door, set it on the table as well. Then brought her cup over and sat herself down.

"You said it was something behind the greenhouse?" he asked. "I saw a mark on the path, leading away from the tree. The ground was scorched, like something had exploded there." He took a sip of tea and promptly burned his tongue.

"I do not know about that," she said. "Smoczek was behind the greenhouse, and then he was in the tree. It was terrible. What kind of a thing could do that?"

It was odd, the way she said *thing*, but he didn't pursue it. He could tell she was holding something back. Years of flying with all kinds of passengers, from reticent to belligerent, gave him a sense of when to push to find out more and when to stop and wait. She had obviously seen or imagined something. Some *thing*. And she was frightened, maybe in shock.

A small brass picture frame caught his eye. It was perched at the rear of the kitchen table, up against the wall. He picked it up, looked at the old black-and-white photo placed within it—slightly crooked, not quite the right size. The old woman was much younger, with a stern, distinguished man. There was no visible affection between them, but sometimes old photos were like that.

"Is this your husband?" he asked.

She nodded. "He is gone. He has been gone for many years." She dabbed at the corners of her eyes. "Everything is taken eventually. One thing after another, until you have nothing."

"I'm sorry," he said, setting the frame back in place. He wanted to ask more about him, more about the park, the dog, but he didn't want to set her off. She had only just regained her composure. "Do you want me to stay while you make the call? To the vet?"

She shook her head, sipped from her tea. "No, thank you. I will do it. You are good to ask." She made a show of checking the clock. "You should go, I have kept you too long."

He nodded, slid his chair away from the table. Before he could stand, she leapt up abruptly, scurried across the room, opened one of the cupboard drawers, and rooted around inside for something.

"Take this," she said. She pulled out something small and shiny, a silver patron saint medal, and pushed it into his hand. "It belonged to Marek, my husband."

He recognized the shape and size from his childhood, though not the name: Benedict of Nursia. A grim bearded man in a cloak. He looked like he'd seen some things. He turned the medal over to find a circle of letters inscribed on the back, surrounding a cross made of more letters. Prompts for prayers and recitations. If he ever knew them, they were now long forgotten.

"Oh no, I can't," he said. "It's really not necessary. You should keep it in your husband's memory." He started to give it back to her, but she refused.

"No, no, you must, I want you to have it. It was very dear to him. We have no children, I have no one to pass it to." She pressed her hand over his, over the medal in his palm. "Please. It will help to protect you."

"Protect me from what?"

"Many things. You will see."

It was clear she was determined that he take it, so he relented. She stood behind him and fastened it around his neck, gave it a tiny tug.

"There," she said. "My husband wore it every day. You should do the same." She placed her hand on his shoulder.

He touched the small silver disc hanging from his neck. *I wonder how well it protected Marek.*

"You did see something, didn't you," he said. Not a question.

"No, nothing." She withdrew her hand. "I saw nothing."

He nodded. The dog, gasping and swinging in the tree; the blackened path; the strange smell; the terror on her face, the screams.

"Well, thank you again," he said as they walked up the hallway to the front door. He pulled on his coat, tossed the knapsack over his shoulder. They both paused at the living room doorway. He could smell it before he saw it, the still, small, burnt body of the dog under the towel. Against the blue of the rug, it was like a small, soft cloud in an otherwise empty sky. He wanted to pull the towel off, confront her with the obscenity of it, confirm it for himself. Throw her little church gift shop pendant down on the blackened corpse.

But he didn't. "I'm sorry about—Smoczek," he said instead.

"Yes," she replied. "He was a good boy. Thank you for helping me."

As Trevor stepped out the door and onto her porch, she reached over and gave his arm a gentle pat. "Do not go back to the park. Do not go back to the tree." And then she pulled the door shut before he could reply. He realized too late that she had never mentioned her name.

Elke walked back down the hallway, into the kitchen, and reheated the kettle for another cup of tea. She would call the animal doctor and ask for someone to come and get the body. She had seen what was in the park, she had seen what had murdered her dog. She did not want to see it again, and she did not want it to see her.

Another cup of tea, and then she would call.

It had been a mistake to come to this country, and even more so as newlyweds. She had told Marek often in their first few years here: too hot and then too cold, too many strange faces and sounds, too much vulgarity and stupidity and inefficiency. Everything took forever, and nothing was right. He nodded and made little sounds, feigning sympathy and agreement. *Yes, yes, I know, but what can we do, we are here now, try to make the best of it.*

Within a few weeks of their arrival, he was hired as a night clerk at the Westbury, a sleek new luxury hotel that had recently opened on Yonge Street near the College subway station. He got on well with his employers, which was good, and they increased both his hours and his responsibilities, which was not. Within just a few months, he became quieter, less intimate, more withdrawn and distant. A shadow of the man she had married. He started leaving for work hours early and coming home hours late. She had fretted that there might be another woman, and cried herself to sleep more than once. But then came the night when she woke up to find him sitting at the foot of the bed, on the corner closest to the door, his face slashed by a sliver of moonlight.

"Marek, what is it?" she whispered.

"Wróbli," he whispered back. *Sparrows*. He turned to face her. She saw that he held a handkerchief to the top of his head, swollen with blood from a gash on his scalp.

She threw back the covers and turned on the bedside lamp. He had several such wounds on his forehead and neck, and his ear was bleeding as well. *Sparrows. Impossible. He must have been beaten, he must have fallen.* She rushed to the bathroom and soaked a face cloth in cold water, took the peroxide out of the medicine cabinet, and hurried back to his side. She pulled up her vanity chair and tended to his wounds, but it was as if she wasn't there. He just sat in silence and stared at the window, and when she finished, he stood up and went downstairs and sat in his living room chair until sunrise.

Marek called in sick that morning, but he didn't stay home. He went to a nearby church, the Paroisse du Sacré-Coeur, to attend morning mass and give confession. He had not been to a church since their wedding, and not since he was a child before that. She offered to go with him, but he insisted on going alone. She changed the dressing on his forehead, helped him into a freshly ironed white shirt and suit pants. She wondered if he had a concussion, if he'd had a stroke. That could change a person. He was so different from who he had been just a few days before.

He returned to the church several times over the weekend, and each time, he brought home tokens of his new-found faith: framed pictures of Christ to hang near the front and back doors, statuettes for the knick-knack shelves and china cabinet, a religious calendar to hang on the door to the basement. The Lord's many miracles. More than once, she had come downstairs in the night to find him sleeping on the couch or sitting by the window, watching the backyard. Once, she found that he had left the house completely. He told her the next morning that he had gone for a walk through the park to be alone with his thoughts.

The following week, he returned to work, this time to the day shift. On the Wednesday, while she was dusting and vacuuming upstairs, she moved the bed aside to clean underneath and found the small brown cardboard box. She lifted the lid. Magazines, photographs, postcards. Titles leapt out at her: *Colt, Champions, Tiger Man, Stallion, Drum, Body Beautiful* ("Studies in Masculine Art"). Perhaps she was meant to find them, perhaps it was his way of forcing an issue that neither of them could raise.

She looked at the first photo, two men on a motel-room bed with their mouths on each other while a third man sat nearby touching himself, and she could not help herself—she felt the disgust rise in her chest and throat like bile. She wanted to vomit. The next was a naked man posing proudly on the beach, clean-shaven and sturdy, squinting up towards the sun. His penis jutted out in front of him. Was this what Marek wanted, wanted instead of her? She looked at every photo, forced herself to set her eyes on every single image.

When she lifted the last magazine out of the box, she found the tattered red notebook, girdled with the Benedict medal as if it was trapping something inside. The medal and the chain were new—another token from the church, no doubt. She carefully removed it and set it aside, then turned the book over in her hand, weighing its age, its origin. No title, no author. Where he got it, and how, she could not begin to imagine. There were pages in Russian and French and Italian and English, in languages she did not know and that looked like no language at all.

What she read and saw there frightened her. There were drawings and poems, confessions and pleas, written and printed and scratched and scrawled by different people at different times. Animals dancing, men in flames. Some of the pages seemed blank at first, but then she caught faint glimpses of lines and figures twisting and writhing across them. Others were filled with tiny crosses marked in what looked and smelled like old blood. It was disgusting, dangerous.

She slammed the book shut, placed it back in the box, dropped the medal on top of it, then left the box in the centre of the bed.

She made the evening meal and dined with Marek when he arrived home from work, as if nothing had happened. They watched television, *Gunsmoke*, *Peyton Place*, another western she couldn't recall, and then he went upstairs to go to sleep. She turned off the television and cleaned up in the kitchen, taking the dishes from the rack and tucking them back into the cupboard.

When she ascended the stairs, she saw the dim light from the bedroom. He had left the lamp on by her side of the bed and had turned to face away from it. She could tell he was awake. She undressed and slipped on her nightgown, then slid into bed beside him. The box full of horrors was nowhere to be seen. Had he disposed of it, or just hidden it away somewhere else? She turned off the lamp, and a long moment passed.

"I am sorry," he sighed.

She had no answer. Elke maintained her distance under the covers— just a few inches, though it felt like a chasm between them. He placed his hand on her shoulder. She stiffened. He stopped and limply pulled it away. She closed her eyes and willed herself to sleep.

The next morning, she woke up alone, late. Marek had already left. It was an hour later when his supervisor called and asked to speak with him, assuming that he had fallen sick again. She immediately grew fearful, and the poor gentleman did his best to calm her. He offered to contact the police, to help check the hospitals. She declined and thanked him, promised she would let him know more when she knew more herself. And then she called, and called, and took notes, and asked questions, and thanked everyone she spoke to, but she knew even before she began that she would not find him. And she did not.

She waited three long days just to be certain, then confirmed his absence to the police, and the bank, and then to the government. It was 1968, and she had been wise to have her name on the bank accounts and on the deed to the house; it was not the common practice. Still, it took many months before she received all the papers declaring her house and money and possessions to be hers alone. She moved herself into the spare room and cleaned out the master bedroom, fearful that the box was still somewhere hidden away, in the back of the closet, under the mattress, beneath the floor.

She finally found it behind the chest of drawers, held against the wall by the heavy wood. She took the magazines and photographs and burned them in the bathtub, then flushed the ashes down the toilet. She took the silver medal and hid it in the kitchen drawer. She would have destroyed the red book, but it was nowhere to be found. Why would he take that and leave everything else?

A few weeks after his departure, just before Easter, at the time of night when the world was cold and still, Elke awoke to what sounded like a high, soft whistle, just one note, a whistle or a squeal as if from an old iron gate or a porch swing gently swaying, metal twisting on metal. It was coming from outside the window behind her, from the back garden. She reached for the bedside lamp, then stopped herself. She stood up, pulled her dressing gown around her waist, then approached the window, moving forward in small steps until she could see the garden below.

As her eyes adjusted, she could see that someone was standing there. *Marek?* No, this person was lean and narrow, tensed like a trap, like an animal kept strong and hungry and vicious. He stood there, breathing in and out, the air rasping through his teeth. She watched him, a shadow among the shadows, and then she saw him change. Like someone had taken a stick of coal and had scrawled all over him, until he was something else, something larger, darker. And then he was gone.

She stood frozen for a moment, sure that what she had seen could not have been real, and then fled back to the bed, under the covers, awake and afraid until dawn.

A few days later, in the early spring sunshine on a Sunday afternoon, Elke was seated at the dining room table with a glass of juice and a fresh butter biscuit when, out of the edge of her eye, she saw something move in the backyard near the fence. *Wolf*, she thought first, then *wolf-bear*, though of course that was absurd. But it felt that large to her, huge and black and predatory and it could *see her*, it was standing and staring at her, watching and waiting. She turned her head to get a better look and saw that the yard was empty. There was nothing near the back fence. The garden was filled with warm, dappled light. And yet, when she turned her head towards the cup, the plate, she could still see it standing there, a dark, cold, angry presence. A giant fist, clenched, poised, waiting.

She stood and went to the dining room window, turning her face one way then another until she could almost see the beast, could almost feel its eyes trained upon her. She peered up at the cloudless sky, looked into the neighbours' yards, then along the alley, trying to see what could have cast such a shadow. Then a small brown bird slammed into the glass right in front of her face and fell to the ground, making her gasp and recoil. She stood there with one hand on the door jamb, the other on her chest, pressed to her racing heart, and thought she heard the same soft whistle as before, but this time in short, sharp bursts, laughing at her, mocking her.

Wróbli.

Months passed, years passed. There were times in her brief marriage when she had felt she was living with a ghost; now, even the ghost was gone. She repainted and refurnished the master bedroom, then rented it out to a series of students, usually young women, often in the arts. She received many small paintings and sketches and ornaments over the years as gifts from her tenants. And that was how she lived her life—until that morning in the park with Smoczek, and the helpful young man, and the sycamore tree, and the thing behind the conservatory.

After running home and changing his clothes, Trevor called Crew Scheduling to say he would be late because of a family emergency, only to discover that his flight was delayed two hours and might be delayed again, because of a storm out east. *Perfect.* He pulled on his coat and boots, picked up the backpack, and headed over to the house on Pembroke Street.

It was the right half of a three-floor red-brick duplex behind a plain wrought iron gate. He stepped up to the glass-and-aluminum door; BELL BROKEN was scrawled on a piece of paper taped beside it in watery felt-tip pen. Below it was the broken doorbell, which looked like it had been beaten with a shoe. He knocked, waited a few moments, then knocked louder. The deadbolt turned with a clunk and the door swung open, revealing a short olive-skinned woman in a lemon cardigan and straight-leg jeans with shot-out knees. The warmth in her eyes dimmed as they darted from his face to the backpack.

"Where did you get that?" she asked sharply.

"Hi, um, I'm Trevor," he said nervously. "I live about a half a dozen blocks from here." He gestured vaguely to the north and east. "I was out for a run this morning and I found this in the snow in Allan Gardens, down near the greenhouse. Is Julian home?"

"No," she said bluntly, then softened somewhat. "Sorry. Karyn. I'm one of his roommates. He's not home, I'm not sure when he was here last. I was just trying to figure that out myself. Did you find anything else? Did you see anything?"

"No, not really," Trevor replied noncommittally, deciding to keep the morning's drama to himself. "But—I don't know, has anything strange been going on in the park over the last little while?"

She seemed struck with a sudden realization. "The cops. They've been trolling the park since the fall. Maybe he's been arrested?"

Trevor recalled hearing that the police chief wanted the park cleaned up, that it was supposedly a haven for sex-seeking gays, drug users, and the homeless.

"I don't know. I didn't see any police around when I was there. I guess you'd have to give them a call."

Karyn made a face. She was clearly not thrilled at the prospect. "Where in the park did you find it?" she asked. "I should go see if anything else is there."

Trevor tried not to show the horror he suddenly felt. "It was, um, at the south end of the old greenhouse, where they're doing the construction. The bag was there, half-covered in snow. I didn't see anything else around it. But maybe the police can check. Or park security."

"Oh, okay. If you're sure." She seemed puzzled by his insistence. "I'd invite you in, but the house is kind of a mess."

"That's all right, I'm already late for work. But here's my number, if I can help." He handed her the backpack, then pulled one of his airline business cards out of his wallet. It already had his home number written on the back in case a hot, handsome passenger needed some personal assistance.

She took it from him, looked it over. "How did you know to bring it here?"

He pointed out the backpack's small side pocket. "There's an address tag in here. I didn't look through anything else. The whole thing already felt kind of creepy."

"Kind of," she replied. "Okay, well, thanks. And thanks for the number. If we need anything, we'll call." She pushed a cat back from the door with her foot and then closed it with a shove.

Trevor stepped back off the porch, down to the front walk, then turned to look up at the house. He thought he saw something move behind the third-floor window, but he decided he was mistaken. No one was there.

❧

"It's ten after," Leon said.

"I know," Karyn replied. "I thought she'd be home by five, but I guess not."

Karyn was annoyed that Salem was not back from the library, but she couldn't wait any longer—they would have to start without her. It was weird seeing Julian's backpack on the kitchen table; he never went anywhere without it. It was like a tiny body awaiting an autopsy, a comparison that made her shiver for even thinking it.

"I've already checked," Leon said. "There's not much in it. Nothing that tells us when he disappeared or where he might be."

Karyn and Leon had been together for nearly two years, both bi, both poly, both exhausted. They kept and paid for separate rooms in the house so that Karyn could sleep with her ex from time to time and Leon could snore.

"He could still be perfectly safe somewhere," Jared said. "We shouldn't call the cops if we can avoid it." Jared's long hair and scraggly beard, rotating collection of concert T-shirts and hoodies, and the vague green haze of weed that followed him wherever he went made him a particular target for authority figures of every kind.

"I think we'd all like to avoid that if we can," Karyn agreed. She had called 51 Division earlier, but they had no record of anyone picking up Julian, and no particular interest in his whereabouts. "Who was the last one to see him here in the house?" She looked at Leon, then Jared. They both looked like they were struggling with some difficult math problem. "I saw him Friday night at dinner," she prompted.

"I wasn't here Friday night, but I saw him Saturday morning," said Leon. "He was making breakfast when I went out to the library. By the time I got back, he was gone for the day. And I think I was out the door on Sunday before he woke up. I haven't seen him since."

"Okay," Karyn said, jotting down LEON – SAT MORN on the note-pad she kept by the phone. "Jared?"

"I guess for me it was Friday. We were all here for dinner, right? That was the last time. He just read and ate, didn't say much really, and then went up to his room after."

"Okay, Jared and Karyn, Friday dinner," she said, writing it out in block letters on the pad. Thinking back, she realized that Julian had barely spoken at dinner, and had barely eaten. Something had been bothering him. Was he in some kind of trouble?

"Wait," Jared said. "There's something else. I got up a little after midnight to go to the bathroom, and I could hear him talking to some-one, I could hear him from the hallway."

"So, you saw him Friday at midnight," Karyn confirmed, noting it down.

"Well, I didn't actually see him. But yeah. Who would he be talking to? Everyone else was either in bed or out somewhere, and no one else came by. So maybe—to himself?"

"It might have been a tape recorder," Leon suggested. "He could have been listening to a lecture, or dictating some notes."

"I did think that at first," Jared replied. "But now, I don't know, it was more like an actual conversation—or half of one. Which doesn't make sense. There's no phone up there."

The front door swung open and Salem burst in, holding the EMERGENCY HOUSE MEETING 7 PM sign that had been taped to the door. "Sorry I'm late!" she shouted, then began to divest herself of her bright-red down-filled parka, her various woolly scarves, her bulky hand-knit mittens, her chunky polar snow boots. She shook out her wheat-blond hair and gave her rosy-red cheeks and nose a rub to warm them up as she hurried into the kitchen. "What is it? What's going on?"

"Julian is missing," Karyn said. "Like, 'more than twenty-four hours' missing. We're just trying to figure out who was the last to see him."

"Oh, okay, weird," she said, lifting the teapot on the table and peeking inside to see what was brewing. "Um, I saw him Sunday? Like, Sunday night? You were there," she said to Karyn, and Karyn shook her head.

"Yeah, I was here with you on Sunday, but Julian wasn't. He never came home after his meeting." Karyn drew a little round face with little devil horns on the notepad for no particular reason.

"Of course he did, he came right through the front door, all bundled up," Salem said as she pulled a blue ceramic mug out of the cupboard, gave it a rinse. "You were on the couch, I was in the blue chair watching *Murder, She Wrote*. I said hello and everything."

"Right," Karyn replied. "You ate all my pickles."

"I thought they were house pickles, not private pickles," Salem sighed. "Anyway. You probably didn't see him because you were knee-deep in *The Art of Courtly Love*." She poured some tea into her mug, leaning in to breathe some of the floral-scented steam.

"Did he say anything back?" Leon asked.

"No, I don't think he even looked at me, he just went upstairs. He's been in a mood for weeks."

Leon stared at her blankly. "Then how do you know it was him?"

The four of them looked at each other as the implications of Leon's question sank in.

A loud thud came from somewhere upstairs, making everyone jump a foot.

"It must be Marbles crashing around," said Jared, his heart racing. "Nothing to get excited about."

"Marbles is under the table," Salem said. Everyone peered under at once to find Marbles, a cozy cat with tortoiseshell fur, looking curiously back up at them.

"Then we should go up and see what it is," Karyn said, looking at Jared and Leon. "Or at least some of us should."

Another thud from upstairs, this one even louder. All four of them leapt to their feet and looked at each other. "Fine, I'll go first," Karyn said, sighing, and led the group through the front hallway towards the stairs, then turned and saw that Leon was grabbing the oven mitts from beside the stove.

"Just in case," he said, pulling them on. "I don't want to get bitten by anything."

One after the other, they crept up the stairs until they were all standing in the second-floor hallway. Julian's bedroom was on the third floor at the front of the house, facing out onto the street. A swirl of cool air played with Karyn's hair. "Is his window open?"

"It wasn't earlier," Jared answered. His room was also on the third floor, across from Julian's, facing the alley.

Leon rolled his eyes. "Then something broke the glass. Hold on." He moved to the front and started onto the stairs. "Jared, you're the tallest. Go get a bath towel and hold it like a net." A bat had found its way into Leon's parents' house when he was a child, causing two hours of mayhem that he didn't want to relive.

Jared ran around to the washroom and hurried back with a large wine-coloured bath sheet clutched in his hands. Leon motioned for him to hold two corners in each hand and spread his arms wide, then turned around, made his way to the top-floor landing, and placed his hand on the door. Ice-cold.

He opened the door a crack, slipped his hand inside, flicked on the light switch. Nothing. He let out a groan. "I'm going in," he whispered. "Everyone else stay back." He threw the door open, quickly stepped inside, and closed it behind him. Then turned around to face the room.

It was a shambles.

"Holy shit," he exclaimed.

"What is it?" Karyn asked from the other side of the door.

"Nothing, just—wait. Don't come in." Leon knew that Karyn was famously squeamish. She couldn't squash a bug; this would send her over the edge.

He inched into the room, stepping carefully to avoid the glass on the floor but otherwise taking everything in.

The upper pane of the window was shattered; how they hadn't heard it was anyone's guess. And there were spatters of blood and muck everywhere—the walls, the bed, the door. Books were out of their shelves, papers were off the desk and all over the floor, Julian's huge shrink-wrapped Hockney poster was torn, the ceiling light was smashed. *What the hell did all this?*

On the floor, among the books, were the partial remains of a small animal, gutted, maybe a chipmunk. The head and one of the legs were missing; the rest was shredded, matted with blood. A kestrel or a merlin, he guessed. They lived in the eaves and nested on rooftops all over downtown. They mostly went after pigeons, but the larger ones caught rodents, sometimes even small dogs. Death from above. Something must have chased it right through the glass—another larger hawk, or possibly an owl. Everything was hungry at this time of year. From what he could tell, it crashed through the window, flew around in a daze banging into everything, prey in its claws, and then somehow flew back out. He carefully peered out the window into the twilight. Bits of glass glinted on the roof, on the front walk. Nothing on the lawn or in the street beyond.

He turned back, pulled off the oven mitts, knelt down, and picked up the book on the floor next to the corpse. It was an old journal of some kind, red leather binding, faded gold on the spine. It felt, and smelled, like something you'd find in a grave. He opened the cover, held it up to the light from the window. It was all handwritten, but not by Julian—or anyone who still walked the earth, it seemed. The first few pages looked strange, a language he didn't know. Numbered sections, like lessons or verses. Then some French, some English and Spanish. A half-dozen blank pages. Then a few lines of German.

Ich liebe dich, mich reizt deine schöne Gestalt;
Und bist du nicht willig, so brauch ich Gewalt.

A terrified scream made Leon jump to his feet, clutching the book to his chest. He spun around to find the door open, where Jared and Salem were holding Karyn, who had collapsed in some kind of shock. Jared helped her lie down on the floor in the entryway and told Salem to get her a glass of water and a cool, damp cloth.

Leon knelt down beside her. "Why are you in here? I told you all to stay out!"

"I saw him," Karyn said, wide-eyed. "Right there, right there on the bed, he was naked and—"

"Who was on the bed?" Jared asked.

"*Julian*, he was—open—screaming—his insides, everywhere, and—"

"It was the blood," said Jared. "She saw it on the wall and the floor and, I don't know, she fell back on top of me—"

"*I saw him!*" she shouted. "And someone else too. Next to you," she whispered sharply at Leon. "This—thing on his head, a hood, or a mask, like an animal, he was—reaching for you, he—" She began to gasp and gasp, her chest heaving, her eyes like saucers.

"Jesus Christ," Leon snapped, then shouted: "Salem, grab her puffer, it's on her dresser!"

Salem raced up the stairs, holding out the little brown cylinder like a baton. Leon grabbed it and placed it in Karyn's mouth, helped her squeeze it, helped her breathe. Instinctively, the others breathed along with her, in and out, in and out, until everyone grew quiet.

Jared cleared his throat. "I guess now's a good time to tell you all that I'm moving."

Once they helped Karyn back to her bedroom, they all agreed to sit with her in shifts in case the asthma returned. She insisted she was fine, refused to go to the hospital, but also claimed she couldn't remember anything that had happened in Julian's bedroom or in the hallway upstairs. She had blacked out. It was just as well.

Leon relieved Salem just after eleven, and was surprised to find Karyn still awake. "I cleaned up Julian's room," he said. "Taped some plastic over the window. I'll call the police tomorrow. It doesn't seem like we have much choice."

"You'll tell them about the backpack?" she asked.

"It's really the only thing we have," he answered. "I'll tell them it was found in the park. Maybe there's something else there under the snow."

"Or maybe they arrested him. Or he might be in the hospital."

"Yeah," he said. "Lots of possibilities."

She let out a long yawn, put her hands under the pillow, turned away from the light of the bedside lamp. "I love you," she sighed. "I'm sorry I scared everyone." He could barely hear her.

"I love you too," he whispered back. "And that's okay, we were all scared. I hope somebody finds him."

"Me too," she said sleepily, "but I don't think they will."

"What makes you say that?" he asked, but she didn't answer. A silence fell between them, and a few moments later she was sound asleep.

He sat watching her until one thirty, when Jared came to relieve him. Then Salem and then Leon once again, and by then the sun was just starting to rise.

When Salem came down around noon, Leon was at the kitchen table waiting for her with the red notebook. "Hey, you know more about this stuff than I do. What do you make of this?" he asked. "Different handwriting on every page, a lot of different languages. It must be a hundred years old."

She took it from him, looked at the front, the back, the spine. "Oh wow," she said. "Where did this come from?" It had been beautiful once, but now looked like it had been kicked around the block about fifty times. And it smelled—musty and acidic. Water had gotten to it at some point; the boards were strangely spongy underneath the thin red leather covers.

"Julian's room. It was on the floor in all the mess. It's not from school or the library. Can you make out anything inside?"

She opened it, flipped through it, wrinkled her nose. "It looks like some kind of commonplace book," she answered. "Normally, you'd just see one person's writing, but this looks like it's been passed around. German, Italian, this looks like Greek. This at the front could be Gaelic. I don't know a ton, though I should, my family's full of fucking leprechauns." She held it under the light, looking at the page more closely. "Let's see. Glas is lock—doras is door—and iuchair, I think, is key. So, I'm going to say: 'Every door has a lock, every lock has a key.'" She turned a few more pages, stopping to look at one then another. "Any idea where he got it?"

Leon shook his head. "I bet it would be worth something if it wasn't in terrible shape."

She flipped a few more pages, stopped at a passage in French. The writing was tiny and cramped, and strangely difficult to focus on. She read it out loud, feeling her way through the words:

Ce monstre horrible à double têtes
Passant ne t'effraye il pout
Et toute-fois o grosse bête
Tu las a tes côtés allez souvent conjoint

"It's something about a beast with two heads, right?" Leon asked.

She nodded. "'This horrible monster with two heads, passing by, does it not frighten you? But, great beast, your two sides are often married.' Connected. Conjoined. Something." She handed it back to him.

Leon opened it to what looked like an old English poem or song. "'D'ye ken that bitch whose tongue was death? D'ye ken her sons of peerless faith?' I have no idea what that is." The next page was blank, and the one after was covered with tiny red crosses, dozens and dozens of them, crushed up against the margins, crashing and careening down to the bottom edge. The following page had just one huge crimson *X*, scrawled and gouged from corner to corner, taking up the entire surface, piercing it, tearing through it. Whatever the smell was, blood or infection or the sick, sweet smell of carrion, it was coming from this page. Something about it felt alive, awake. Curious.

He ran his fingers over it and the ink spread to them, staining them. The tiny shreds of paper uncurled at his touch. Words and letters crawled out from under the other pages like insects, crawled up and onto his hands.

"Leon?" Salem half shouted, shocking him back into the moment.

He looked back down at his fingers. They were dry, unmarked. And the page itself was clean and blank except for a few water stains along the ragged edge. *Jesus. Did I sleep at all last night?*

"Sorry, I lost you there," she said.

"No no, it's okay," he replied. He could still feel the prickliness on his hands, like bugs just under the skin. *Pins and needles.* He rubbed his palms together and the feeling slowly subsided.

"I wanted to know if I could hold on to it for a while," Salem said. "The book. There are a few things in there that I'd like to transcribe. We can put it back in his room when I'm done. Or I can just give it back to you."

"Uh, yeah," he said, handing the book back to her. "Sure. No rush. Take your time."

The next day was Salem's trans support meeting at the 519 with her friends Trace and Sydney. Every once in a while, someone new showed up, but mostly it was the three of them. It didn't help that Trace kept changing the name of the group. This month, it was Genderation X. In December, it was TransCanada Truck Stop. Sydney was knitting yet another scarf, this time for Trace, so it was in greens and blues and blacks—"blowfly colours," at her request—and Trace was up at the flip chart listing trans movie and TV role models, arguing that *Dynasty's* Krystle Carrington as played by Linda Evans was definitely covertly MTF. The other role models were Martine Beswick in *Dr. Jekyll and Sister Hyde*, Tura Satana in *Faster, Pussycat! Kill! Kill!*, the secretary in *Ferris Bueller's Day Off* ("Edie McClurg!" Sydney shouted), and Jodie Foster in *Candleshoe*. Really, it was just an excuse for them to hang out, eat different flavours of chips, compare notes on their various doctors and employers and housemates, and fool around with fruit-scented markers.

"Sydney," Salem asked, "you lived in Berlin for a year once, didn't you? How much German do you know?"

"Not as much as Nina Hagen. Why do you ask?"

True to form, Trace wrote NINA HAGEN on the list of trans role models.

Salem turned around to take the old red book out of her shoulder bag and saw that the bag was unzipped, wide open, and the book was no longer inside it. "Oh, shit," she said as she reached in and felt around the sides and bottom.

"What's wrong?" Sydney asked. "Did you lose something?"

"Yeah, I think so. Bloody hell." Her wallet was there, her little plaid makeup case, her three pairs of sunglasses, her keys, her school work, her Vi Subversa mixtape, her *Everywoman's Almanac* with the turtle on the cover. "There was this weird old notebook that I wanted to show you. We found it in Julian's bedroom. But I guess the zipper came open." She'd have to tell Leon as soon as she got home. He was probably going to be pissed. She doubted the book had anything to do with Julian's disappearance, but it might've meant something to him.

"Our time's pretty much up. Should we head out and look for it?" Trace asked. "Get some hot chocolate along the way?"

Salem nodded. Even if they could retrace her steps, it was unlikely they would find it. It was probably long gone by now. But a cup of hot chocolate with whipped cream and sprinkles and those little marshmallows did sound like a good idea.

❧

The first warm spring weekend in the Village was a colourful, chatty event. Everyone who had been cooped up inside over the winter or smothered in parkas and snow boots was out and about to stretch their legs, see who was around, and catch up, even if it was still cold enough to see your breath.

Trevor was sitting out in front of Second Cup, finishing his first coffee of the day. The steps were already crowded with guys cruising and gossiping, recounting the drama from the bars the previous night and making plans for the evening to come. He stared out across the street towards the video store and, next to it, Bar 501. Bedelia Bidet, one of the city's more popular queens, was standing on the stage in the window, and a small crowd had gathered outside to watch. Dirty Bingo. "Under the O, sixtynine!" she shouted. When he was growing up, a gay bar with street-level windows was out of the question. Now, a mother and daughter joined the crowd to watch; she must have been about ten years old. Bedelia waved to her sweetly, and said, "Eat all your vegetables or you'll end up like me!"

Couples and trios darted in and out of bookstores and butcher shops, bags of groceries in one hand, bundles of tulips in the other. It seemed like fully a third of the businesses on Church Street had changed since Christmas. Now it was gay bar, gay card shop, gay café, gay diner, florist, fruit market, wine store, with Coming Soon! signs posted in a few empty restaurants and storefronts, no doubt in anticipation of Pride weekend. Every other window had a rainbow sticker in its bottom corner. Some had black stickers with pink triangles stating "Silence = Death."

Trevor was watching two couples try to untangle their terriers' leashes when Robin sat down beside him, regal in her age-old leather biker jacket, vintage pleated tuxedo shirt, cuffed Levi's, and black Frye boots.

"Are you warm enough in that?" he asked. "We can go inside."

"I'm fine, I generate my own heat," Robin replied. "I'll go grab something in a few minutes, I just need to catch my breath."

Trevor moved aside to let a pair of moms squeeze past with their stroller. "What have you been up to since New Year's? How was Vancouver?"

"Warmer, rainy, of course. Good venue, the place was packed. It was a circuit party, so, you know. But nobody asked to touch my hair. Nobody called security. And I got about two hundred dollars in tips, so a great night all-round. There's not much out there for women like me, though, just wispy New Age types named Willow and Aspen and boys, boys, boys."

"I should move," Trevor replied.

She gave him a smack on the shoulder. "What about you? How did you survive the winter? Did you at least get some decent flights?"

"Mexico, Cuba, and Saint Lucia. And I took a week for myself in Puerto Vallarta, where every man I met was from Toronto." He rolled his eyes. "But that was just January and February, and now my tan's all gone and so are the men."

"So, speaking of travel, I have some news," Robin said.

Trevor studied her face but couldn't tell if the news was good or bad.

"Paulo, you remember Paulo."

"I slept with Paulo, but yes, I also remember Paulo," Trevor answered.

"Right, well, he came out to Vancouver and saw my set, which is literally his job, but let's not talk about that. It turns out—he got me a gig in Ibiza, at Space—which, I can tell you don't know what that is, it's one of the biggest clubs in the world, and it's such a huge deal."

"Oh, cool." Trevor's expression was slightly off—happy because he knew he should be, but also tense, anxious. "When does all this happen?"

"I'm going to play a few nights in early June," she said, "and if they like me, I might get some more gigs and maybe a shot on their terrace, which could lead to other gigs all over Europe. Okay, say you're excited for me."

"I'm excited for you," Trevor replied. "I thought Ibiza was all rich kids and Eurotrash. And straight people."

"Okay, try to be a little more excited," Robin said. "Seriously, this is big. It may not be the whole summer. It might only be a few weeks. But if it works out, I could really make a name for myself."

"I'm excited, really I am," Trevor replied. "The summer won't be the same without you. But it sounds really great and you deserve every good thing that happens there."

"It's only one night so far, let's not get too ahead of ourselves. Besides, you don't need me to have a great summer." She looked over at him and saw something pass over his face. "Is everything all right? I need to know that we're cool. Are we cool?"

"We will always be cool," Trevor replied. "We are the coolest."

"That's why I love you best," Robin said, pulling him in for a hug. "Did you want a coffee? I'm getting a coffee."

"No, no," said Trevor as he stood up, "I'll get the coffee. I have their little punch card. How do you want it?"

"Tall, black, sweet—like me." Robin gave Trevor an extra squeeze, then sat back down on the step as Trevor ducked into the shop. She could tell he was feeling conflicted, that her news had come out of left field. These last few months had been hard; they had rarely been in the same city. Maybe he worried they were drifting apart, which was the last thing she wanted him to feel.

Trevor reappeared, handed the taller cup to Robin, sat back down beside her. Something was up. "Okay, so. I also have some news. Some less happy news." He let out a short, sharp sigh. "I was tested a few weeks ago, and it came back positive."

"Oh shit, Trevor. I'm so sorry," said Robin, reaching for him and pulling him close. "And here I am babbling all my nonsense. Are you all right? What do the doctors say? Have they put you on medication?"

"That's just it. All we have is AZT, and it sucks. Most people can only go on it for a year, and then it becomes too toxic. You might as well drink bleach. So, the other news is—I'm entering a drug trial. Like, immediately. From what I can tell, I'd be taking a combination of drugs, instead of just one. It looks promising, though I guess they all do at the start."

"That's great news," she exclaimed. "They wouldn't try these things if they didn't think it might help. But listen, I can just do the one gig and come back. Or do one in June, and one or two others over the summer. And if you want me to come back, I will. One call and I'm on the next plane."

"Oh, come on, you can't do that," he sighed. "Like you said, this could be the turning point. I'd still be here when you got back."

"Of course you will," she said. "It's only a few months, and maybe not even that."

"I'll be okay." He shrugged. "I'm set up with a counsellor, and my doctor suggested a discussion group thing. I might try that. I just don't want to end up like Victor."

Robin nodded, let the moment unfold. Trevor's lover, Victor, had found out he was positive two years ago, and had come apart completely. Robin and Trevor sat with him the day he was diagnosed as he just cried and cried. "What about my job?" he asked. "What about my family?" Trevor didn't know what to say. Victor had always been the strong one, the resilient one, the one who had his life together. Other people came to him for advice, for support, sometimes even for under-the-table jobs and loans that turned into gifts. He was so afraid of being judged, of having to depend on other people. He couldn't see how he could still be strong in the face of this. Ten days later, he just disappeared. On his birthday. Some joggers came across his clothes by the edge of the water. His body was never found.

"You're not going to end up like Victor," she said. "You're already not like him. He lost hope the moment they told him, and he never really got it back. If you start thinking like that, I will fly back here and kick your ass."

"My ass is pale and skinny and you would break it to bits. But don't screw up your career over me, or I'll be kicking yours." Trevor put his arm around her, and her head settled on his shoulder. "Hey, check it out," he said suddenly. "Somebody likes you."

Robin scanned the area where Trevor was looking and saw a brooding young guy standing across the street, next to the bar, just standing there and staring back. *You see me.* Black hair, old boots, grey trousers, suspenders, baggy white shirt. Something about him was familiar.

"Yeah, he's not my type," she said tartly. "And I doubt that I'm his."

"Never say never," Trevor said teasingly. He looked back across the street. "Ah, you missed your chance, he's gone."

Sure enough, the boy wasn't where he'd been standing, wasn't with the crowd by the window. Wasn't anywhere on the street. Poof, like a magic trick.

"Yeah, well. The Village is a small town in a big city," she replied. "Everyone sees everyone sooner or later. Besides, if someone really wants me, I'm not that hard to find."

Late that night, as the owls flew up from the valley, their eyes wide and their ears attuned to their prey, Robin quietly shifted box upon box in her storage closet, not wanting to wake her already hypersensitive neighbours downstairs. The closet had no light of its own, and she didn't have a flashlight even though she needed one roughly three times a year, so she relied on the thin slice of light cast from the hallway to aid her search.

Finally, in the far back corner, she uncovered a black nylon organizer full of cassette tapes. She pulled it out, unzipped the sides, and flipped it open. Twilight Zone, the Chez, the Rose, Stages, Club Z, Empire, BamBoo. All the slots but one were filled. She looked around on the floor, in the box below, then back at the tapes in the organizer. Every single slot had a tape tucked into it, except for the one that had held the dub she made for Ryan at Boots all those years ago. That slot was empty. The tape she wanted was gone.

Again. They were here again, outside my bedroom window.
I heard them, saw their shadows on the curtain. I pulled
it back--nothing. No one. Then all night, whispers and
scrapings and whistles and sighs, no sleep at all.
And this morning, just for a moment, in the garden, I
thought I saw it, tattered and red, glints of gold, but
I know that can't be true.

I was not a well child, nor a strong one. Shorter and
thinner than the other boys at school, I suffered a
litany of frustrating, isolating illnesses--bronchitis,
digestive disorders, ringworm from someone's cat--that
further alienated me from my classmates and threw my
oddness and queerness into high relief. My pediatrician
was skilled at soothing my mother's concerns, but clumsy
and callous when it came to the countless invasive pro-
cedures that our visits required, like administering
booster shots and digging out deep-rooted moles.

While I dreaded every visit to his office, I developed an unusual fascination, nearly an obsession, with
a Christian-themed children's book of bedtime stories
in his waiting room, and looked forward to reading it
whenever I could. We were not a religious family. I
knew what Christmas was, and Easter, but we never went
to church or said grace unless we had company, and we
talked little of God in our day-to-day lives. But in
this book, I remember one story where a young boy is
struck by a car and taken to the hospital. It's clear
he's going to die. He wants to know how Jesus will know
it's time to come take him to Heaven, and he's told by
another child that he should just raise his arm when the

time is right and Jesus will see him. And later that
night, the boy dies with his arm upraised in hope that
Jesus will come. This passage was accompanied by a vivid
illustration of the boy in his hospital bed, his head
and left arm wrapped in bandages, his eyes closed, his
right arm propped up, his hand hanging limply, while
Jesus stands at the side and reaches for it.

I had nightmares for years because of that story and
that image, nightmares where something came for me as
I raised my hand, as I lay dying, while Jesus stood back
in the shadows. And yet I read it every time I sat in
that waiting room, and stared at that picture until my
name was called. A few years ago, I found the book online
and ordered it, then promptly mislaid it. Possibly on
purpose. It's around the apartment somewhere.

Fear has always fascinated me, especially my own.
I'm afraid of practically everything: water, heights,
crowds, enclosed spaces, open spaces, loud noises,
flying, driving, the dark, birds, dolls, babies, flying
and jumping insects and spiders, being lost, being
watched. I am an anxious person, ever since I was an
anxious child. High-strung, I think was the term they
used then.

I enjoy being scared in relative safety, where I have
some measure of control. I love to watch horror movies
and read horror stories, to plummet down roller coasters
and cower through spooky amusement park rides. I have

mined my own fears in my writing, aware that exploring and immersing myself in them can sometimes fuel
them, can increase their power and their hold on my mind
rather than diminish it. And yet, for some reason, it's
irresistible to me. Many people try to ignore or deny
or suppress their fears. I find myself drawn to mine,
worrying them, troubling them, like a tongue against a
tooth clinging to sore and bloody gums. I want to understand where my fears come from, and why, and how they
have such a grip on me.

I remember taking a trip downtown with my mother when I
was five or six. We must have been shopping for clothes
for the start of school. All the seats on the bus were
taken, so we had to stand. There was a man a few feet
behind my mother--she didn't see him, but I did. He
looked at me and smiled, and made funny faces that
were supposed to make me laugh--crossed eyes, clownish
mouth--but they didn't. The faces frightened me, and his
regular face--ordinary, mildly handsome--for some reason
scared me more. There was something about him that made
me feel odd inside, and that feeling seemed wrong somehow. I was being singled out for attention, a kind of
attention that troubled me. Plus, he was a stranger,
which made it even worse.

Soon, it was time to get off the bus, so my mother and
I stepped through the gate and down the two steps and
out onto the street. I stopped and turned back to try
to see him, but I couldn't, the bus had pulled away too
quickly. For a moment, I thought he might have gotten
off with us, that he might try to follow us, but he was

nowhere to be seen. And then my mother yelled for me and
I ran to catch up with her.

After this, I was always afraid of strange men following us, or following me, watching me, in the store or
at the playground or on my way to and from school. As I
grew older, this fear of strange men and what they might
do (never articulated, only ever hinted at) evolved
into a fear of gay men--of being pursued by them, of
being associated with them, of being teased or arrested
or assaulted or killed along with them. Of course, the
flip side of fear is desire, isn't it? It's remarkable
how many of my fears are queer. Anxiety in gay spaces,
in sexual or sexualized spaces. Strip bars, back rooms,
bathhouses, public washrooms, parks at night. The over-
whelming crowds at Pride. An internalized, and sometimes
externalized, homophobia.

But my life in fear really began when I was about eleven
years old, when I woke up early on a Sunday morning to
find myself fully paralyzed from head to toe, barely
able to breathe, and unable to make a sound.

I had travelled alone with my father to visit his
family on the outskirts of Sandy Lake, about two hundred miles outside Winnipeg. It was the year after my
father's brother Nick died. He had been much younger
than my father, handsome like a matinee idol, and had
recently become a professor with a Ph.D. in Chemistry at
the University of Manitoba. Unmarried, no girlfriend,

a very private person, lonely in the same way that I
was. He was my earliest crush. He brought gifts, he
gave me books, he answered my questions about how the
world worked. He had given me a cigar box full of little
treasures when he'd last visited: a large, sharp bear
tooth (it could have been from a dog), a pearl-handled
penknife, a tiger's eye marble, a red toy car from his
childhood, a brown, glasslike stone he said was obsid-
ian. He was just thirty-one when he was killed in a car
accident, a head-on collision in winter, an hour before
dawn. The other driver was uninjured. I was too young to
go to the funeral, and spent the day crying at my cousins' place instead. I was haunted by his sudden absence,
wondered if somehow I was to blame, if I could have
said something or done something, given him something,
learned something from him, that would have sent him on
a different trajectory, towards life, towards us.

It must have been May or June, after the snow was
gone. My father and I would have driven up early on
a Saturday, with the intention of spending the night
and returning around suppertime on Sunday. My younger
brother refused to go--there were no other children to
play with and there was nothing on TV, as they didn't
have cable--which meant my mother had to stay home with
him (something they may have both preferred). So Dad
and I packed ourselves into our old two-tone mint-blue
Oldsmobile and made our way out of the city and into the
gently sloping countryside. We stopped at Sandy Lake
Cemetery along the way, and visited Nick's grave, which
had a sparkly grey granite stone and his name written in
Ukrainian: Миколая--Mykolya, or Nicholas. I had brought

the toy car with me, and when my dad was on his way back to the parking lot and was calling back to me to stop dawdling, I took it out of my pocket and set it at the bottom of the gravestone.

It's a bit more modern now, but back then Sandy Lake was a small, old-fashioned Ukrainian farming town, with many of the same stores, silos, houses, and barns you'd have seen in the thirties. The older generation spoke little or no English, and relied on their children and grand-children to help them deal with the outside world--with calls and letters and forms from the government, with strangers looking for directions, with men from the city wanting to buy up their land. There were few other kids my brother's age or mine, mostly cousins who came in for holiday weekends the way we did, or visited for special reasons. Dad was in to kill chickens and to help with some repairs, plus some semi-annual chores around the house that required extra hands: mending fences, mowing and baling hay, cleaning and organizing the barn, taking equipment into town for maintenance, helping my grand-mother prepare the house for the inevitable visits from aunts and uncles and cousins.

Everyone at the farm was friendly to me, but my grand-mother spoke maybe a dozen words of English (though she understood much more) and my grandfather spoke none at all. My uncle Tony spoke English well and could be charm-ing, but he had the most work to do, so we didn't spend much time together. Mostly I was on my own, exploring around the barn and the outbuildings, visiting the cows and pigs and chickens, or walking the mile-long road that led into town. This was back when a boy my age could walk alone in the country and no one would think twice about it. Cars and trucks and tractors drove past; none ever stopped or slowed or called out to ask if I was okay. And so, to escape the screeching and flapping of the chickens, the thud of the axe, I would make my way to the general store, which had torn-open boxes of nails and screws, bolts of burlap and cotton ticking, some basic groceries, a few cheap but colourful plastic toys and dusty old board games, and a counter full of chocolate bars and gumballs and Tootsie Rolls and Dum Dums. That store was probably my favourite place on earth. After visiting, I would sit on the stoop and eat a Lowney's Cherry Blossom, or some Mackintosh's Toffee that would tear my fillings out if I wasn't careful, or a giant jawbreaker that would colour my fingers and stain my tongue blue, and then I would wander back home.

We likely had a big supper that night--my grandmother and grandfather, Tony, my father and me--and went to bed fairly early, as my grandfather would have been back by the barn or out in the field before dawn. I was on the living room floor with my father on a spare mattress he carried in from Nick's room, and we were under a heavy feather coverlet that poked me with quills from time to time and made me itch. It got dark fast in the country; the sky was strewn with stars we never saw in the city, and the moon was huge and filled every room with cold, clear light.

I must have woken up around four thirty or five, the house dark and silent as everyone slept. I was trapped

under the covers and overheating and unable to push
them aside. My body was stiff and sore, my arms and
legs drained of strength. Something was terribly wrong.
I tried to call out and could only huff, and it was then
that I realized I was unable to pull air into my lungs,
and, only making things worse, I began to gasp and gasp.

I discovered I could move my back, my spine--an inch or
two one way and an inch or two the other--and that with
tremendous effort and determination I could shift my
shoulders and hips like a lizard and squirm my way out
from under the covers and onto the floor. It took ten or
fifteen minutes, but felt like forever. Once I was on
the floor and felt how cold it was, with just my pyjamas
and bare feet, I realized I had made a mistake and had
to figure out what to do next. I couldn't get back onto
the mattress; at five or six inches, it was too high off
the ground for me to wriggle back up onto it. I still
couldn't use my hands, arms, or legs. So instead, I again
wormed my way towards the couch, hoping that by the time
I reached it, someone would have woken up and found me,
or that at least my voice would have returned.

My best guess is that I was on the floor shivering and
gasping for at least thirty minutes before my grandfather's alarm began to ring and then abruptly stopped.
A few minutes later, he emerged from his bedroom in his
work shirt and grey striped overalls, walking directly
towards me, then suddenly turned in to the kitchen. He
hadn't heard me, hadn't seen me. I tried to cry out and
could only find a whisper. And then he was running water
for the kettle, and then more into a pot for porridge.

He set the pot on the stove with a clang, and after a
few moments, the water began to simmer. Tears streamed
down my face. Every sound seemed deafening. I knew
I would never be heard above them.

A few minutes later, my grandmother tottered out in
her nightgown and her sheepskin slippers, tying her
pink striped robe around herself. She too walked up
the hall towards me, not seeing me, not knowing that
I desperately needed to be seen. With all my effort,
I clenched the muscles on my right side and my arm
twitched outward, catching her eye. She let out a yelp
and then shouted my father's name: "Wasyl!"

He awoke with a start, sat up, and saw me on the floor.
By then, my teeth were chattering and my arms and legs
were lashed with sharp, searing pain. He threw the
feather comforter aside and rushed over, lifted me up,
and put me on the couch, feeling my forehead, my cheeks,
my hands, while my grandmother shouted things that I
couldn't understand. I tried to say a few words, but
could barely conjure a sigh. My dad leaned in to hear me
and I managed to croak out, "Hot bath."

He picked me up, carried me to the bathroom, pulled
off my clothes and put me in the tub, and began to run
increasingly hot water over me. I could feel the warmth
returning to my body, and with it came terrible pain.
I started to keen and wail. My dad reached into the water
and massaged my arms and legs, and tears were streaming
down his face too. My father rarely touched me--we were
just not that kind of family--and now to be touched at

a time like this. My grandmother stood in the doorway
watching, and I could see how frightened she was.

After about ten minutes, Dad drained the tub and helped
me sit up so that he could dry me off. I still couldn't
stand without help, so he laid another towel on the bath
mat and sat me down on it, then brought me back to the
living room to help me get dressed. Uncle Tony was up
now as well, and he and my dad and my grandparents all
talked rapidly in Ukrainian, I guess about what to do
with me. Dad turned and started packing up our things,
and that made me start to cry again. I loved being at
the farm; I didn't want to go back to the city, or to
the doctor, or to a hospital.

By this time, my hands and arms were regaining some of
their strength. I tried to move my legs, but, aside from
the soreness, they were still like heavy stones. My grandmother came in holding her beaded change purse and, to my
mortification, took out a ten-dollar bill for me. *Oh no,
she thinks that I don't want to be at the farm, that I
want to go home, she thinks I don't love them.* I tried to
refuse, but she kept pushing it into my hand. Tears were
welling at the corners of her eyes too, so I finally took
the money and clutched it as tight as I could while Dad
helped me out of the house and into the car.

We drove back in relative silence, the Sunday morning
worship shows cutting in and out on the radio as we
hurtled down the highway towards home. By the time
we arrived, the pain had subsided significantly and
I could walk on my own, albeit like Frankenstein's

monster. I went straight up to bed, leaving my dad to explain to my mother what had happened. She kept me home from school the following day and took me to the doctor. He checked me over, asked if anything still hurt, had me grip his finger tightly, made me push against his hands with my hands, my feet. Everything was fine. I was perfectly fine.

There was a dog, I remember that now. The graveyard had a gate, but the fence was just posts strung with chains. It must have slipped under, a mutt of some kind, lean and sleek, pacing among the stones and panting, squinting, hungry and probably wild. Nobody's dog. Burrs on the backs of its legs and its tail. My dad told me to get back in the car so I wouldn't get bitten. He picked up an old hockey stick from outside the gate, held it up in front of him, and shooed the dog out and across the road into the brush. It must've been beaten at one time or another--it knew what a stick was for.

The attacks continued, sometimes partial, sometimes total, throughout my adolescence and into my twenties and thirties. At forty, during a particularly intense and frightening episode, when my heart rate fell by half over a few hours to forty-five beats per minute, my then-boyfriend rushed me to the ER at St. Michael's Hospital and I was finally diagnosed with hypokalemic periodic paralysis--a rare genetic neuromuscular dis-order, potentially fatal, that affects one in 100,000 people, most of them Asian. Typically, the paralysis begins in the extremities and inexorably makes its way towards the core--the throat, bowels, lungs, and heart.

The killer is in the house, I thought to myself as I lay there. I still think it today.

My hypokalemia is largely controllable through diet and medication. ("Perogies are a side dish, not an entree," my hospital-assigned dietitian once sternly informed me.) Yet it remains my constant companion and my greatest threat. I have at least two or three attacks a week, sometimes as many as five or six. Even as I sit here, typing on the keyboard in my lap, I can feel my legs stiffen from the meal I had a few hours ago. Something in my body is a traitor, an adversary, a monster. It is my own Michael Myers, my Freddy Krueger, my Jason Voorhees. It's coming for me. I cannot escape. And one night, while I am lost in the maze of my dreams, it may finally catch me.

2000

That was the year that Devon Sawa reached his *Final Destination*, Madonna's retro-inflected *Music* was tearing up the dance floor, and *Buffy* was back to back with *Angel* on The WB. Most Internet users were still on dial-up and the cellphone of choice was a Nokia.

The city's LGBTQ communities were enraged over two police raids in the previous twelve months—the first on the Bijou, a controversial porno bar, and the second at the Club Baths during a queer women's event called the Pussy Palace (later known as the Pleasure Palace). All charges were dropped in both cases, raising questions about the policing of queer sexual spaces, the perception of queer sex as inherently criminal and adjacent to other criminal acts, and the deteriorating trust between the queer community and the police force and local government.

That was also the year two gay men went missing—Michael Larose, forty-six, and Suda Sabaratnam, thirty-seven. Though hardly anyone noticed.

❦

In the days leading up to Halloween, the air was cool and crisp, the leaves crunching underfoot. A few stray flakes of snow fell from the lead-grey skies throughout the week, causing typical Torontonian panic before they touched the ground and promptly melted. The businesses along Church were preparing for the annual street party that would close several blocks to traffic and pack the bars and clubs well past last call. Halloween brought out all the drag queens and costume fanatics, individually and in groups; some would charge for impromptu photo ops while others would hop from contest to contest hoping to score a cash prize or two.

The original Halloween parades of drag queens down Yonge Street in the sixties and seventies were pelted with eggs and ink and threatened with physical violence. Everyone had a story about a friend or lover who had been chased or beaten or worse. More than twenty years later, clubgoers were still encouraged to leave the Village in small groups and to take cabs or public transit. Bar patrons leaving with strangers were still advised to tell a friend where they'd be. Those looking for some post-party fun were encouraged to go to the baths instead of parks and other cruising grounds where they might be targeted by queer-bashers, the police, or both. The more we were accepted and embraced, the more a persistent hateful minority wanted to see us suffer.

Suda was twisting and turning in his sleep, caught in the clutches of a horrible dream. He was in a gay bar, huddling in a storage closet not much smaller than the space he rented in a rooming house on the edge of St. James Town. He could hear the police outside the door, but was more frightened by what was in the darkness with him.

Suda had arrived in Canada two years earlier, sponsored by his wife's brother to come on a visitor's visa to work in his restaurant. When the brother-in-law learned he was meeting men via the staff computer, he threw Suda into the street with a green garbage bag stuffed with all his possessions. He knew little English, had no other family, had made no real friends. He was pleasant but distant with his co-workers at the financial tower where he got a job cleaning offices and at the diner where he washed dishes for cash. The half-dozen men he'd met online, all of them white, all of them older, had enjoyed his company but made no attempt to meet a second time. Even with eight other residents in the rooming house, with a shared kitchen, bathrooms, living room, and laundry, Suda lived his life alone.

He had been swept up in the police raid on the Bijou sixteen months ago, and the resulting nightmares had steadily increased in their frequency and potency. In his dream, as on that night, Suda walked up Church Street and turned down the alley that led to the Bijou's entrance. There was a short lineup of men waiting to pay the cover charge and receive their wrist stamp. When his turn came to pay, he held out his wrist, but the doorman just waved him through. "We only have red ink tonight," he had said. "It won't show up on you." The doorman gave him a pat on the shoulder. "It's okay, I'll know who you are." His words were meant to be friendly and personal, but they had bothered him. Suda didn't want to be known. He didn't want to be seen.

Once he was buzzed through the door, he entered a dark, cavernous room with a dance area on the left and a bar straight ahead. Above it hung one of many large screens scattered throughout the space. Suda stood for a moment and watched the grainy, soundless video of a younger man on his knees sucking an older, muscled daddy type who was seated beside a fireplace. The younger man was half out of his tuxedo, satin bow tie hanging about his neck—his wedding day, presumably. Suda normally enjoyed porn, but something about the scene made him uneasy. He always found weddings to be the least erotic and most effortful events in one's life. Bad weather, terrible clothes, snide comments, tantrums, children always underfoot, parents and aunties so demanding, so much work and expense, and never a moment alone. And the last person he would want to have sex with was a relative.

A bartender waved Suda over to take his order. He didn't drink, which sometimes made him unpopular in bars, even with a cover charge. He had learned over time that it was best to order a ginger ale or a soda water and then leave a larger tip to compensate. Drink in hand, he stepped around the bar towards the back, where several viewing areas were set up—some with seating in rows like miniature movie theatres, some like conversation pits. Men were milling about, furtively checking each other. Nobody looked at him. Off to the side was the most notorious feature of the Bijou, the slurp ramp, an elevated area where several men could stand at glory holes cut into a plywood barrier while other men standing below could suck their cocks. It was a popular attraction, especially later in the evening, with men jerking themselves as they stood in line, but it was much too public for Suda. After completing his circle of the room, he left his drink at a nearby cocktail table and made his way to the one place where he felt comfortable: the dark room.

Most of the bathhouses and even a few of the bars had them (the Cellar, a Wellesley Street bathhouse hidden behind a black, unmarked door and down a treacherous flight of stairs, was essentially one large dark room), but few were as large and lightless as the one at the Bijou. Suda could stand at the door and look through to the far end and see nothing inside but vague shapes and silhouettes. He knelt down to tie his shoelace and, while doing so, slipped his wallet out of his pocket and into the leg of his sock. He loosened his belt, unfastened the top button of his jeans, and walked forward into the waiting darkness—free of his face, free of his skin, free of his jobs, his wife and parents and brother back in Colombo. He made it a kind of game in these rooms, to see how far he could walk before someone stopped him. This time, it was just over halfway. Cold, clammy hands slipped under his jacket and shirt to touch his densely furred chest, pulled down his pants to clutch the curve of his ass, the hardening mass in his crotch. They smelled like they had dug their way up and out of the earth to reach him. Two men, three men, they pulled him off to the side, against the rough, raw trunk of a tall, thick tree, pushed his mouth onto one cock and then another, the stars whirling across the night sky above the arching branches, the canopy of leaves, the ruined bodies of the long-dead emerging from behind bushes, pushing aside the tall grasses, the eyes of a thousand animals glittering in the darkness, and then two slimy, mouldering fingers pushed into him, reaching and probing, opening him, readying him—

"Police!" someone yelled in the distance, and the nightmare began in earnest. A flurry of confusion, more shouts. Glass smashing on the floor. Someone grabbed Suda by the hand and pulled him to the dark room's exit, pants and briefs still around his knees, hobbling him, house lights bursting on, blinding him, the hand pulling him out and around and into a cleaner's closet, a bolt snapping into place. More shouts. Shadows cutting back and forth across the crack of light at the bottom of the door. The acrid scents of bleach and ammonia, and something else. Burning flesh.

"Hello?" Suda whispered.

"*Shhhhh*," his rescuer breathed, soft and soothing. A tenderness washed over him, a feeling of safety, of belonging. Whoever was in here, he had known that Suda was alone, had needed help, and now was watching over him.

Footsteps just outside the door. One man, then another. "There was a little brown bastard," the first voice said, anger coiling like a snake. "He came past here, I saw him. When I find him, I'm going to fuck his throat with this."

"Hank, put the gun away," said the other voice, weak and pleading. "They've called it in, we're wrapping up. They've got who they need." A silence, then a sigh. "Come on, let's go."

Footsteps away from the door, chaos fading into silence. The light outside snapped off.

"Thank you," Suda whispered.

"Don't thank me," the voice whispered back. And then something around them changed, the room changed, no longer a room, warmer, humid, dripping, viscous, Suda reached for the door, reached for the wall, soft and lush and moist, guarded by a row of slick, sharp objects, the floor slippery and spongy, lifting him up and pulling him back and down, tumbling now, back through a huge, wet, hungry mouth and into an endless swallowing throat.

Suda's eyes sprang open. He threw his bedclothes to the side, gasping, lurching out of the bed, bare feet on the linoleum, heart thrashing, and he stood there, afraid to move, *not alone*, stood there, until the grey morning light crept in through the dirt-mottled window. In a few hours, he would start his shift at one of the tall towers, where he'd be vacuuming carpets, emptying wastebaskets, and scrubbing sinks and toilets from 6 a.m. till noon. These shifts were mercifully uneventful. But two days before, the last time he was in the building, he'd found an old red-covered notebook in one of the bathroom stalls. He picked it up, flipped through it, saw different words in different languages, and decided to leave it next to the sink, where the owner would hopefully see it. Near the back of the book, he was surprised to find a sentence in Tamil.

என்னிடம் வாருங்கள்.
Come to me.

❧

Michael Larose, known to many as Mikey, was sleeping in a laneway a few yards west of Church and Alexander when a piercing bright light shone in his eyes, waking him, and a pair of heavy, rough hands pulled him up out of his sleeping bag and onto his feet. *What now?* he thought, squinting against the glare. He was wearing one old battered running shoe, a half size too large, the other lost days before in a scuffle with some asshole who knocked his cup of change all over the street. He looked away from the light and saw a police car parked just a few feet away. He sighed. Swiftly, his hands were pulled behind his back, his wrists snapped into biting steel cuffs. He was pushed towards the cruiser until he fell on his knees, then his face, and then was picked up and dragged to the rear door and thrown on the seat. The officers never said a word, never showed ID. He never saw their faces.

Mikey had been arrested three times before for sleeping in public places and once for public intoxication. He had been taken to the drunk tank at 51 Division, the detox centre on Queen Street, Seaton House, and the Scott Mission. He'd been treated badly from time to time, shoved and kicked and sworn at and told to move along. He always obeyed as best he could, gathering his belongings and moving somewhere out of sight. *If you don't make trouble, you don't get trouble.* But now he had trouble, and he didn't know why.

He lay on the seat, his face hanging over the edge, afraid to move, afraid to speak. His nose was bleeding, drop after drop, down onto the rubber mat on the floor of the cruiser and trickling off to the carpet just under the seat. With one eye, he could watch the spill from the street lights race across the car's interior, could count the lights as they were passing, count the number of stops they made at signs and crossings. It was a long drive, every turn taking them farther east and south. He already knew what that meant. They were heading to Cherry Beach.

Mikey had heard about Cherry Beach even before he ended up on the street. An isolated strip of lakeshore in an industrial area at the eastern end of the city, it was one of those places where guys hooked up with each other, in the bushes and in their cars, and it was one of those places where police roughed up queer people, homeless people, anybody who needed to be taught a lesson. He remembered a song on the radio, years ago, a catchy pop song about the brutality that went on there, "Cherry Beach Express." The cops tried to get it taken off the air. Mikey had never been down there, but he had known guys over the years, some women too, who were taken in the middle of the night, beaten senseless, and left to walk back to the nearest hospital, more than an hour away on foot. He guessed that he had been lucky all this time, and now his luck had run out.

He felt a low metallic grumble under the wheels. The cruiser was crossing the Cherry Street Bridge. They were only a few minutes away.

Police Constable J. Henry Harris, known to his colleagues as Hank, sometimes Hank the Tank, slowed the cruiser as he reached the parking lot off Regatta Road, turned onto the gravel, stopped in front of a capped-off steel pipe sprayed with a red primer *X*, and gave the siren a brief blast. *That should drive those faggots out of the bushes.* No prying eyes. He nodded to his partner, Constable Tony Tosaro. Tony's instructions were to stay in the car and watch and listen for signs of trouble: lost or wandering civilians, emergency calls, visits from other cops. Dispatch listened in on their radios, so Tony had a signal, three clicks on the walkie, that he was supposed to use if anything went pear-shaped. But they'd never had a problem. Hank never spent more than fifteen minutes with these guys, and always came out alone.

Tony opened the glove compartment, pulled out a steel flask, took a swig. Offered it to Hank, who shook his head. Hank pulled a dark-blue bandana out from under his jacket collar, tugged it up over the bottom half of his face. Tony did the same. Hank stepped out of the vehicle, slammed the driver's door shut, opened the rear door and reached into the back seat, pulled the rubby out by his shabby plaid overshirt, and half pushed, half dragged him away from the lot, down to the old Quonset hut where the trees met the shore. Tony had watched Hank do this at least a dozen times; a few times, he'd come back to the car wiping blood off his hands. He never asked what Hank did to these guys down there. He didn't want to know. *Proactive deterrence*, he called it one night at the bar, and his buddies all laughed. Tony didn't laugh. Hank had what a shrink might call "unresolved anger issues," and he wasn't picky about where he expressed them. He was a good guy, Hank was, and a good partner, but sometimes he wasn't.

Tony switched on the FM, turned the dial to Q107. Bon Jovi was singing "It's My Life" and Tony couldn't help singing along. He reached over to turn it up louder, and something poked him in the thigh. He reached into his pocket and pulled out a red ludo playing piece. Angelo must have tucked it in there; he was all about hiding things now, strange things in strange places. Tony had found a dead bird in his shoe the other day. He didn't say anything to Ella, but maybe he should have. He'd mention it to her once he got home, if she was still awake. Maybe she knew what was going on with him.

Once Hank was finished, he wiped himself off, pulled his pants up, tucked in his shirt, unfastened the cuffs, took his belt from around the bum's neck, and slipped it back around his waist. A rush of dizziness washed over him, and he put his hand onto a nearby tree to catch his breath. He was getting old, no doubt about it, he couldn't fuck up a punk the way he did even a few years ago, but he still did pretty all right for himself. Finished with a nice donkey punch, that was good. Give the little fucker credit, he barely made a sound. Tough little bitch right to the end. Hank did like a bit of noise, a grunt and a groan, a whimper or two, liked to know he was making an impact. He looked down and saw he had a smear of blood on the toe of his shoe and wiped it across the rubby's naked ass, then gave him a nudge with it. Nudged him again. Gave his head a little push. And then leaned in close with his flashlight.

Fucker's not breathing.

Shit.

And DNA fucking everywhere, just fucking great.

Hank looked around. He had to think fast, stay cool, *focus*. He had about five minutes tops before Tony started clicking the radio and then maybe came down here after him. The water, from where they were, was maybe thirty feet away, and some of that in the deep shadows of the willows. He could just carry the body down in behind the hut and dump it there. The water over here wasn't safe to swim in, there'd been signs up all summer long, so no one was likely to find him or even see him. And some storms were coming over the next few days; they'd likely drag him out away from the shore.

Hank pulled off his shoes and socks, roughly rolled up his pant legs, then picked up the body—*it's true what they say about dead weight*—and carried it through the maze of cattails and marsh grass down to the sand and then behind the hut. He knelt and dropped the body into the water with a gentle splash, then shoved him out farther with the flat of his foot, waded in a bit and shoved him farther still. Just then, the three clicks came, and Hank almost dropped the walkie into the lake in his rush to answer. "On my way," he growled, then looked back at the body. It was under the surface, a shapeless shadow, barely visible. The fish would find it soon enough. He turned and started walking back to where he'd left his shoes and socks, and stopped.

A boy was standing there, right where Hank and the rubby had just been. He was standing on their mess of blood and piss and shit and cum. Just standing there, staring at him. Thick black hair, white shirt, grey pants, suspenders. Not dressed for the cold. Eighteen, nineteen, not much older. Just staring, curious, defiant even. *Jesus Christ, he's seen the whole fucking thing. What do we do now?*

"Hey," Hank called out. "Police officer. Come down from there."

The boy just stood, watching intently.

"I said police officer. I'm going to need to see some ID."

Three more clicks. Hank grabbed the radio, barked into it: "I said I'll be right there." He looked back at the boy and saw—what could you call it? A ripple in the air, all around him, in the light shining down from the waxing moon, and for a moment, he was both a boy and a *not-boy*, something dark, animal, feral. A jittery blur of ears and snouts and mouths and teeth and tongues. Something hungry.

"You took something of mine," the boy said.

Hank felt light-headed and wondered if he was sick, if the shock of the rubby's death had jarred him somehow. It was like that wooziness he once felt a few minutes before an earthquake.

"The shit are you talking about?" He slid his hand down his Glock 22, felt its reassuring weight, touched his finger to the trigger. "I'm not fucking around here, this gun is loaded."

The boy/*not-boy* kept staring, not moving, the shimmer between them like what radiated off the sidewalk in the dead heat of summer. He was solid, he was real, not a ghost—*Why would I even think that?*—but maybe something else, something more, and he was watching, waiting, his left hand moving to the front of his pants, stroking himself with his thumb, growing visibly hard.

"You take something from me," he said, "I take something from you."

Hank looked from the boy's crotch to his face, and the dizziness flooded his head till he thought he'd have to sit down. "Don't make me come over there," he tried to say, but his mouth felt swollen, the words mangled. Something was wrong here, terribly wrong. Hank's thick, sticky cock hardened as if on command. He wanted to step forward, wanted to touch the boy, to feel the heat of his breath, to smell the blood on it, to bare his throat and offer it without knowing why.

Nicholas. Did the boy say it? It felt forced into his head, some kind of a magic trick. Hank looked across at him, struggled to focus on his strange changing face, and saw the corners of his lips pull back in a faint, cold smile.

Now drowsy and heavy-eyed, caught in a waking dream, Hank lifted his gun out of its holster, then let his arm dangle down at his side with it as he watched the beast-boy arouse himself. A flickering flash behind the boy revealed a vast tunnel of arching trees, and under their bending boughs Hank saw dozens, hundreds of boys and men, mauled and mangled, naked and yearning. Another flash and the vision was gone. *I've been drugged. That fucking rubby bit me and now I have rabies.*

The boy turned his attention to Hank's weapon, gazed at it fiercely. Hank barely noticed as his arm, his hand jerked up and out on a puppeteer's strings, lifting and lowering the gun, moving it forward and back, until it was level with his head, his face, his chin. Hank's puppet jaw dropped. He barely realized he was welcoming the gun's barrel into his dust-dry mouth, only faintly realized he was squeezing the trigger, until he saw the boy's delicious grin, heard the shot ring out inside his head, and felt everything he had ever known and wished and dreamed explode out onto the side of the Quonset hut and into the green-grey sludge that lapped at his wet bare feet.

Tony heard the shot and flung himself out of the cruiser and halfway down to the shore before its last echo had faded. *Jesus Christ, Hank, what now?* He burst through the trees, gun drawn, looking around wildly. It was so fucking dark. "Hank? Hank?" he whispered. He couldn't hear anything, could barely see anything. The rubby must've run off.

Then he saw the faint beam of light shining down from the corner of the hut, like watered-down milk, with a rumpled, dark shape beside it. He rushed over, knelt down, found his partner dead on the ground, his gun in his hand.

Oh fuck oh fuck what the fuck is this. He recoiled and jumped to his feet, his knees weak and wobbly, and he staggered back up to the cruiser to call in for help.

As he did so, Michael Larose, forty-six, of no fixed address, floated out as if he was being tugged by his shirt collar, gently but insistently, and slowly sank to the lake's sandy floor.

Crystal Lake was walking briskly along Maitland Street pulling a plaid carry-on bag when she saw the police cruiser up at the end of the block. Known around town as Toronto's Scream Queen, Crystal had just finished the Every Day Is Halloween show at Trax and was twenty minutes past her scheduled start time at Bedelia's Hoes of Horrors show at Bar 501. Even so, she slowed down and watched carefully as the officers picked up the handcuffed homeless man from the sidewalk where he'd fallen, threw him into the back of the car, seated themselves in the front, and drove off. *Shit, they've got Mikey.* She thought about trying to stop them or even ask what he'd done, but she was wearing sky-high red heels, a tight black skirt, and a black-and-white-striped blouse and fur jacket, and had a bloody plastic axe jutting out of her blond bouffant wig. Not the best ensemble for a police confrontation.

She had known Mikey for as long as she'd lived in the neighbour- hood and had dropped him some spare change whenever she could. Sometimes she'd stop to chat when she was on her way home from a show, or bring him some leftovers from whatever fast food she'd picked up for dinner. He had been a fixture for a few years at least, and never seemed to cause any serious trouble. He moved from grate to bench to stoop to vestibule all over Church Street, but she most often saw him on Alexander or on Maitland, next to the Super Freshmart, sometimes with a sleeping bag, sometimes with a bundle buggy full of odd items, sometimes with nothing but the clothes on his back.

She stopped at the corner, knelt down, and gathered his things into a small, neat pile: a sweatshirt from a long-shuttered clothing store in the east end; a cigarette pack with two mismatched smokes inside; a bat- tered paperback copy of *Interview with the Vampire*; a ratty old red diary of some kind; and a messed-up deck of cards rattling around in an old cardboard box. Mikey collected playing cards that he found on streets and sidewalks and in alleys all over downtown—he'd joke that he almost had a full deck. Under all this was the blue nylon sleeping bag, which she folded neatly and tucked off to one side, where she hoped he would find it. She opened her red vinyl clutch, pulled out a twenty, stuffed it into the cigarette pack so that he would have something good to come back to, then tottered off to her show, hoping the cops were just taking Mikey in somewhere to sober up. She hadn't liked the look of what she'd seen.

The bar's bouncer pulled the door open for her as soon as she arrived. The place was packed and Bedelia was up on the stage dressed as Elvira. "Oh look," she shouted into the microphone. "It's Crystal

Late!" Crystal waved at the stage without looking—she didn't dare get caught in Bedelia's basilisk glare—and wove her way through the crowd towards the back, to the glorified broom closet the queens used for a dressing room. She shoved her bag into the corner, pulled out a clear vinyl zip case, and then turned to the mirror to do a quick touch-up. Someone had drawn a huge *X* on it from corner to corner with what looked like the original 1994 MAC Viva Glam lipstick. *Atmospheric.* She jumped a little as the shower curtain pulled open behind her, revealing sometime co-star Anita Drinq in a long white bath towel and shower cap with a bloodied butcher knife in her hand. "I did two extra numbers to cover for you. You can pay me back later. You're welcome." And then she pulled the curtain shut.

Crystal heard Bedelia's bellowing from the front of the bar. "And now, here she is—back from the dead!" That was her cue to move it.

She took a custom-burned CD out of her bag, whirled back out of the little room, stopped quickly at the bar as Bedelia continued to slag her from the stage, and leaned in to the bartender to hand off the disc. "Track two," she half shouted into the bartender's ear. He nodded, turned, slipped the disc into the player, and hit the track, then Crystal made her way up onto the stage as an eerie, stripped-down instrumental of "Every Breath You Take" rumbled from the speakers. She grabbed the microphone from Bedelia and gave her the finger, then growled the first few lines of the song at the crowd. They clapped and cheered, pushed closer to the stage, and started waving five-dollar bills at her. Halloween really was her favourite time of year.

After two songs on her own and a duet with Anita, Crystal handed the mic to Bedelia, who called a fifteen-minute break. Crystal hopped off the stage and sped to the ladies' room, as the gin-and-sevens from earlier in the evening required immediate attention. She threw herself into one of the stalls, slammed the door shut, untucked, and sat down, and felt several kinds of sweet relief as she peed. Glancing around the cubicle, she saw a sprinkling of standard-issue graffiti, likely left by other queens, at least those who could spell. She was amused to find herself mentioned on the door of the stall: CRYSTAL LAKE IS POLLUTED, nestled in a toxic cloud.

A pair of old black leather boots, worn and dusty, shuffled into view just outside the stall. Someone was standing there, just inches from the door. She must've been lost in thought—she didn't remember hearing anyone come in or seeing the boots approach. Yet here they were, presumably with feet inside them.

"Girl, there are two other toilets in here. You don't need to wait for me."

The boots didn't move. She rolled her eyes, let out a huff. *What bullshit is this?* If someone out there wanted to pick a fight with her, she was ready to bring it.

"Are you afraid?" came a voice, young, male, Scottish maybe, from directly above the boots. "Afraid of being alone?"

"Why don't you fuck off, and we'll both find out."

No response. The boots didn't move. Crystal's grandmother had been from Edinburgh; this accent sounded like hers, but even thicker.

"I said go away and leave me alone."

The owner of the voice pressed his mouth close to the crack in the stall door. "You put on a brave face," he said. "But I see who you really are—your shame, your anger, your fear. Unable to be yourself, not wanting to be seen. I see you, I see all of you. I can almost taste you."

"Kiss my ass and see what that tastes like. You don't know anything about me." Crystal was not in the mood. She was not about to be menaced by some nameless, faceless creep, and especially not in a bar where she was doing a show.

"Lady, what's going on back there? Did you fall in again?"

Anita had stepped into the room and it sounded like she was standing by the sinks. *Good.* Crystal looked down to the bottom of the stall door and saw that the old worn boots had vanished.

"Anita! Stay there—don't move." Crystal stood up, flushed, retucked herself, made herself presentable, and opened the stall door. Anita was standing there in her platinum bob and black latex catsuit, visibly unimpressed. "Did you see that asshole? Where did he go?" She looked across at the row of mirrors above the sinks. She could see the other stalls were empty, the whole room was empty. She and Anita were alone.

"You've been in here muttering to yourself for ten minutes," Anita said. "I thought you were in a k-hole. I tell all you girls not to leave your drinks around, put them somewhere safe, and then I come in here and find you climbing the fucking walls."

"There was this guy back here, he was creeping me out," Crystal said, baffled. "You didn't see him?"

"Oh—wait a minute," Anita replied, tapping her finger on her chin. "I do remember someone. Tall guy? Deep voice? Big dick? Yeah, he crawled up my hole and died there. *Sorry.* Now get your shit together and get out there, these people paid to be miserable and you're our only hope."

Just before last call, as Crystal was standing in the bar window singing a mash-up of "If I Could Turn Back Time" and "Bela Lugosi's Dead" ("Undead! Undead! Undead!" shouted the crowd), she turned and thought she saw a boy in the waving, swaying mass of men, darkly handsome, black shock of hair, a familiar face she couldn't quite place. He always seemed to be at the corner of her eye, but when she turned her head to look, he was suddenly somewhere else. Someone from her past—maybe a bad date? Or a bad date's worst boyfriend? Even though he kept his distance, his being there made her uneasy.

Her Cher impersonation skills were negligible—a few exaggerated mouth movements and an approximation of her trademark hair flip— but her Peter Murphy was spot-on. As she held the mic in front of her mouth and intoned the final lines of the song in her booming baritone, she saw the boy right down at the front of the stage, practically at her feet. At his side were two other men that she was sure she knew, two men she had gone out with several years apart, Rick and Lyle, two men she had loved and who were dead, had been dead for many years. She watched as they embraced, kissed each other, then slowly and tenderly began to bite into each other's face, ripping chunks of meat from each other's cheeks and tongue and throat.

Crystal looked over at Bedelia in terror and Bedelia, realizing something was wrong but unsure of what it could be, stepped up onto the stage and stood beside her, leading the crowd in their "Undead!" chant. Crystal put her hand on Bedelia's shoulder pad, steadying herself, then looked down and saw that the contagion had spread, that the two ravenous men were now five, and then twelve, and then thirty, clawing at each other and shrieking, then fifty, and then the whole room, gouging out eyes and consuming them like pale plums, gnawing off ears and fingers, tearing open chests and bellies, devouring fistfuls of squirming, glistening viscera. The black-haired boy remained at the front of the stage, in front of Crystal, unscathed and smiling, reaching up towards her. She recoiled and fell backwards, one heel skidding and slipping out from under her, and slammed her head onto the stage with a crash. As the room whirled and strobed around her, she could hear Anita shouting from the back, over the crowd, "A k-hole! I knew it! I tell these girls!" and then Crystal fell farther, as if the stage were a deep pool of water, she fell back and back, back into darkness.

"Haunted. Haunted. A little bit haunted. Very haunted. Definitely haunted."

Salem pointed at the various houses and buildings along Alexander Street. Some had pumpkins out on their porches or in front windows, others had displays made of seated scarecrows, dangling witches, and cobwebs hanging from the trees. Robin walked alongside her, trying not to slip and fall in her impractical new split-sole Pradas.

"That's Vaseline Tower," Robin said. The cylindrical twenty-storey high-rise just off Church Street had long been compared to a giant sex toy. "It can't be haunted, it's not even fifty years old."

"*Exceptionally* haunted," Salem replied. "I don't know about the other two towers, but—a little bit haunted. Probably."

Robin was horrified to see that some of the balconies were freshly strung with Christmas lights. "What makes you so sure?" she asked, trying to find some traction amid the ice and fresh-fallen snow. "Do you have psychic superpowers?"

"No, not superpowers. At least, not psychic ones. Just vibes."

"Vibes, hmm." Robin smiled. "I'm good with vibes."

Salem grinned back. "I bet you say that to all the girls."

And then, there they were at Church Street. Before Robin could respond, Salem had turned the corner and was striding up towards Maitland.

I'm not falling for anyone, it's too soon, I've only been single for six months, I'm not chasing after anyone, and yet here she was, chasing after Salem, tall and blonde and bratty and kind of hilarious and now scampering up the street to the corner. "Salem!" Robin called out, pulling her coat collar tight around her neck. "Slow down, there's ice everywhere!"

Salem gave a little wave without turning around and without slowing down. Robin shrugged and relaxed her pace, watching the sidewalk in front of her. She would catch up eventually. She was not going to kill herself running after some flirty smartass. Not tonight, anyway.

After nearly twenty years, Robin had finally reached a stage in her career where she could take it easy in the off-season, stay close to home, slide her suitcases under the bed, and hang out with friends. The last few years had been exhilarating but exhausting: top spots at both Black & Blue in Montreal and the Easter weekend White Party in Palm Springs, a month of Sundays at Fabric in London, a surprise invitation to spin at Junior's Arena night at the Palladium, followed by a guest spot at Twilo with its mind-blowing sound system, then a one-month residency at Amnesia back in Ibiza in a DJ booth suspended over the teeming, whirling crowd, and headlining the AMF arena event for forty thousand fans at ADE in Amsterdam.

It was good to be home long enough to unpack. She was offered a biweekly series of gigs over the winter at Industry, a cavernous space on the west side that brought together an eclectic crowd: gay and straight, house and hip hop, trance and techno. And on her free nights, she was a street check volunteer at the 519. From October to April for the past three years, she and a partner had been going out once a week to check on people in the neighbourhood who were living on the streets and, for whatever reason, were unwilling or unable to seek shelter at the nearby missions, instead spending their nights on grates and benches, in doorways and alleyways. She was usually scheduled for Thursdays or Sundays with her more gregarious friend Andrea, who worked at three different bookstores and was in a perennial state of postgrad crisis. However, Andrea had been down with the flu since the middle of the month, so Robin was paired with Salem, a teaching assistant at the University of Toronto who knew something like six languages and was apparently single and frisky in all of them.

Salem was the first to see Mikey's possessions folded up and set aside against the wall of the Super Freshmart. It was unusual to see a sleeping bag unattended; they were rare to start with, and among the first things to be taken, especially once winter had arrived. She turned and looked back to see Robin manoeuvring around some black patches on the sidewalk. "Robin, Mikey's stuff is here, but he's not. Could you gather his things while I look around for him?"

Robin carefully crouched down and checked over the pile of items nested on the folded fabric: a beat-up box of playing cards, a few creased paperbacks, a tattered old red journal, a partly crushed cigarette pack with a twenty-dollar bill tucked inside, a stubby pencil, a coupon for some free fries at one of the new places up the street. She pulled an old HMV bag out of her inside jacket pocket and started filling it, brushing the snow off each item before she dropped it in. Maybe he'd had to use a washroom? Even so, he'd have taken his stuff with him, or left it all with someone he knew.

Also, why would he leave twenty bucks?

"Robin." Salem was standing right at the edge of the sidewalk, looking down at the snow-dusted pavement. Her brow was furrowed. She was very still.

Robin tucked the smaller items into the bag and picked up the sleeping bag to bring to Salem. A few homeless men had gone missing over the past few years. More than a few. No one she knew, but— She stopped and stood next to Salem and followed her gaze to the ground.

A smear of blood, or what looked like blood.

"I checked up and down the sidewalk and into the street," Salem said evenly. "This was all I saw. Do you think he was mugged?"

"Someone probably just spilled some wine, sneaking around with it while they were having a smoke." Robin tried to sound confident, but a slight tremble snuck into her voice by the end.

"You're probably right," Salem answered. "It doesn't even go anywhere, it just stops at the curb."

"He probably just wandered off somewhere, mooching a meal," Robin continued. "It's too late to drop this stuff off at the 519, though. Let's bring it back to my place. Maybe call St. Mike's and Toronto General." She pushed the sleeping bag into Salem's chest. Reluctantly, she put her arms around it. It smelled like urine, stale smoke, and Aqua Velva.

Robin turned, started walking north against a tide of noisy gay men bouncing from bar to bar. Salem followed close behind, trying not to be sick. *He could have been mugged*, Robin decided. *Or maybe he got clipped by a car.* Mikey did get loaded from time to time, and the drivers downtown were for shit. She peeked into the bag and saw a grubby dog-eared copy of *Interview with the Vampire* looking back up at her. The battered box of playing cards bounced around on top of it. The old red notebook was somewhere at the bottom. She really hoped that nothing had happened to him. He was one of the few guys they checked on whom she actually liked.

Their walk to Robin's was a largely silent one, their sparky banter muted by their growing dread, their fears for Mikey creeping over them as they made their way to a cluster of towers on Gloucester along the Village's edge. The frightful decorations they'd seen just a few blocks south were less in evidence here. A damp, dull mist muffled the sounds of the night, leaching the colour out of the streetscape as if they had just stepped into an old photograph. Robin was reminded of the time she'd spent in London, in Highgate, minding a record producer's house while he and his partner were in France for a month. The nights there had been thick with fog, veiling the houses and trees, playing tricks with the sounds of footsteps. She was transported back a hundred years in a moment.

"These houses over here," Robin said, pointing to a pair of red-brick Victorian bay-and-gable townhouses.

"Haunted," Salem replied.

"I figured you'd say that." Robin smiled. "They've been carved up into offices, they're actually quite nice. Expensive as hell, though. I checked them out a few months back, but I ended up picking a place down on John Street instead."

"Probably also haunted," Salem replied.

"Mmm." She nodded. "It wouldn't surprise me."

A moment passed between them. "So, what do you do exactly?" Salem asked. "I know, typical Toronto. You don't have to answer if I'm being too nosy."

"No no, it's a fair question," Robin replied. "I'm a DJ. Old school— turntables, crates of vinyl, the whole thing. That's why I got the office, I finally moved all my stuff out of the living room."

"Awww, like for weddings?" Salem exclaimed. "That's so cute! I love music, that would be a great job. As long as you don't get a ton of requests for corny country songs and Céline Dion."

"Actually, not that many," Robin said with a grin.

"Good, I wouldn't be able to handle it. Hey, come look at this," Salem said, examining some flyers taped to a light standard. As she drew closer, she saw that in amongst some posters for yard sales and lost pets were a few seeking information about missing men, missing from around the Village. One was at least four or five years old, the packing tape that wrapped it around the pole yellowed and fragile. Some of the names rang a bell, but most did not. Their faces weren't familiar. "Do you think it's true, what they say," she asked, "that someone around here is doing this?"

Robin shook her head. She had heard stories like this for as long as she could remember, about Toronto, Montreal, New York, London, Berlin. Every big city seemed to have one. "It's an urban legend. We look for patterns where there aren't any, and then we try to explain them away. Sometimes people just disappear. Or they just take off and die, and they're never found." *But Victor loved Trevor. He may have been depressed, he may have needed help, but he would never have killed himself.* "Or they're found, eventually," she added, "and we never hear about it because we're on to the next thing. Mysteries are less interesting once they're solved."

A fluttering up in a tree across the street caught her eye. She and Salem looked and both quietly gasped. Perched on the bare branch of a maple was a snowy owl, ghostly and imperious, and it was looking right at them.

"Wow," Salem whispered. "What's that doing here?"

"I don't know," Robin said uneasily. Robin didn't like birds, especially large ones. She was afraid of their randomness, afraid of them taking flight and swooping down towards her face. She was once attacked by a red-winged blackbird protecting its nest, and it had taken her weeks to get over it. She looked over at Salem, her companion's fascination and delight obvious. *Why can't I be more like her?* "Come on, we should get going." She took Salem by the hand and together they kept walking up the street, the owl watching them intently as they passed.

The pair arrived at Robin's apartment a few minutes later—a pre-Depression three-floor walk-up squatting amongst the delicately decaying sixties high-rises and stolid century-old houses that lined the street. "I'm sorry, I left the place in a mess, I didn't know I'd be having company."

"It can't be any worse than mine," Salem replied. "I haven't cleaned since I defended my thesis, and that was six years ago. Everything is still in little piles plastered with sticky notes, all around the edge of my room."

As she and Salem approached the building, Robin saw a light glowing in her living room window, a light she hadn't left on. *Lovely, someone's broken in.*

She sighed, unlocked the heavy front door, and the two of them made their way up to the third floor, down the hall to her unit. She held her finger up to her lips and Salem nodded, not entirely sure what was happening. Farther up the hall, someone was watching a late night talk show, the shrill, spiky laughter spilling out into the hallway. Would anyone hear them if they shouted for help?

Robin gently tried the apartment door. It was locked. She slid her key in, turned it, then pushed the door open with her foot. It clunked against the inside wall.

"Hello?" she called out. Then, in a firmer tone: "I'm not alone."

Another burst of tinny laughter from up the hall. Otherwise, silence.

Robin stepped into the front hallway, peered around. Aside from the warm pool of light surrounding the lamp in the window, the rest of the apartment was swallowed in shadow. Maybe she *had* left the light on? Something caught her eye on the desk at the window, just under the lamp, something small and odd.

Salem reached in and switched on the hallway light, then set the sleeping bag on the floor and went from kitchen to bedroom to bathroom, turning on every light in the apartment. As she wandered, she spotted colourful framed posters for concerts and parties and music festivals, a bulletin board with clusters of event tickets pinned to it. The knob on the bedroom door was strung with dozens of neon and iridescent backstage passes.

The wall adjacent had maybe twenty snapshots and Polaroids tucked between sheets of glass. Flashlit Robin in VIP rooms and on crowded dance floors, and sunlit Robin on sunny, summery terraces with her arms around smiling, laughing people in expensively shabby clothes. A few of them had names and places printed underneath in fine-tip marker: *Carole and Dusty at Joy. Angel at Stereo. Carl Cox. Nick and Paul. Sonique at the Brits*, the two of them peering over their matching red-rimmed sunglasses. *Sasha & Digweed. Kylie—I should be so lucky! Frankie Knuckles*, looking like a proud dad. *Junior, Missy, Madonna—holy shit*. Holy shit was right. Robin was the biggest star that Salem had never heard of.

Weddings. Good job, Salem.

The final shot—or maybe the first?—was of Robin standing over an array of turntables and music decks and soundboards, headphones held to one ear, spotlights criss-crossing and dry ice blowing, in front of hundreds of people with their arms in the air: *My Summer in Space—Ibiza.*

Salem circled back to the living room and started to ask Robin about what she'd found, but slowed as she saw her seated in the chair by the desk. She was holding something in her hand, holding it as if it were a living thing, a peculiar insect, fragile and venomous.

"Robin?" Salem asked, and then came closer.

It was a playing card, creased and stained, part of one corner peeled away. It was just like the cards that Mikey had found in the street, that he was using to build his deck. Robin held it up to show her. Jack of Spades.

"It was just sitting there," Robin said, her expression blank.

"Mikey?" Salem asked.

Robin turned the card this way and that.

"Could someone have let him in?"

"The super has keys, but she lives out in the east end," Robin replied, thinking through every possibility. "No balcony, no fire escape." Mikey could barely climb a flight of stairs; there was no way that he had scaled the side of a building.

"Where did you put the bag with Mikey's things?" Salem asked.

Robin pointed to the HMV bag by the doorway. Salem went to it, lifted and upturned it, and spilled the contents out on the front hallway floor.

"Is this everything?" she asked.

Robin nodded—then stopped, frowned, shook her head slightly. "There was a book. An old red notebook. A diary maybe? It must've fallen out somewhere."

An old red diary.

Salem looked around on the floor, checked the bottom of the bag, *nothing*, then did a quick scan of the room. *It can't be, it's just not possible.* "The diary, what did it look like? Did you open it? Did you read it?"

Robin looked at her, confused. "No, I just picked it up and put it in the bag. It was an old red book, no name or anything, faded cover, falling apart. Why?"

"Nothing. Just a weird feeling. Déjà vu." Salem tucked the playing cards back into the bag. "Listen, I . . . don't think you should stay here tonight. If someone was in here, they might come back. We have, like, six hotels around us, I'm sure we can find you a room." Robin stood silent, stood still. "We can deal with everything else in the morning."

"Where do you live?" Robin asked.

"I—live on the west side, me and a few friends," Salem replied. "A regular den o' dykes." She smiled and Robin smiled. "Did you want to come stay with me?"

"Yes, actually," Robin answered. "If that's okay." She stood up, reached down to Salem to help her up.

"Of course," Salem said, then: "What do we do about Mikey?"

"We can make a few calls," Robin said. "Sometimes it's better to wait until the morning shift arrives." She didn't intend it, but there was a dark, sad edge to her voice. Whatever was going on, whatever any of it meant, it felt like Mikey was no longer part of it.

They opened the door and left the apartment, left it just as it was, walked down the stairs and out of the building, turned the corner, and crossed the street.

If they had stopped before turning the corner, if they had looked back at the window just for a moment, they might have seen it: a tiny knot of darkness releasing itself, unfurled and freed like a thin tangle of smoke. A spark leaping from the frayed cord of the lamp in the window onto one of the pages on the surface of the desk.

Caught.

Lit.

Curled.

Spread.

Dancing from tinder to kindling, licking greedily at greeting cards, magazines, thrift store curtains, wicker baskets and bamboo rods, blistering, blackening wallpaper, hand-me-down furniture, and overstuffed bookshelves.

Within minutes, the place was engulfed, and the alarms began to ring.

Trevor stopped dead in his tracks as he felt the faint rumble of the subway beneath him. The ground rippled and swayed under his feet. Annoyed pedestrians brushed past him as he stood rigid in their path. He didn't know what to do. He could taste his morning meal clawing its way up to the back of his throat. He looked down through the long rectangular grate on the edge of the pavement and felt a whirl of vertigo as flashes of the subway train passed below.

"What's happening? Are you okay?" Sergio asked, putting his arm around his shoulder and guiding him back onto the pavement.

Trevor nodded, feeling foolish. He motioned for Sergio to step around the corner with him, out of harm's way, and then he leaned against the building to take a few deep breaths.

"That's it, just breathe," Sergio said. "We can go sit down somewhere. The hotel has a coffee shop."

Trevor looked across at what had once been the elegant Westbury Hotel and was now a cheap and cheerful Marriott Courtyard. He hadn't seen them exactly, and he couldn't bring himself to tell Sergio about them, but he'd had the sensation as he walked over the metal grid that people were trapped underneath, hundreds of them, trapped and screaming, their eyes wide, faces bloodied, fingers reaching up through the tiny holes, he could feel them clinging to his feet. A hallucination? Premonition? Maybe his medications were doing a number on him. What he'd seen wasn't real, he knew that, it was stupid, but it unnerved him, unbalanced him. If he couldn't trust his eyes and ears, if any corner he turned could reveal some new horror, what was he supposed to do?

"Okay, sure. Just for a minute." Trevor let Sergio take his hand, and together they walked up to the hotel entrance. *This used to be such a nice place.*

Trevor had met Sergio on Manline at the end of summer the year before. Dating sites were a new and somewhat strange thing for him, but arguably an improvement over bars and clubs where he increasingly felt too old, too tired, too hard of hearing, and too impatient. He had experienced a string of no-shows and weirdos before messaging Sergio, and had thought he was ready for anything. Yet when he and Sergio hooked up, he was surprised by the urgency that fuelled their sex, like they were running for a train that was late leaving the station. There was a fierceness, but also a certain tenderness, a haunted quality. Trevor wondered if he might have lost a partner too; at times, it was as if someone else was in the bed with them, another pair of lips as they kissed, another pair of hands as they touched and held each other.

In the afterglow, Trevor asked Sergio if he'd consider going out for a date. His online ad had repeatedly and emphatically said "no strings."

Sergio turned his head to face him. "Okay. So. I'm starting treatment for lymphoma, I'm just waiting to hear what stage and how we're going to deal with it. It's complicated, I don't want to get into it, and you don't need to help. I don't want to hear about fights and battles. That's not how it is for me. But." He looked away, looked down at his hands on the sheet over his lap. "But if you can handle that, and you want to grab a drink or something, I would like that."

The drink turned to dinner, turned into a night together. One date turned into two, and then into five. Sometimes the pub around the corner, sometimes just ordering takeout. The lymphoma was at stage three, it turned out, aggressive but not hopeless. *How do you love someone in danger?* Trevor had wondered. Do you hang back just in case, protect yourself, keep your feelings tight and close? Or do you go all in? Trevor went all in, accompanying Sergio to appointments and helping him understand treatment options and side effects, sitting with him in the hospital and caring for him at home, prepping meals and cleaning up vomit. Every day, he was afraid that Sergio would be taken from him— that the phone would ring, they'd be called into an emergency meeting, shown spots or growths on scans or X-rays, would be told "untreatable" or "incurable." But, after a round of radiation and a gruelling bout of chemo, the heavy black curtain that Sergio had hung around himself began to disintegrate, and the odd shaft of sunlight would peek through to his clouded face. They moved in together at six months, and after a year, Sergio was declared to be in remission.

Now, Sergio set a warm can of ginger ale and a straw down in front of Trevor, then sat down across from him with a plastic cup full of icy cappuccino slush. "Is this better?"

Trevor nodded, eyes on the surface of the table, not saying anything.

Sergio let out a sigh, looked around the room. "I haven't been in here for years," he said. "My grandfather used to bring me here. Did I tell you about him? Amazing guy."

"Yeah, I think so," Trevor answered. "He died a while back, didn't he?" He felt tired, irritable. The anxiety pulsed and thrummed, underscoring everything.

Sergio reached over and held his hand, warming his chilly fingers. "He did. I admired him so much. He was a builder, he made me want to build things—be an architect or an engineer. But I guess it wasn't for me." Sergio gestured around the room. "He brought us here for an early Christmas dinner once. The place was gorgeous then, a luxury hotel, mid-century modern, and the restaurant was fancy, though maybe I just remember it that way because I was so small. The whole room was red—the chairs, the tablecloths, even the carpet, I think. Everything but the wood. Some of the waiters knew him by name and came over to say hello and shake his hand, which made me think he was famous. It was because he had overseen the subway construction, just outside of here, and he and some of the other men were regulars here for years."

The subway. *Faces. Fingers. Screaming.* Trevor wiped the sweat from his brow with his forearm. He clicked open the can, slid the straw in, and sipped the ginger ale, hoping it would soothe his jumpy stomach. Someone had furiously scratched a message onto the wooden tabletop near his wrist: HAVE YOU SEEN HIM.

"He did a lot of work on this section just out here." Sergio pointed towards the hotel's entrance, at the rear of the building. "He told us once that his crew found this box, this large iron box, or at least pieces of it. More than a hundred years old, he said. Right alongside where the tunnel was being dug. See, south of us," he pointed again, "the subway runs under the middle of the street, but here, there's a bend in the line. The tunnel cuts past the hotel and then curves up and runs north from there."

The whole room was red, everything red. Trevor was trembling, he could feel the ginger ale sloshing around in the can. He carefully placed it back on the table and kept his hand on it, anchoring it.

"He said that when he was down where the tunnel was being dug, one of the workmen called him over to part of the eastern wall. They had dug through to something that looked like a sculpture or carving. The workmen thought they'd uncovered some buried treasure, something that was going to make them rich. But it was just the side of this old iron box, all broken up, under the ground." Sergio pointed up towards the hotel. "Somewhere over there."

"An old iron box," Trevor repeated.

Sergio nodded. "It would have been very old, from before the city was a city. This was all a forest two hundred years ago. Woods and farmlands and fields. The middle of nowhere." He sipped from his iced cappuccino. "They got someone to come in from the museum, pull out the pieces they could reach, take a few photos. Then they just filled in the wall with clay, covered it with plastic sheeting, inserted some struts to hold it in place. And then they sealed it up. He kept a small piece of it, or so he told me." He stopped, looked over at Trevor. "Are you feeling better? Is the ginger ale helping?"

"Yeah, it's good. I'm just a bit dizzy." Trevor closed his eyes and found he could imagine himself inside the iron box, could see the four walls, could almost touch them. He could feel that someone or something else was in there with him, someone he couldn't see, pulling him into a suffocating embrace. "Was someone buried in it? Does anyone know?"

"Buried? No." Sergio shook his head. "He never said anything like that, he just talked about the pieces of iron. My father has some of Papa's things—maybe it's in there with them. But, you know, we don't really talk."

"I thought I saw something—" Trevor started, then corrected himself. "I mean, I thought I read something, about bodies buried near here."

"There was a cemetery up north of here," Sergio explained. "A potter's field, up where the subway lines cross. They still keep finding graves and bodies whenever they build something there." He caught himself, realized he'd been a little too loud. Should they even be talking about this? Trevor's sleep had been ruined by nightmares lately. It seemed like the kind of thing that would just upset him more.

A clatter of glasses startled him, and he turned and saw the server behind the counter was watching them. At the other end of the room, some punked-out teens were looking their way. Guests leaving the hotel glanced through the window in their direction as they wheeled their luggage out towards Yonge Street. "Do you want another ginger ale? Maybe some water?"

Trevor closed his eyes and he was back in the tomb once more. The walls were cracking from the pressure of the clay, crumpling against the weight of it, and then suddenly it tore into hundreds of pieces, cold and sharp like knives, collapsing and crushing him. *If he reaches for you, then he's already caught you.*

"I—I need to get to the washroom," he said thickly, acid burning in the back of his throat.

Sergio hurried to the server and asked for the key, came back and helped Trevor to his feet, helped him to the alcove where the restrooms were. He couldn't make it as far as the stall and threw up into the sink, retching and coughing until his eyes were wet and stinging and his nose running. He instantly felt better, if still a little light-headed. Might have been food poisoning after all. Sergio ran some water over a few paper towels he had tugged from the dispenser, handed them to him, and then started rinsing the sink and wiping it down while Trevor cleaned up his face.

"Let's find you somewhere to sit in the lobby. I'll go to the front desk and call us a taxi," Sergio said.

Trevor tossed the paper towels into the nearby bin. "I'll be right there, I just need a minute."

Sergio gave him a look that said *Are you sure?* but Trevor motioned towards the exit. As Sergio left the restroom and the door thudded shut behind him, Trevor turned, placed his palms on either side of the sink, and looked in the mirror.

He closed his eyes.

Nothing. Just blackness.

He opened his eyes, and then closed them again.

Nothing.

HAVE YOU SEEN HIM

He ran a little cool water in the sink, let it stream over his wrists. Splashed some onto his face and the back of his neck. Something under the sink caught his eye. He bent down, picked up a crumpled old playing card leaning up against the wall. Jack of Spades. He tucked it into his back pocket. Maybe it was good luck.

As he opened the restroom door, he walked right into Sergio, who was just about to come looking for him. "The cab is here," he said. "Do you have any cash?"

"I can get us home," Trevor replied as they stepped back into the coffee shop. "Do you smell something burning?"

"Like toast?" Sergio asked. All he needed was for Trevor to be having a seizure.

Trevor shook his head. "Maybe something happened in the restaurant."

"Maybe," Sergio said, looking doubtful. He didn't smell anything at all. He stepped into the revolving door, and by the time they climbed into the cab, he had steered them onto another subject entirely: a follow-up story on the *Sun's* front page about a cop who had killed himself at Cherry Beach.

Four and twenty naughty boys. Sergio turned over, squinted out into the darkness. Instinctively, he reached across the width of the mattress. The sheets were smooth and cool. He was alone. Trevor wasn't in the bed, or in the low-slung lounge chair he sometimes moved to if he got too warm or if Sergio was snoring. He switched on the small, dim lamp beside the bed. His watch said 2:33. Maybe Trevor was in the kitchen? Or was he sick again?

He swung his legs out from under the covers, stood and turned, and abruptly slammed into the side of a drawer. All three drawers of the chest were open, clothing shoved and strewn about. Then he heard the sound from the spare room—more drawers sliding open and then banging shut. "Trevor?" he called out. No response. Maybe he was sleep-walking. Sergio gently pushed the dresser drawers shut, then made his way to the spare room. "Trevor?"

Trevor was standing there, naked, his skin prickled with goose-bumps. The heat was turned down in this room and it was almost cold enough to see your breath. "Have you seen the St. Benedict medal?" Trevor asked, his voice edged with fear and frustration.

"I don't know what that is," Sergio said, baffled. "It's the middle of the night, come back to bed."

"The medal, the little silver medal, I need to find it now." He opened another drawer, felt around—front to back, side to side—shoved it back into the dresser.

Sergio sighed. "I don't know, it could be down in the storage locker, I cleared out some stuff and packed it away for the winter. We have too much shit to keep it all up here. Why, what's going on?"

Trevor looked down and away, his face filled with shadows. "I don't know."

"Come back to bed, it's cold in here. We'll go downstairs tomorrow and see if we can find it." Sergio held his arms open and Trevor came to him, allowed himself to be held. He was sweating and shivering, and limp like an old doll. "Hey, I'm sorry, I should have asked you first."

"I'm sorry too," Trevor whispered.

Sergio led him out of the spare room and into the bedroom, then back under the covers. It was probably just the last of the food poisoning, shaking itself out of him. *We should be more careful of what we eat.* "What is that medal, anyway—are you becoming a Catholic?"

"Protection," Trevor answered, his voice hoarse, his syllables slow. "To keep us safe."

"Ah," said Sergio. "Brujería. I should have known. It's okay, don't worry. We're safe with each other." But he couldn't be sure that Trevor had heard him. He was already fast asleep.

Screaming.

Tony winced, stretched, opened his bleary eyes. Pallid grey light filled the room. *Faces. Eyes.* What was that? A dream he'd shaken off? A thin shard of memory, something he'd tried to erase?

He blinked and blinked, trying to pull the room around him into focus. Maroon silk curtains, cream damask wallpaper. His mother-in-law's house. He was in her house, on her diamond-tufted floral velvet couch, and his son Angelo with his black, curly hair and wide, serious eyes was standing next to him, staring into his face. He wore a yellow rubber rain jacket with an orange sun visor and shiny black-and-white eyes on the sides that made him look like a large, curious duckling.

"Jesus, kid, don't scare me like that. You'll give your old man a heart attack. Where's your mom?"

"Getting dressed," the young boy said. "It's raining outside."

"Ella," Tony called out.

"Yeah," came a voice from two rooms away. She sounded tired. Glass clanking against metal—dishes in the sink. And then the jingle of keys being grabbed off the table.

"It's all right, I'm awake, I can take him," Tony said.

"No, it's okay, you stay there," Ella called back, then popped her head into the doorway. "Angie, you leave your dad alone, he's not feeling well."

"I feel fine," he called back to her. Then to Angelo: "I feel fine."

"He smells funny," Angelo shouted to his mother, wrinkling his nose.

"Yeah, well, you smell funny too," Tony answered. "Come give your dad a kiss."

Angelo wrinkled his nose again and gave Tony a peck on his forehead. Tony felt something wet smudge up above his eyebrow. He reached up, touched it, knew before he even looked at his fingertips that it was blood. The scent of it, the tang of it. He pulled back. A thin trickle of red ran down from Angelo's nose over his lip. He stuck out his tongue to taste it.

"Hey, buddy, be careful," Tony said. He dug a wrinkled tissue out of his shirt pocket and used it to wipe his son's face. "How did that happen?"

He shrugged. "I saw Uncle Hank in the yard today. He had one, and then I had one too."

Hank.

Hank is dead. He had forgotten for a moment, and now he remembered all over again, as if the last few weeks just happened in the last ten seconds. *Hank is dead.*

"You say you saw who?" Tony asked, keeping his voice steady.

"Uncle Hank," Angelo said shyly, looking down at his fingers. There was dirt, blood, under his nails. Kid never washed his hands.

Hank is dead.

"Now Angie, I told you," Tony cautioned. "Uncle Hank had to go away for a while. You can't be making up stories."

"I saw him," the boy said. "He came back." He kept his eyes away from Tony, still looking at his hands.

Tony couldn't really blame him. They hadn't properly explained Hank's sudden absence, hadn't really known what to say. Angelo had seen dead squirrels and birds, he seemed to understand what death was and how it worked, but when it came to people, well, you couldn't be sure. Who knew what he heard or saw, or what sense he tried to make of it.

"Hey, I found something of yours." Tony reached into his pocket, pulled out the red ludo playing piece.

Angelo looked up at it, squinted. "That's not mine," he said quietly.

Faces. Fingers. What the hell was that? Something was teasing him from the darkest corner of his brain. His head was starting to throb, he could feel his pulse in his temples. He was sweaty and chilly. The hangover he was fearing had descended with a crash.

"Time to go, Ange," Ella said as she appeared in the doorway in a knee-length green raincoat belted around the middle. Angelo spun around like a toy and bumbled across the floor in his blue rubber boots to join her. "I'm going to pick up some groceries on the way back," she said, checking through her purse. "Want anything special for dinner?"

"No, no, it's okay, whatever looks good." Groceries were normally Tony's job, lately the only contribution he'd been making to the household, so clearly she was pissed. She was hiding it well enough from their son, but it was coming through loud and clear to him. He pulled himself upright, took a sharp breath. His head was pounding. "Do you need some money?"

She shook her head. "I'll take a look at the fish, or else maybe some pork chops. Ma's had breakfast, she should sleep till noon. Angie, stop kicking things." Angie kept kicking things. "Okay, we're going. See if you can try for a shower today." She gave him a tight, bitter smile, then took Angelo by the hand and stepped into the hallway and then out the front door with a slam.

Great.

Tony sat for a moment, his knees spread wide, the blanket pulled over his boxer shorts, and stared straight ahead, trying to wrangle his thoughts. *Fucking Hank. Who shoots themselves in the middle of a shift? Where did the fucking rubby go?* It had been just over two weeks since Hank's death: two weeks of administrative leave, no guns or weapons, no word on what was happening or when he'd be back on duty. Phil from the union had been right by his side that whole first night and day, asking for the lawyer to be called. The lawyer, Steve, came to the station at 8:45 a.m. and by then Ella was sick with worry and not getting any answers. After a few more hours, Tony was released into Steve's care with the usual cautions and admonitions: check in daily, always be reachable, no leaving town, avoid the news, and be ready to come back in for questioning at any time. HR had offered a referral to a counsellor, but Steve had pushed the card away before Tony had even had a chance to speak. No shrinks, no drugs, no help. And no telling anyone about what had happened that night, not even his wife.

Steve had driven Ella and Tony home in silence, and once he'd left, the silence continued. Check-ins with Steve quickly became check-ins with his answering service. Phil stopped picking up his calls, letting the phone ring and ring. He couldn't understand what the problem was; everyone could see that he hadn't done anything wrong. From time to time, he looked out the front window and saw an unmarked car sitting outside his house, a pair of plainclothes officers from another division sitting there drinking coffee, listening to the radio, flipping through the morning paper. Tony waved to them once, but they pretended not to see. He yanked the curtain shut and hid himself in the deepest part of the house, down in the rec room, away from everyone, hoping to be forgotten.

Three clicks, like we said. I shouldn't have waited. I should have gone to him. I could have stopped him.

Tony had always liked to drink, and now he liked it even more. Ella wouldn't buy him anything stronger than Bud, though, and only a two-four to last the week, which was crazy. But Santo, who owned the No Frills next to the liquor store—his kid did deliveries for both. He came by every other day with a brown paper bag for Tony with rye or J&B and refused to take a tip, all bashful in the face of Tony's compliments. There was no need to be shy, he was a good-looking boy, played sports probably, or maybe worked out at the school gym, a shame he couldn't come in even for a few minutes while he was on the job. It's not like he was going to bite the little fucker.

So Tony sat in the basement alone, with his rye or his J&B for company, straight-up, and sometimes he'd watch the old movies on Telelatino, sometimes music videos or cooking shows, sometimes he'd sit in silence and jerk off to one of the magazines he had hidden under the old leather couch down there. If Ella knew about them, she never said anything. They barely had a sex life anymore, not since Angelo was born, so maybe it was a relief for her. She didn't know about his visits to the video store, how he had waited in one of the booths for someone to join him, how the feeling of someone's hands and mouth on him had brought him close to tears. It was all he could do when he was drunk not to head over there and spend the whole day, risking everything, ready to bring it all crashing down around him. But he couldn't, not anymore. He had to keep it together for Angie, for Ella, for their families, for Hank. But now Hank was gone *fucking Hank* and he still didn't understand how, or why.

Keeping them in line. That's what Hank had said once, years ago, when they were out at the Brass Rail for drinks after a shift, shafts of pink-and-blue light washing over the impossibly round breasts of the strippers on the platforms. Back then, it was maybe three or four times a year, something would just get into him, he'd be driving down one street or another and he'd point and say, "That one." Maybe he'd had a fight at home, maybe he'd been dressed down back at the station, got shit for something. He couldn't say or do anything then, so he'd hold it in, keep it in, maybe for days, and then, out of the blue: "That one." Once, after a beating, one that left Hank's knuckles red and raw like meat, they'd ended up at the Rail and Tony asked, *Why are we doing this?* and Hank said, *We're keeping them in line,* and Tony went to say something else and Hank banged his glass on the table and said, *Don't fucking talk to me,* heads swivelled, they heard him three tables over. You don't raise your voice in a strip club, not unless you want to get bounced. So Tony kept quiet, never raised it again.

I could have stopped him. No, he couldn't have stopped him. He would have just had to stand there and watch.

Tony picked up his glass from the coffee table, went to take it to the kitchen for a refill, when an odd jingly sound rose up, stopping him in his tracks. Some kind of music from somewhere in the house, somewhere upstairs. But he was alone. Well, except for his mother-in-law, but she was basically bedridden. She did have a radio, but she couldn't reach it. Tony set the glass back down in the sink then walked softly through the front hallway, stood at the foot of the stairs, looked up and listened. It was definitely music, and it was coming from her room. Maybe Ella had left it on? She was talking a few days ago about old people, people with dementia, responding to music from when they were younger.

Tony made his way up the stairs, step by step, straining to make out the singer, the song. The sound was harsh and distorted, futzing in and out as if travelling from outer space or the bowels of the earth. As he reached the top step, he was surprised to find that the old woman's door was shut tight. Ella would never have left it that way. Had the care worker been over while he was passed out? What else had he missed? No wonder his wife was busting his balls.

He tapped the door with his knuckle. "Vivi?"

The odd crackling continued, spewing out a string of chaotic sounds, and then snapped into sudden clarity. *I just want to live while*

I'm alive. The song, the singer, were instantly, impossibly clear: Bon Jovi, "It's My Life."

"Viviana?" He knocked harder but sounded less certain, more frightened, as if he was still back asleep on the couch and the slim, dark fingers of a nightmare were slipping up the back of his neck. He turned the knob, pushed the door open, and jumped back a foot: Viviana was standing at the window, in her pale-pink cotton nightgown, her hands and face pressed against the glass.

What in Christ's name is this?

"Vivi, what are you doing? How did you get out of bed?" He placed his hand on her shoulder, tugged gently to lead her back, but she wouldn't move, wouldn't take her eyes off the yard below.

"He was here, Tony. He was looking for you." She pressed her forehead against the glass, rubbing it in a circle, hard, as if she was trying to stop a headache, or force her thoughts back into her brain.

Mary, Mother of God, this was the first time she'd spoken in weeks. "Who was here?" he asked. One of the guys from the station, or maybe a reporter? They had shown up over the first few days, hopping fences, tapping on windows, acting like old school chums, scaring the shit out of Ella, making Angelo cry. But how would she know if they were looking for him? Was somebody out there yelling for him? Was that how Angelo got a bloody nose?

"It was the boy," she said, "the boy who was with Hank," and Tony thought he'd misheard, thought his mind was still caught on his previous thoughts and hadn't let the words in, hadn't strung them together in a way that made sense.

"Jesus, Viv, what's going on? What's Ella been telling you?" He tried to peer past her down into the yard. "There's nobody out there, there is no boy. Stop it, Vivi, you'll hurt yourself." Maybe she meant Santo's kid? Tony pulled her away from the window and looked down through the rain to the wrought iron fence, the frozen fountain, the ice-glazed plants and bushes, the patches of brown-green grass peeking through the snow. There was no boy—not in the garden, not at the beach. What was she talking about?

"He wants to see you." She turned and looked him in the eye. She hadn't been this lucid in months, but she was also clearly lost. "He came such a long way."

"Viv, stop it, you're hurting yourself." He looked over at the radio and realized it was off. But the music was coming from somewhere. "Come on, you have to get back into bed. Ella's gonna shit herself."

"So many—an army—right under our feet." And with a sharp jerk, Viviana smashed her head against the window, drew back and smashed it again, pushed her face through the glass and began to slice and shred and flay herself on the broken pane, peeling the flesh off her cheeks, slashing into her neck, blood coursing down to the sill and then onto the floor.

"No!" Tony shouted as he pulled her back, away from the window and down onto the rose-coloured carpet, spattering the ceiling and walls as she fell.

Shouts erupted outside, followed by a burst of footsteps on the porch and loud banging on the front door. Tony pulled himself up and stumbled into the hallway and down the stairs, pulled the door open to see four shocked people standing there—the two plainclothes officers from the car up the street, Joe Belasco from his station, and a pretty but stern brunette in a dark suit that he knew to be another lawyer with the Police Association. Not Steve. Where was Steve?

"Call an ambulance," he gasped. "My mother-in-law, up in her room, she just tried to kill herself."

With that, one of the plainclothes officers pushed past him and ran up the stairs, then made a noise that sounded like "Holy shit," and the other ran back to the car to call in for help.

"I, uh— Do you want to come inside?" Tony asked.

Joe and the lawyer looked at each other awkwardly, shook their heads. "No," Joe said, "we'll stay out here. This won't take long."

"Tony," the lawyer interrupted, "you don't have to say anything. Do not say anything."

Joe continued as if ignoring a buzzing fly. "Tony, the investigative team has looked at your notes, and they've looked back at some other incidents—"

"Tony, I repeat, do not say anything," the lawyer warned.

The howl of sirens slowly rose in the distance.

"—disappearances that happened while you and Hank were on shift in that area."

Tony tried to follow what they were saying, and then, in that moment, the first plainclothes officer was standing at his side, blood all over his hands and sleeves.

"Sir, I'm sorry, I— The lady upstairs. She's dead." He glanced nervously at Tony, then back at Joe and the lawyer. "It looks like her head was pushed through the window."

Joe, the lawyer, everyone looked at Tony. His eyes widened. *What the fuck is happening?*

"I didn't do it, she did it herself!" Tony shouted. "She hasn't been in her right mind for years. Ella will tell you, we can't leave her alone for a minute!"

"Is Ella home?" Joe asked.

The second plainclothes officer bounded up the sidewalk as the sirens grew louder.

"No, thank god, she took Angelo to school and then she was going shopping. She'll be back any time." He looked at his wrist and realized he wasn't wearing his watch, was just standing there in a T-shirt and boxers with blood all over himself. He was lucky his dick wasn't hanging out.

"Inspector," the first officer said, peering down the hallway, "I think there's someone in the kitchen."

Joe nodded, and the first officer went back inside.

Finally. Ella must've come in through the back with the groceries. He turned and started to call out her name, but stopped when he saw the plainclothesman standing on the checkerboard floor over two motionless figures, drenched in blood, one much smaller than the other.

"Ella?" he whispered. "Angie?"

"It looks like they've been here for hours," the officer said, "maybe even since last night."

Tony felt his hands pull back, the cuffs snap sharply around his wrists, nipping into his skin.

"But—I just, I just saw them—I just talked to them, I—"

"Tony, I'm sorry," Joe said. "You're under arrest. We'll figure this out at the station."

"There was some kid, she saw him in the garden. He's the one who did this, not me!" Tony twisted, pulled his arms free from Joe's grasp, wrestled himself away from the others. "Where's Steve! Goddammit, I want to talk to Steve!"

He just wanted to say something, he just wanted to tell them, but then a shot exploded behind him and then another and he went blind with shattering pain, and a long black tunnel opened up before him, and through it a road of bright white stones, and above it a bower of bare white trees, their trunks and branches fashioned from bones, picked clean, bleached dry, weathered and worn. At the end of the white stone road was a giant black dog, who was very far away and then suddenly close, close enough that Tony could feel its hot, coppery breath on his face, in his mouth, and the dog reached out to Tony, beckoning him, but instead of a paw, it held out a hand, the hand of a pale young boy.

⁊⁊

A week after his last nightmare, Suda left for his under-the-counter shift at the twenty-four-hour diner, but of course he never arrived. He took a shortcut through the alley behind what was once the Hotel Selby, now a Howard Johnson; it happened just a few feet away from where the patio used to be. No one saw it, and even if they had, they wouldn't have understood.

Within a few hours, his clothes and belongings, folded up neatly next to a rust-coloured dumpster, were picked over by passersby, and were gone by mid-afternoon. Ill-fitting blue jeans, white briefs, black socks, a second-hand green polo shirt, cheap white canvas sneakers, navy-blue windbreaker. Sudharshan Sabaratnam, thirty-seven, of 515 Ontario Street, Unit 8, was never found.

I have laid myself open to ridicule & malevolence,
which I know not how to meet; that the thing will
be made the subject of mirth and a handle to my
enemies for a sneer I have every reason to expect.
                                                    --A.W.

Alexander Wood, gay pioneer, whose eight-foot-tall
bronze statue was erected in Toronto's Church-Wellesley
village in 2005, was a troubled, and troubling, man.

Wood came to Upper Canada from Scotland in 1793, when
he was just twenty-one years old, first to Kingston and
then, a few years later, to the Town of York (later
known as Toronto). A young entrepreneur with a sense
of adventure--or a desperate need to escape--he became
one of the town's leading merchants, and was one of
the few of his stature accepted among the local elite,
most notably by the Family Compact led by Judge William
Dummer Powell, George Crookshank, and the Reverend John
Strachan. They were a small group of conservative men
who fashioned themselves and their families into the
aristocracy of Upper Canada, and Wood was one of their
most loyal disciples. Though York was sparsely inhabited
when Wood first arrived, it quickly grew both in popula-
tion and in influence, and he grew more prominent within
it. He became a ranking officer of the York militia, was
appointed magistrate and a small-courts judge, and was
involved in a number of the town's social and community
organizations. As Wood ascended, he cleaved ever closer
to the men of the Compact, and to Reverend Strachan in
particular. A number of York's business owners came to

resent his intimacy with the local leaders, and turned their attention to his ambition, his slavishness, and his conspicuous bachelorhood.

From what we know of Wood's early years, we do not see a man we would describe as a hedonist or a libertine, flouting religion or the law or social conventions in order to carve out his own true path. Indeed, the impression given is one of a pious young man, conformist in nature, respectful and restrained. If he saw something deviant in himself, he may well have been ashamed of it, tormented by it. He may have considered it a corruption of the soul or an indelible stain on his moral character. It could be what motivated him to place himself beyond temptation, or so he hoped, by crossing the sea to a new land and redeeming himself with a life of tireless hard work and public service.

However.

In 1810, at the height of his success, a devastating scandal threatened everything he had worked for. Stories began to spread that he had inappropriately fondled several young men while investigating a supposed accusation of rape. It was said that the victim of the attack, a Miss Bailey, claimed she had scratched the genitals of her assailant, and during Wood's examinations of possible perpetrators, it was these scratches he claimed to be searching for. Soon after, the entire account of the rape was called into question (including the existence of the victim), and the rumours suggested that "Molly" Wood was

a sodomite using the investigation as a pretext for his
sexual impropriety.

When confronted about the situation by Judge Powell,
Alexander Wood admitted to his friend that he had indeed
conducted the examinations, and that the gossip circulating about them left him vulnerable to attack from
those who resented his rise beyond his station. The evidence was submitted to the public prosecutor, but Powell
agreed not to pursue the case if Wood left the country.
In October 1810, Wood departed to Scotland, leaving his
shop for his clerk to manage in his absence.

It has been suggested that a small group of towns-
people may have fabricated the rape story in order to
entrap Wood into intimately and inappropriately examining the suspects, thereby incriminating himself, but
his own admission of guilt to Judge Powell seems to
contradict this.

We know little of Wood's return to his home country,
other than his introduction into a circle of influential
men who frequented the Beggar's Benison, a gentlemen's
club in the town of Anstruther. The Benison was devoted
to "the convivial celebration of male sexuality." The
beggar's "benison"--or blessing--of its name referred
to an old expression: "May prick nor purse ne'er fail
you." It was a notable example of what was known at that
time as a Hellfire Club, providing its membership with
certain social and sexual outlets not readily available to the lower classes. It was here that Wood found

fellowship among the region's nobility and gentry--lords
and earls, ministers and bishops, military officers,
lawyers and doctors, musicians and artists. He learned
to hunt, to drink, to debate. He confronted and embraced
his desires. He turned away from one god and knelt
before other, more ancient ones.

His exposure to the denizens of the Benison, their
beliefs and their rituals, as well as the activities
within its hidden Green Wing, transformed him utterly,
and set him on a course of self-realization, erotic
abandon, and unlikely redemption.

Wide awake all night, darkness crushing me. Once again
the voices, the scratching and tapping, first outside,
then inside. Doors open, doors close, footsteps in the
hall. The television snaps on, full volume, shouting
about chairlifts and walk-in showers, but when I leave
the bedroom to investigate, the set is black and silent
and cool to the touch. Little things. One clock stopped,
another turned hours ahead. Books moved from room to
room. Photos placed face down, medicine cabinet left open,
a mirror facing the wall. A fast-food napkin, angrily
defaced: *Have you seen him.* Little pieces of paper everywhere, under plates and cups, behind cushions, tucked
into pockets. Index cards covered with tiny printing
and sometimes just one word scrawled over the others.
Did I write those? And then, in the dark, the hushing,
the whispers, they come and stand over me, dark figures
around my bed, shadowed hands touching me, caressing me,

I can't move, I can't shout, I can't breathe, my heart in my throat. Is this me? Am I here? Am I writing this now?

It was sometime close to nine in the evening on the first of July 1812 when Alexander Wood opened the door of his lodgings in Fife to find one of Lord Newark's men standing there with a hastily scrawled letter requesting his attendance at the Beggar's Benison on a most urgent matter. Shortly after eleven, Wood arrived at the Benison in his carriage to find Lord Ogilvie waiting outside the door, the building empty, the rooms darkened save for one in the eastmost corner of the Green Wing. "Newark's inside," he said to Wood. "It's best that you see for yourself."

It is difficult to imagine what ran through Alexander Wood's mind when Ogilvie led him into the one lit room in the Benison's Green Wing, and then asked the favour that would change the course of his life. And yet, my role here is to do so. Wood was two years into his exile from Upper Canada, likely at his lowest since the eruption of the scandal that forced him across the ocean. He was barred from his family home in Fetteresso and provided with a punishingly small allowance to pay for his room and board elsewhere. He relied heavily on the generosity of his friends Newark and Ogilvie, who remained well-connected with the members of the Compact in Upper Canada. His life, his ambitions, his ascent were all at a standstill. And then, he and Ogilvie reached the pale-green door. Ogilvie pulled out his handkerchief and held it over his mouth and nose, gestured for Wood to do the same, then knocked and announced himself. The lock tumbled and turned. The stink of the abattoir burst out, sickening them both. Wood pushed the cloth tight against his face, all but useless. He pinched his nose and clenched his teeth, stepped inside.

The bed had been stripped, but the blood and shit and piss had soaked through the ticking. Newark stood there, grey and grim. "Mr. Wood. I am profoundly grateful. We have a most delicate issue to discuss."

Wood looked at him, then looked past him. On the floor, a boy crouched in the corner, quivering, wet-eyed, encrusted in filth and gore. He lifted his face, met Wood's gaze with his own. *Help me*.

As repulsed as he may have been, sickened by what he smelled and saw, I can't help but wonder if Wood took it all in and thought to himself: *At last*.

A selection of correspondence between Lord Ogilvie and another of the Benison's members, Andrew MacVicar, collected in the archives at the University of St. Andrews, confirms the circumstances of Wood's return to York, albeit in spare detail. An "incident" at the Benison prompted Lord Newark to call upon Wood for assistance. A servant boy had apparently been injured in a violent disagreement with one of the guests. Wide-eyed and motionless, he did not respond to questions, had no reaction when called by name: Nicholas. Ogilvie told Wood that the boy was in

grave danger, and was to be taken out of the country as
quickly as possible. His plan was for Wood to take the boy
back to his rooms, and then down to the port at Kirkcaldy.
Ogilvie had prepared a small trunk for the boy's journey,
as well as a significant purse to ease any challenges they
might face in their travels. He also drafted a letter of
passage in lieu of personal documentation, so that the
boy's departure would be unhindered. Newark assured him
that he would be welcomed and protected by those who were
friends of the Benison, principally the Reverend Strachan,
and that the boy had certain talents that Strachan's
Compact could deploy against their detractors.

The documentation for the merchant ship *Apostle*, which
departed from Kirkcaldy on July 3, 1812, listed both
Alexander Wood and his young attendant as requiring
special passage at the request of Lord Ogilvie. Captain
Philip Watson later noted in the ship's log the disappearance of two crew members named Hartley and Steed. It
seemed that they were swept overboard during a calamitous
storm, perhaps while engaged in an altercation on deck,
as no other explanation presented itself. The voyage otherwise proceeded without incident, and the *Apostle* made
its landing at the Port of Quebec on August 19.

From there, Wood and his young ward travelled by coach
to the Town of York over a period of six days, arriv-
ing on August 25--just as U.S. president James Madison
declared war on the British and the colonists in their
territories. Wood's reputation remained tarnished, but

his powerful friendships were a great asset in restor-
ing him to his former positions. He returned to his
shop, resumed his social and community activities, and
regained his post as magistrate.

Soon after Wood's return with the boy, four of the
Compact's opponents were found dead on the outskirts of
town--savaged, it seemed, by wild animals. As the war
encroached on Upper Canada, Wood fought in several battles, including the Battle of York in 1813. Through it
all, he was able to maintain the flow of supplies into
his establishment, though he never again achieved the
level of prosperity or popularity he had enjoyed before
his fall. Friends no longer spoke to him; once-loyal
customers withheld their patronage. Even so, he continued to lead an active public life, while his private
affairs remained cloaked in mystery.

Little was recorded about young Nicholas Boyd. He
remained a fixture of the Wood household for at least
two decades, but he was rarely seen and seldom spoke.
One of Wood's remaining faithful clients noted in
a letter to her mother that she had caught several
glimpses of Boyd over her many visits, and described him
as "the ghostly young man who. . . . lives in a room in
the cellar, in the dark and damp, and only goes out at
night," and that in ten years he had barely aged a day.

Peter Wells, miller, 1813; Jean Lariviere, labourer, 1814;
Daniel Wallace, carpenter, 1816; John Ferriman, joiner,

1817; David Edgar, clerk, 1820; Richard Mercer, mer-
chant, 1821; Roger Tonkin, cabinetmaker, 1821; Michel
Fortier, labourer, 1823; Paul Andrew Hill, brewer, 1824;
Duncan Jones, weaver, 1825.

In 1826, Wood purchased a fifty-acre parcel of wood-
land north of the town, which soon became known as
Molly Wood's Bush. The area had long been a clandestine
meeting spot for men in search of momentary companion-
ship, and Wood's purchase rendered it private property.
Although it was beyond the reach of the York constabulary, the area was investigated three times in ten years
for disappearances, violent incidents, and other strange
occurrences. Chief among these were sightings of a black
dog or wolf "with the stature and comportment of a large
brown bear." Hunting parties combed the woods, but no
such creature was found. The officers did, however,
discover numerous items of a sexual and sacrilegious
nature, including a crude St. Andrew's cross fashioned
from forest maple. The items were removed from the site,
taken out to a nearby field, and destroyed.

In 1842, Wood visited Scotland with the intention of
eventually returning to Upper Canada, but he died there
intestate in 1844. All of his brothers and sisters had
predeceased him. Despite more than four decades in
Canada, the courts determined that Wood had been a resi-
dent of Scotland, and by Scottish law, his large estate--
including his shop, his house, and his woodlands north
of the town--passed to a first cousin once removed, "of

whose existence he was most likely ignorant." Without the protection of its prominent owner and his allies, Molly Wood's Bush became increasingly dangerous for the men who congregated there, facing violence from police and gangs of townsmen, as well as from predators whose territory was being encroached upon. A few years later, when Wood's store was finally closed and his property sold, his long-time employees were cited for their years of service in the *Upper Canada Gazette*, but no mention was made of Nicholas Boyd. It was as if he had never existed.

"Ah, look who's here," he whispered. "I'm so glad. I hope you will join me for dinner?" His voice was rough and cracked, his language oddly formal. And the accent: English? Scottish? "Well. Come closer. Don't be afraid of the big bad wolf."

At last, I slept, for the first time in days. I felt myself sink into it like warm water in an old claw-footed tub. I didn't even try to get to the bed, I just moved the laptop off the couch and curled up with my head on a toss cushion. I closed my eyes, I opened them. I didn't know where I was.

A small, tight tunnel of hard, damp clay, maybe two feet of space above and a foot on each side--enough room to crawl forward but not to turn around, with a dim light in the distance but no sense of how I had gotten there or how far I had to go to get out.

I found I could move by shifting my hips back and
forth, scuttling onward the way a lizard does on its
belly. At one point, something crawled over my hand and
I stopped, fought off the urge to be sick as a long
stream of wiggling, clattering legs rushed past. A
clutch of centipedes.

Eventually, the dim light grew closer and brighter, and
the air in the tunnel grew sharper and colder, until I
reached a sudden steep incline and slid forward, hands
out, fingers splayed, eyes clenched shut, and then
straight down onto a hard and unforgiving surface.

I touched the cool metal floor, embossed with an elaborate floral pattern, broken in places, rusted and crumbling in others, dotted with soft mud and pale round
mushrooms and restless, wide-bodied beetles. In the
closest corner, a trio of candles drooled speckled
beeswax into each other. I pulled the tallest one loose
and held it aloft, looking from floor to walls to ceiling. I was in a small earthen chamber, naturally formed
or painstakingly dug, some distance under the ground.
It was just barely tall enough to stand in, lined with
mossy timbers, soft with rot, the clay walls studded with swirling vines and leaves fashioned out of the
bones and skulls of small animals and birds. Here and
there, thick, gnarly roots poked out like pale, hairy
fingers. Sharp metallic fragments the size of my hand
jutted out in odd places; I had to be careful not to
slice myself. Above, a starry, moonlit sky whose con-
stellations, I saw, were made from human teeth.

Then I sensed I was not alone. With me in the chamber, in the farthest corner, a figure sat cross-legged on the floor. He cradled in his lap a speckled enamel bowl, and in it was a jumble of glistening organs and meat-covered bones, raw and red and wet. He held up one of the bones, a slender curve of modest size that might have been a rib, and tore at the flesh with his teeth. He looked up and into my eyes. His face seemed to move and shift and change from human to canine to something even more monstrous.

"I know who you are," I said. I had imagined this boy, but not *this* boy. This was not a boy at all, not any-thing human. His nose and mouth were strange, misshapen, sometimes more of a snout, changing from moment to moment, and the whole of his jaw and neck and chest were soaked with clotting blood.

"And I know who you are," the creature replied. "The book has wound you in its web and drawn you here to me." He waved me over with his furry hand and gestured to a place across from him. "Come, sit with me. Make this a quiet interlude in your night-journey. I shall share my tale with you. I know how you love stories."

He drank deeply from a dark clay cup of even darker wine, cleared his throat, and then he began.

"I once knew love," the beast-boy said. "My one true love, an Irish lad. His name was Tommy. He loved music, he played the violin, like your uncle did. Is this why you were brought to me? We will have to see. All this

was back in the land I once called home, before my
rescue by Master Wood. Before Wood and I escaped to this
wretched country.

"A bright young boy was our Tommy, his life sold out
from under him. A mill owner named Wilkes had fallen
into debt and offered the lad to Lord Newark, in
exchange for relief from his obligations. Newark asked
young Tommy what he could do and he answered that he
could work as a hall boy, emptying chamberpots, cleaning
boots and running errands, fiddling tunes, plus he knew
a few tricks with the cards, and could suck a prick the
size of a rat until it was spent.

"Wilkes went red like a bushel of beets, much to
Newark's delight. He accepted the offer and took Tommy
in. He'd have plenty of work for the boy's mouth, and
some for the rest of him as well. You must understand,
the mill had been a punishing place--beatings, hunger,
dangerous machines, and days that stretched to sixteen,
sometimes eighteen hours. The molly house was a palace
by comparison, and the madges who met us there doted
upon us like pets. But whereas I had come to the house
seeking shelter, Tommy and the others were catamites,
playthings in a private nursery. Yet he and I were as
brothers, and sometimes more."

I cast my eyes around the room, the grotesque bone mosa-
ics on the walls and ceiling pulsing in the candlelight.
The beast-boy was talking more to himself than to me. I
could only listen in confusion and watch his gruesome
meal congeal between us.

"The mollies were an aged lot, and some could hardly
pop a twig, so ofttimes it was Tommy and I who played
while they watched and frigged themselves or each other.
He spied the silver ring that dangled from my neck and
asked if I was joined or owned. I laughed and said the
only ring to marry me was his own when he o'er-bent.
Just then he bowed and spread his cheeks and asked,
'Give me your finger, then, if not your hand entire.'
The mollies whooped and howled and we gave them quite a
show. It was in this way that we entangled, inseparable,
like the branches of twinned trees."

The creature picked a kidney out of the bowl, lush and
livid, and popped it into his mouth. He ground his teeth
into it, making a gristly sound, then swallowed it with
a gulp. A fresh trickle of blood snuck down from the
corner of his smile.

"Now, I say we were well treated, but there was one man--
we knew him as Acton. A colleague of Lord Newark's, an
Examiner with the Court of Chancery. He stepped over our
threshold twice a year, and that was twice too many. He
had a vicious streak which widened when he drank. Once he
dug his claws in you, he would not release you until the
sheets bloomed red."

The beast-boy set the bowl aside, lifted the hem of his
shirt, and wiped the caked and crusted gore from across
his face and neck.

"Acton had received word of 'the new lad' and had come
to see for himself. Our Tommy was brought out, and a

dark look drew over Acton's face like a heavy cloud,
then just as quickly vanished. I was sure that something
had passed between the two before, but Tommy seemed not
to know the man nor register his demeanour.

"Acton brought out a deck of playing cards, and Tommy
proposed a game of Pick the Punk--cheekily stating that
if Acton couldn't find the punk, then he would have to
become it. Tommy had a cock like a baby's arm holding a plum, so this was no idle threat. Mind you, many
a madge would be keen to play, with the hope of happily
losing." The creature held the curved bone aloft between
his forefingers to show the full size. "Acton would have
waddled for weeks to take a prick so big. But he nodded
and took the dare, and the mollies laughed and cheered
while Newark and I grew unsettled. Are you all right, my
good man? You look a bit pale."

"Thank you, I'm fine," I answered, though I was growing queasier as each moment passed, made worse by the
grasping shadows cast by the guttering candles, the soft
scuttling of the insects in the encroaching darkness. The
room seemed to be drawing itself around us like a cloak.

"The two men stood at a small parlour table and Tommy
put the punk into play. The saucy Jack, who had seemed
so easy to find at the start, proved elusive once the
chase was on. Five separate tries, and all five times
he escaped. Acton observed that he was being made not a
punk but a fool, and suggested that the game was neither
free nor fair. Lord Newark assured him it was all in
good fun, and Acton gave an icy smile in response--then

took a hefty purse from the depths of his coat. 'I would like a moment with the boy, to learn the secret of his clever trick, and to show him one of my own.'

"I moved to step in and join, but Newark held me back, taking the sack of coin and coaxing Tommy and Acton into an adjoining room. Tommy was confused, and looked to me pleadingly as the heavy oak door closed between us. Their first few moments were quiet murmurings, and then the sound of a slap like a thunder crack, a smash of glass, and then cries and shrieks that quickly grew unbearable. I struggled in Newark's arms, but he was strong and fearful and his terror infected me. After a quarter-hour passed, every second of which seemed an eternity, the heavy oak door reopened. Acton emerged, spattered and splashed with blood not his own. Wiping his hands and face on Tommy's shirt, he declared the wager won: he had picked the punk after all. He stepped away from the door to let Newark through, and I followed. I should never have seen what I saw at that moment. We found Tommy face down on the bed--his face and body beaten, his life's blood pooling around him. He was dead, of course. Belt tight around his neck. Across his freckled back, from shoulders to tailbone, a large, bloody cross was carved deep into his flesh, and in the centre lay a playing card. The prancing punk himself, the Jack of Spades.

"I spun round to launch myself at Acton. I felt the beast-rage rising within me. But Newark held me by the shoulder and said five words that stopped me cold: 'He is the boy's father.'

"Acton, Tommy's father. An officer of the court who sired a boy with one of his servants, under his wife's thrice-broken nose, and then sold the child away. And now he'd found his son, a bugger boy, and murdered him.

"Newark had me stay with Tommy as he helped Acton with his hat and coat then led him down to his horse and carriage. Their voices were just below our window. 'Mutual discretion,' I heard Acton say, then the horses cried out as they lunged forward and pulled the carriage away. I knew I had only a moment.

"I took Tommy's hand in mine and sent a surge of life into him, and took a piece of his death back into me. It is a dark talent of our kind and we do not use it lightly. It is like taking poison. His eyes fluttered and opened, blind. 'What has happened?' he whispered. 'Have I been killed?' I told him yes, then asked if it was true, if Acton was his father. 'It is, though I only know it now,' he sighed. 'Cursed from birth I was, and all my life, but let this be the end of it. I lived more than many twice my age. And of all the monsters I have known, it was you I wept for, and it was you who wept for me.'

"Then, he sighed, a last shuddering sigh, and once again he succumbed.

"In those last moments, before Newark flew back through the door, I did what I have always done, what I will always do: bit by bit, from top to toe, I swallowed him up. My tiny, perfect Tommy.

"And this is how his shade came to join me in the everwood. As they all do, for a while. But spectres fade in
time, fade or wander. Even into your waking world."

He picked up the rib bone once more, drew it through
his teeth, scraping it clean before dropping it back in
the bowl with a clatter. I felt like I was being crushed
by the darkness, the dirt, the rage and despair. *I must
wake up. I must find the light.*

"So sad about poor Acton," the beast-boy sighed.
"That very night, he died in his bed--imagine! His
throat torn out, his body rent limb from limb and half
devoured. 'A ravenous beast,' they said, one that
had terrorized the countryside for ten generations or
more. 'Crept in like a cat,' it did, when the night
was at its blackest, and then it took him--and shook
him--and ate him all up. All while his wife, his children, his servants slept safe in their rooms. They
heard not the tiniest sound."

"Why am I here?" I asked.

"Why indeed." The creature cocked his head slightly,
then smiled. "You may know better than I. Something you
touched, or someone you loved, has left my mark on you."
With that, he stood and pulled my face up to his. I could
almost taste the thick black blood on his lips. "The day
will come when I reach for you," he said. "And you may yet
reach for me." He held up from the bowl a single glistening eyeball, a tangle of ganglia dripping down from it.
"I--have my eye--on you." He peered into it curiously,

then popped the tidbit into his mouth and crushed it, the vitreous spewing out and spattering my cheek.

I woke up wide-eyed, frantic, unable to catch my breath, like something had been sitting on my chest and crushing my windpipe. I grabbed the pen and paper on the coffee table, wrote down one word before I rushed into the kitchen to vomit.

Nicholas.

Awake, asleep, awake. I dressed, I walked. I sat down in the park at 3 a.m. and I waited, but he never came. I was there for more than an hour, and nothing. I think I passed out on the bench for a moment, a dangerous thing to do. When I opened my eyes, someone else was standing there in torn, baggy jeans, no shirt, and a navy-blue hoodie. He must have been freezing. I asked if he'd come to see the world below, but he just turned away and took a piss, so I waited a few minutes more and then I got up and left.

> *Black and chill are Their nights on the wold*
> *And They live so long and They feel no pain*
> *I shall grow up, but never grow old*
> *I shall always, always be very cold*
> *I shall never come back again*

2008

Aaron Tate was crashing.

It was a Thursday night, or Friday morning, just after 1 a.m. He was at the very back of the last subway car, in the double seat next to the conductor's cab, on the last northbound train, and the bright lights and the jostling and the noise and the smells were making him sick. He felt like he was being watched, like the person on the other side of the grey metal door was peering at him through the black oval window, their hand hovering over the alarm. He'd been clean for forty-two days, his longest break since Christmas, and had careened between euphoria, despair, and exhaustion, had found himself standing in front of the bathroom cabinet mirror searching his face for any sign of the Aaron he used to know, used to be. His eyes were hollow and sunken, his skin grey and scattered with pimples, his hair thinning so that you could see the scabs on his scalp. Back in the day, heads would turn when he walked into a room. Nobody looked at him now. *Assholes.*

He had opened every drawer, checked every pocket, felt around under the bed, nothing, not even a cough drop. And then he'd said screw it, he'd pulled on his pants and rain jacket and taken his bike to the loft down near the water where his ex pushed out little packets of crack and Molly and Tina. They'd hung out and blown some clouds together, did a few lines, fucked around a little, ordered a pizza and forgot about it, and then Aaron staggered out onto the street to find that his bike had been stolen, the U-lock snipped in half with bolt cutters. Then it was a race to get up to the subway and onto that last train, and every jump and lurch in the line made his stomach clench like a fist. *Faces. Fingers. Screaming.* He wasn't sure what was worse, closing his eyes or forcing them open.

By the time he arrived at College station, the high he'd been riding earlier had gone rancid, leaving him shaky and teary and hopeless. His legs were weak and rubbery, it took all his mental energy to make them carry him forward out the sliding doors of the subway car. As hard as he was concentrating, careful and focused, he still nearly stumbled into a clutter of plastic sheeting, wooden barriers, and small orange sandbags on the platform. It seemed like the area had been hastily prepped for an urgent repair. A brownish-red substance was leaking out from behind a few of the large ochre wall tiles and was starting to pool on the platform's granite floor. The whole section would need to be removed, something that would probably take weeks if not months. "This fucking city," he muttered. Sometimes it felt like everything was collapsing all around him, and he wasn't far behind.

Off to the right were two heavy steel doors, leading to a storage or electrical room. Roughly scratched into the grey enamel on the right-hand door was the figure of an animal, walking upright, a wolf or a bear, a long tongue curling out of its sawtoothed mouth. On the floor beneath, a sodden copy of *Xtra!* from the first week of April, its front cover shouting SOMETHING IS WRONG IN THE VILLAGE. Below that, a photo of an anxious young Hispanic man, grimacing into the camera, his face half in shadow. ACTIVISTS "DISAPPEAR," GO UNDERGROUND IN FEDERAL CRACKDOWN ON LGBT REFUGEES.

A little cough just to his left made him almost jump out of his skin. He turned and saw a guy, a younger guy, bomber jacket and tight jeans, smiling back at him. Weird—he had been the only passenger in his car, just him and an off-duty conductor in his sixties, but here was this guy, shorter, huskier, rusty-red hair, pale pink skin dotted with freckles, standing against the wall that led down into the tunnel. Could he have come out of there? Younger; handsome in that boyish way. A little bit damaged, definitely, but that's how he liked them. Cruisy, too, his right thumb hooked into his front pants pocket, his fingers grazing his crotch. He looked like something out of the seventies. *This never happens to me.* Maybe he was a hustler? Aaron had been, back in the day, for close to two years. The money was nice, but he found it exhausting. Bad kissers, bad breath, too many boundary issues, too much emotional labour. He might as well have stayed in the theatre.

"Hi there," Aaron said awkwardly.

The boy smiled invitingly. "Are you here for him?"

"I don't think so?" Aaron ran his hand through his hair. His stomach was still doing flip-flops. "Sorry, I'm a little bit wasted right now. I should be getting home."

"He's here, can't you tell? He is all around us," the boy said, gesturing at the open air. "Do you want to meet him? We can find him together. There's a whole world below us that he wants us to see."

What is this, some kind of cult thing? "Um, listen—I'm not religious or anything like that. No offence, it's just not my scene. And I don't have any money, sorry." Aaron shrugged weakly. *Cute, though.*

The boy held a finger up to his lips—*Shhhhhhh*—and smiled that smile, gestured at Aaron to follow him past the Danger: Do Not Enter sign and into the tunnel. The last train was gone, no others would be coming through. They would be alone in the dark, undisturbed. His insides stilled for a moment, almost as if they were encouraging him.

This is how people get killed.

Aaron started to follow the boy, but then jumped back as a shrieking, grinding noise filled the air. With a metallic screech, the final southbound train plunged into the station, soaring down the tracks on the other side of the divide. It slowed and stopped with another ear-piercing squeal, then threw open its doors and released a scattering of stragglers out into the night.

Aaron turned back to the boy with the rusty-red hair—he'd only looked away for a second—but his new friend was gone. Aaron peered down into the tunnel, looked back up towards the exit. The boy couldn't have passed him, not without walking through the construction debris. Had he gone into the tunnel alone? Was there another way out? Aaron felt a creeping unease, like he was being set up for something. A heavy metal gate slammed shut somewhere up above him, followed by a clamour of thuds and thumps and bangs in quick succession, echoing through the building. The loudspeakers blurted a staticky, unintelligible announcement. The escalator stopped with a groan. Time to go home, home to bed. He didn't want to be rounded up by security.

Then he saw, on the platform near the stairs, a battered old red book. He didn't care much for books, didn't really like reading, but something about it intrigued him. Was it valuable? He couldn't tell. He picked it up, looked it over, flipped through it. A few pages of writing, a few pages of drawings. Somebody's diary? He tossed it back down onto the floor, let out a sigh, and grabbed the handrail to pull himself step by step up to the exit.

Aaron was awakened by the sound of animals yelping and howling. It was still dark, he could barely see across the room. A dog, he thought, or several dogs, setting each other off around the building, their shouts for attention more like screams. Or had he dreamed it? All he could hear now was a distant car alarm, cycling through its honks and wails, then stopping, then starting again. Sirens? A fire? He couldn't smell anything, he couldn't hear anyone.

There had been a dream, not animals, but something. A dream or a memory? Fragments danced just out of reach. *Faces. Eyes.* Faint flecks swirled around in his mind. The park next to the 519, years ago, when the

AIDS Memorial was being built. Cheap wooden hoarding set up all round the space while the stones were being set and the pedestals erected, covered with photocopied pages, pasted, stapled, men's faces and names, *Missing, Last Seen, Do You Know This Man?, Have You Seen Him?*, some highlighted in fluorescent marker to stand out against the others.

Peter Wells, Toronto, 1965–1985; Jean Lariviere, East York, 1940–1983; Daniel Wallace, Toronto, 1961–1984; John Ferriman, Toronto, 1962–1986; David Edgar, Etobicoke, 1955–1985; Richard Mercer, Toronto, 1949–1984; Roger Tonkin, Scarborough, 1966–1987; Michel Fortier, Toronto, 1939–1988; Paul Andrew Hill, 1966–1985; Duncan Jones, Toronto, 1960–1989.

So much loss, so much sorrow. How many friends of his were gone, how many lovers, he couldn't even begin to count. How had he been spared? He had made the same mistakes as all the others, fucked furiously and with abandon, only to burn with shame and regret and terror in the days and weeks afterward. Test after test and always negative and why?

Shadows moved around him in a blur, other people, other men. Fleeting figures, never in focus. No faces. Wait—maybe one face. Away from the others, watching intently. Black hair, heavy dark brows set in a scowl. Icy black eyes. Animal eyes. Fingers clenched into fists.

Aaron grabbed the clock on the nightstand, pulled it closer, groaned. He couldn't have slept more than an hour. It was going to be one of those nights. He leaned over and switched on the blue bedside lamp.

A sound came from somewhere deep in the apartment, a shift or a creak.

It wasn't just the building settling, or someone running their dishwasher at all hours, it wasn't just the blustering wind. He listened, listened harder, till his ears began to ring from the effort.

Yes, he was sure of it. Someone was there. Someone was close.

"Hello?" He cringed as soon as he said it. *Genius move.*

No answer. No sound at all, really. His bedroom was in the southern-most corner of the unit, across from the washroom but uncomfortably far from both the entrance and the sliding glass door that led out onto the balcony. He was nine floors up—could a prowler have broken in next door and then climbed across? Had he left something open, even a crack? He had seen a trailer for a movie a few days ago, three violent teens in masks creeping around Liv Tyler and Scott Speedman's house, moving in and out of shadows. It was the kind of thing that snuck into the back of his mind and lurked there for weeks.

Of course the apartment was empty, of course he was alone. But he'd never get back to sleep unless he checked every room, every door and window, every lock, plus the fridge and stove and the leaky kitchen tap. He'd slept through a flood once in a previous apartment— he couldn't face that again. He threw off the covers, swung his feet down onto the floor, stood up, and made his way to the bedroom door. Stopped. Listened.

Maybe he had mice. He hurried across the hallway into the bath-room, turned on the light. Empty. The shower curtain was pulled back just as he'd left it before getting dressed for work. The clear-vinyl shower mat was ringed with black mildew around the small suction cups that held it in place. He'd have to deal with that soon, the smell in there was terrible. He stopped again, listened. He had moved from panel to panel along the hoarding surrounding the memorial, each panel covered with more posters than the one before. *Missing Missing Missing, Please Help Do You Know Have You Seen.* Pages and pages, pasted on top of each other, stapled, taped, tacked, and nailed. The rain had left some in tat-ters and every few minutes a bird would swoop down, tear off a strip of paper, then fly away to line its nest. But then something changed, the hoarding wasn't around the memorial, not the same park, not the same year. The posters and flyers were all older, decades older, some much older than that, photographs turning into sketches and drawings, pages hand-lettered. He stopped in front of the last of them—*Have You Seen*

Him?—checked the crude sketch printed on it. It was the boy, the glowering black-haired boy, and then it was his own face staring back at him.

Another long creak, from the other end of the apartment. Aaron shook his head to clear it, then picked up the plunger that sat beside the toilet, held it up defensively. Once he got to the kitchen, he'd swap it out for something a bit more effective.

He stepped back into the hallway, where the smell was somehow worse. Rotten, gaseous, foul. Was this what death smelled like? Maybe it *had* been a mouse. He peered around the floor to see if maybe a furry little body, poisoned or injured, had crawled out of a cupboard and died. His neighbour Rosa had once found an injured bat in her front hallway. It had flown in and hidden in one of the closets when she was bringing in plants from the balcony. She had picked up a heavy wooden step stool and dropped it on the creature, crushing it with a yelp, and then was so sickened and horrified that she had thrown up on the floor and then fled to her mother's while the super cleaned up the mess and replaced a patch of parquet.

Dizzied and faintly disgusted, Aaron switched on the living room lights, glanced around quickly. Everything was fine, nothing seemed out of place except for the stink of blood and rotten flesh. Had he forgotten to rinse the dinner dishes, or throw out an old bag of garbage? He peeked into the darkness, flipped the light switch. Nothing there either, not on the floor, not under the sink. He set down the plunger, pulled a roasting fork out of its drawer, held it at the ready.

He re-entered the living room, moved carefully around the couch towards the balcony door. It was closed and locked. He peered through the glass into the darkness. The whole area seemed to be empty, the outdoor furniture was undisturbed. Except the table—he saw something there, it might have fallen from somewhere above. He unlocked the inside door and slid it to the right, squinted through the screen.

It was the book, the old red journal from the subway platform. Why was it out here? And behind it, with his hand on it, seated at the table as if for a meal, was a young man, bare-chested in the cold, with pale skin and black hair—at first staring straight ahead, and then turning his head slowly to lock eyes with him.

The boy from the dream. He was smiling, his teeth sharp and pointed, animal teeth, stained red and wet.

Aaron slammed the door shut and locked it, grabbed the phone, and lifted the receiver. A loud, rapid dial tone blasted into his ear. Out of order. He hammered at the buttons uselessly then threw the phone back down. Movement at the edge of his sight—the young man was standing at the balcony door, right against the glass, the book in his hand, and he was unclothed, his chest and crotch densely furred with coarse black hair, his uncut cock erect. He raised his hand, pressed it to the screen, to the glass, and then pushed his hand through it, as if through a curtain of water. Aaron gasped and ran, ran out the front door and into the hallway. *Shit! I'm naked!* He held the knob tightly, looking left and right, wondering where he could run to, when suddenly the knob turned in his hand and the door swung open, almost pulling him off his feet down onto the floor. The boy stood in the doorway, shifting and changing, slipping in and out of focus.

"Aaron," he said. "You must be freezing. Come back inside."

Aaron rocked backward, steadying himself, brandishing the fork. "Stay away from me! Don't touch me!" He inched backwards towards the end of the hall, the exit into the stairwell. There was a fire pull there. He could wake the whole fucking building.

"There's no need for all this," the young man continued, moving ever forward. "I know how hard it is to live a life alone." His face and body seemed to struggle to remain intact, as if another figure or form was trying to burst through. The air was alive around him, molecules dancing. Not a ghost, not a demon. But a creature, Aaron realized. An actual monster.

The smell was a stench now, vile and putrid, as if an animal had been squashed on the road and left in a ditch for the worms. Aaron pinched his nostrils, covered his mouth. "Stay back!" he shouted, then swung the fork and caught the beast's shoulder, slicing into it. *Flesh and blood. Not a flashback. Not a hallucination.*

The creature recoiled, and glimpses of another form began to emerge: leathery skin and thick black fur and canine eyes and yellowed fangs glistening with drool. Aaron swung the fork again and the monster grabbed his hand, crushing it. It pulled him closer, the thick scent of decay hot on its breath. "No one is here for you, Aaron. No one is coming." The beast snapped Aaron's wrist and pushed him back against the end wall, the fork falling onto the floor with a clatter.

"Please, please don't hurt me," Aaron whispered. He reached up and over with his good hand, felt around—found the fire pull. Dug his fingers into it, yanked down on the lever, breaking the little tube of glass that ran across it.

Nothing. A hollow, mocking silence where the ear-shredding clanging should have been.

The beast loomed over him, then knelt like a forgiving parent. "It's the book, Aaron. It doesn't choose just anyone." He leaned in so close that Aaron could taste the foulness of his breath. "It knows you. It knows how special you are. I was made for you. And you were made for me."

Behind the creature, a shimmer, a shift in the light; for a moment, the walls seemed to melt away. Aaron saw a clearing in a dense old forest, branches waving, leaves fluttering, misshapen figures emerging from the mist. He pulled his gaze away, turned his head. The door to the stairwell was right behind him. He grabbed at the handle with his good hand, turned it, fell backwards as the door swung open, onto the concrete floor of the landing. His legs scrambling, he used his good arm to pull himself backwards until once again he was pinned to a wall. Beside him, stairs led up. The creature was blocking the stairs that led down.

"We can be your family, Aaron. You need never be lonely again. But you must come through me. There is no other door." The beast lifted its foreleg, reached towards Aaron, extended a large, black-furred paw. "Come. Give me your hand."

Another shimmer and the forest rose around them, circled them, embraced them, rich and dark and majestic. The air was wild with the smells of wet, wormy earth, leaf slime, and mould. It was true. He knew and everyone knew: he was alone, he was afraid, now and always. He had felt it every day of his life, ever since he was a child. During one of his parents' drunken fights, when he was just eight years old, as his mother locked herself in the bathroom while his father chased him around the house with a knife, he'd hidden under the bed and squished himself against the far wall, his father cursing and slashing at the air in front of him. Why hadn't he tried harder? Why didn't he just do it?

The shades drew closer, began to gather around him. Some were missing limbs, some had faces stripped of flesh. Eyes were gouged, jaws torn, chests clawed and bellies slashed, innards dragging. They moved stiffly, slowly, like puppets on strings. They reached for him, caressed him, streaking his face and hair and chest with filth and muck and gore. And for the first time in years, for the first time since childhood, Aaron felt like he was coming home.

"Yes," he sighed. "Yes." And he lifted his hand to the beast, touched and then grasped its outstretched limb.

The creature gave the slightest nod, then stood, suddenly taller, its shoulders and back and neck pressed against the underside of the landing above and its huge, slavering mouth opened into a dark, cavernous maw. Aaron could not look away, only faintly felt the hands and fingers and mouths and teeth of his new brothers, his brothers from the glade, now behind and all around him. They dug into his skin and tore him open, peeled him and split him, cracking his bones, clawing and ripping at him, his new brothers lifting him up and offering him to the beast. The creature snapped up his limbs and flesh and organs greedily, licking its lips with its long, coarse tongue, until one of the shades seized Aaron's flayed and hollowed frame and hurled it screaming into the creature's mouth, down and down and down into the blackness. *This is love*, Aaron thought as his life ended. *This is what love is.*

The forest, the figures, the creature all vanished.

The fire bell abruptly stuttered to life, its shrill appeal shattering the silence.

That was the year with the slow-starting spring that had followed a seemingly endless winter. The year when a group of young tourists fell victim to a surprising predator in *The Ruins*, and a ghostly presence gave solace to a fractured family in *Lake Mungo*. Teen girls were adding each other's PINS to their BlackBerrys, Katy Perry kissed a girl, Rihanna took a bow, and Leona Lewis's poignant, ominous "Bleeding Love" was crying out for a club mix. Soaring rents forced some favourite Church Street establishments to close, while a final few teetered on the edge. And the city's Pride festival was about to be rocked by controversy as Queers Against Israeli Apartheid prepared to enter the parade, reclaiming the event as a platform for queer political protest instead of the usual pageant for rainbow-brandishing brands.

That was the year that Aaron Tate, thirty-seven, went missing, and Ryan Wilkes, twenty-four, returned.

§

Nicholas was dying.

In the clearing at the heart of the forest, the beast-boy clutched at himself in a burrow beneath a tangle of roots under the spreading sycamore. The creature twitched and shivered, clenched his teeth. Sweat streamed off his furrowed brow. The ground was splashed with sick just inches from his face. His heart raced like a hundred steeds. He yearned to sleep; he could not sleep. Fractured images danced through his mind, their glittering edges sharp and jagged. He lay on the forest floor weeping in agony, knowing his end was perilously close.

He gripped the old red Book of Shades between his trembling paws. A tendril of smoke floated out from between its pages, a hint of the damage contained within. Faerie books and their owners have an inseparable bond. A wound to one will cause both to bleed. He had been poisoned, and it was his own damned fault.

There were many who thought the creatures of the everwood were immortal, the faeries and nature spirits and elementals who resided there. But all things die, and many can be killed. It was true that those of the wood were immune to human diseases, healed rapidly from common injuries, and could sometimes survive devastating physical damage that would destroy any other creature. But there were certain natural elements that posed great danger to them.

Nicholas had made a terrible mistake. The meat he consumed just a few hours earlier had been tainted somehow, had carried a lethal essence in its flesh, in the blood that had coursed in its veins. The meat named Aaron. *These wretches I feed upon*, he thought as the spasms racking his body escalated in intensity. *My hatred is more love than they deserve.* He should have been more careful, less hurried. He saw the signs but ignored them, thought they were less than they were: the wide black eyes, the scabby lips, the quavering voice, the fidgeting hands. The smell. *Too rushed, too excited. Why was I such a fool? I could have waited a day, or even two.* He moaned and then moaned again, louder, and the animals scattered throughout the wood all trembled at the sound.

As day turned to dusk, the shades emerged ravaged and ruined from among the trees and approached the beast-boy, stood over him in an uncertain vigil. He was direly ill, lost in delirium, oblivious to his surroundings. His power over them had weakened. Memories of their lives above returned to them as if emerging from a fog. The wraiths gazed down at the creature, then turned to each other. *Escape.* Some had slipped away in times past, had followed the beast as he left the wood to feed and had found their way up into the mortal world, and none had ever come back.

Was it a journey into nothingness? The barghest had always warned that no life awaited them outside the everwood, that they would evaporate like mist at the first touch of the sun. For a few, for those whose tie to the waking world was strongest, it was worth the risk to find release.

As the dwindling light filtered through the hushing leaves, the creature shifted, stirred, twitched, and snuffled, as would a dog in a patch of sunlight on its master's floor. He did not have the strength to move even in the realm of dreams. *Robin, where is Robin?* He had hoped the bond he had been building would draw her to his aid. He cast his mind's eye about, trying to catch a glimpse, a whiff . . . Nothing. She was out of reach. But—he sensed another who was nearby, one who had held the book, had opened it, had cast her eyes across its pages. Would she come, if she were called?

"Find her," he whispered. "Bring her to me."

The old red book slid from between the paws onto the lush green grass, crumbled into a fine crimson dust, and then cast itself upon the winds. Each such act weakened him, but he had little choice. Nearby, the shades watched the particles spin and swirl, up and out of the wood and into the land above, and three of them followed, slipping through the crack between the worlds. The creature could do nothing to stop them.

Obediently, the crimson dust—each speck a book, a dream, a passage in its own right—whirled through the rain-washed streets, down and down to the oldest part of the city, steps away from the corner where Master Wood, merchant, once sold his wares to those who imagined themselves his betters. The old red book was not alive, not exactly. It was an instrument, an extension of its owner's will and desires. The dust flew upward along the side of the red-brick wall, through a small, square metal duct, and into the bedroom where Salem lay sleeping, her hand on her cellphone in case Robin called from her hotel in Barcelona.

The red cloud hovered around Salem's face as she softly snored, and then one particle broke away from the others, darted into her nose and up to a cavity behind her eye, planted itself like a seed, and then, like a claret-coloured rose, it bloomed.

Salem was standing at the edge of a dense, dark forest. Before her, on the worn dirt path leading into it, was a wooden door. Red oak, old and heavy, thick, the knob fashioned from faceted glass and set into a mottled brass plate. She reached for it, but before she could touch it, the door slowly swung towards her, clearing the path to let her through.

What happened to my "trans superhero saves the city from venomous wasp women" dream? She cautiously walked along the winding path past ancient trees: flowering hemlocks and spiky tamaracks, enormous bristling pines, ghostly silver birch, and feathery white cedar, some wrapped in vines, others covered over with moss and lichen, buzzing with curious insects. Gentle rustling in the distance suggested she wasn't alone, that someone was lurking just out of sight, watching intently as she made her way through the thickening forest. She came to a clearing dominated by a stark white sycamore. Something lay on the ground beneath it, curled in the crook of the roots, panting and whining. An injured dog, she thought, until she moved closer and saw it was a bizarre jumble of human and animal parts, haphazard patches of flesh and fur, mismatched limbs, jagged teeth, frightened eyes. The dying thing reached out its paw to her and gasped, "Help me."

Salem hesitated, then crouched down and took the paw in her hand. *It's like something out of a folk tale.* She looked down at herself and saw she was wearing her pyjamas, parka, and winter boots. *And typical me, couldn't be bothered to dress for the ball.* Salem looked down and saw that Samson, her five-year-old German shepherd, had appeared at her side, growling tensely. She gave him a skritch on his ear to calm him. *Are we dreaming together?* she wondered.

"What's happening?" she asked the creature. "What can I do?"

"Let your dog closer," he whispered. "Don't worry, I mean him no harm."

Salem watched as Samson approached, sniffing the creature's face, breathing into its snout. The dog pulled its head back, sneezed abruptly, then looked up and out over the wood and bounded off at top speed into the trees.

"Samson!" she shouted. "Samson!"

A high, wild scream pierced the silence. A flock of birds burst out from among the leaves and flew frantically overhead. Another shriek and then another, and then Samson came galloping back through the forest, closer and closer, with something hanging limply from his mouth. Golden brown, black-tipped ears. A hare.

"Oh, Samson, what the hell have you done," she sighed. The animal twitched in his jaws—it was still alive. She jumped back, horrified.

"I'm sorry," the ailing creature said. "You'll have to kill it for me, please. I can't do it myself."

Just a dream, Salem thought. *Just a dream, just a dream.* She reached for Samson's mouth and he dropped the mauled hare into her hand. It was bleeding and its neck was likely broken, but its eyes were wide and its heart was racing. She knelt in the soft grass beside the beast-boy, tightened her fist around the hare's throat until finally it stopped breathing, its heart stopped beating, then placed the bloodied body on the ground in front of the creature's mouth. It lifted its head and snapped at the small brown corpse, gnashing at flesh and fur and blood and bone until only a red, wet stain was left on the dirt. Salem then held its head back and nursed it from a wineskin that was hanging from a nearby branch.

She knew it was a monster, she knew she should be afraid. But she was not. She was sure she had read or heard something about just such a creature. She ran her hand over its fur, from neck to tail, again and again, till the seizing and twitching and panting slowed and it fell into a deep, sound sleep. As the beast calmed and soothed, Salem pulled herself up to her feet, dusted herself off, brushed the blood and dirt off her hands, and motioned for Samson to come join her on the path.

She wasn't more than a dozen steps beyond the glade when she tripped over a gnarly root, tumbled forward, and opened her eyes to find Samson yipping and licking at her face. "Yes, yes, good morning," she laughed. She was surprised at how cold she was—she could see her breath in front of her face. Startled, she looked around and saw that she wasn't in bed at all; she was sitting on a bench in Wellesley Park, a ten-minute walk from the house. *Have I been sleepwalking? Did I bring Samson here and then just zone out?* She had taken a sleeping pill as she was heading to bed, maybe that was to blame. And now here she was in her pyjamas and boots with her parka pulled around herself, and Samson without a leash or collar. She looked at her wrist—no watch. It felt late, well past midnight. The moon was high and bright. *What on earth is wrong with me?*

Her left coat pocket let out a loud, jangling blast and she leapt up from her seat with a gasp. Samson barked and barked. She shushed him, pulled out the cellphone. EUROTEL BCN and a jumble of numbers: it was Robin, using her calling card.

"Oh no, Salem, I'm sorry, you weren't supposed to answer," she said, her voice distant and crackly. "I was going to leave you a message. I thought you'd be asleep."

"No, it's okay, I'm just out with the dog," Salem replied, which wasn't completely untrue. "What was the message?"

"It's beautiful, it's lonely, I wish you were here. That's the message. I'm here in the hotel, in the bed. Missing your voice, missing your smell. Missing your girldick poking into my back while I'm trying to sleep in."

"Really? That's sweet," Salem said. "What about poking it into your front, though?"

"That goes without saying. Sorry, I'm getting these cream puff thingies all over myself."

"Cream puffs for breakfast, I no longer feel bad for you. How is the hotel?"

Robin sighed. "Checking in was a nightmare. It seems they thought I'd be white and male and much less annoyed about it than I turned out to be. They tried to tell me they had no reservation even though I had the confirmation *in my hand.*"

"Jesus, Robin." Samson started to whine and paw at her leg. Salem shushed him and pushed on his bum to get him to sit, then sat back down herself.

"Yeah, I know. I put them on the phone with Paulo, you can imagine what that was like. Anyway, I'm sitting here in my fluffy robe in my upgraded suite with this huge complimentary pastry tray and a jug of coffee that could wake the dead, and I wish you were with me."

Salem shivered all over, pulled the coat tighter around herself. "I wish that twice as much. I'm freezing to death in the park. You'd never know it was spring. No coffee, no pastry tray, no fluffy robe." Samson stared up at her expectantly, wagging his tail. He let out another series of yips as she stood up from the bench. She shushed the dog, then turned back to Robin. "Someone's eager to see you. You're back on Sunday around eight? I'll see if one of us can come pick you up."

"I would love that, but I can always grab a cab. Have you heard from Trevor at all?"

"No, not since before you left," Salem replied. Trevor's father had collapsed a few weeks earlier, a heart attack brought on by a blocked artery. Now Trevor was at his parents' place in the suburbs to help out until they could arrange some home care. He and Sergio never *said* they were taking a break, but—they were pretty obviously taking a break.

"Salem?" Another burst of crackling static. "I'm going to head off for now. I love you, and I love Samson too."

"Love you too, have fun at your gig. We'll see you soon," Salem replied, and then clicked the phone off. She had thought about telling Robin about waking up on the bench, but she didn't want to worry her. She would give her doctor a call on Monday, though, and ask about switching out her medication. She looked down at the dog. "Okay, let's head home. Stick close to me."

Samson went right to her heel and stayed there all the way back to the house, softly whining from time to time. He seemed to be a little bit scared, and she couldn't blame him. The whole way home, she couldn't shake the feeling that they were being followed.

&

"Highland sand bird, five letters," Trevor said. "Second letter is an *i*."

Trevor and his mother were sitting in his father's room on the seventh floor of Etobicoke General, frowning over a newspaper crossword. His mother was dressed in various layers of beige and brown—blouse, vest, cardigan, slacks. Practical shoes.

"Piper. P-I-P-E-R. How are you feeling, Harry?" Trevor's mother asked. "Do you need me to take you to the washroom?"

A long silence passed. Trevor's father had slept most of the day, and now he was tugging at the collar of his blue gown and watching out the window at the late afternoon sky, the gently turning construction cranes, the occasional airplane or helicopter. The heart monitor next to the bed beeped softly and rhythmically. Trevor wondered if his father had heard his mother, or if he was having trouble gathering his thoughts.

"Naughty boys were baked in this," Trevor said. "Three letters, middle letter *y*."

"Pye. P-Y-E."

Trevor looked over at his mother, curious.

"It was a torture device from the Dark Ages," she elaborated. "A metal box like an iron maiden. For heretics, deviants, witches. They would put the person inside and heat it with coals, or throw it on a fire." She shrugged. "I heard it on the CBC."

"Do you have a dog?" his father asked, his voice weak and rough with phlegm.

"Me?" Trevor looked at his mother. "Um. No. I mean, I love dogs. But we live in an apartment, we don't have a lot of room."

"You should get a dog," he said, still looking out the window at the sky, the cranes, the passing jet that could barely be heard through the insulated glass. "It's good to have a dog."

His mother smiled, gave his hand a squeeze. *Humour him*, her smile said, not for the first time. "Lucky was a wonderful dog," she said. "You remember Lucky, don't you, Harry?"

His father didn't answer. Lucky had been a blundering black Lab, lovely and loyal but poorly named—chased by wasps, afraid of cats, hid in the bathtub during thunderstorms. The dog once stole a roast chicken carcass off the kitchen table, ran upstairs with it, and tried to eat it while lying on his parents' bed. There was no forgetting Lucky, though he'd been dead for twenty years.

"I'll ask Sergio, maybe we can get something small and yappy," Trevor suggested. "Or maybe an older dog, one that likes to laze around all day."

"Everyone should have a dog," his father said.

A voice piped up from the doorway behind them. "The doctor will be in shortly, Mrs. Mullin. She has the results from yesterday's tests."

Before Trevor could turn around and look, the nurse had hurried away. He yawned and stood up, his mother's hand pulling away and returning to her lap.

"I'm going to stop in at my place to pick up a few things, maybe grab a bite to eat." He gave his father a pat on the leg. "Dad, I'll be back in the morning."

"Good protection," his father said. "They hear things that we don't hear. They see things that we don't see."

Trevor frowned. "I think those are cats, Dad."

"Fuck cats, you can't trust cats, they only care about themselves. They'll eat your eyes."

Trevor's mother looked down at her pearly-pink manicure, already chipping after only three days. She had three cats, named after the younger Golden Girls. His father had forbidden the addition of a Sophia.

She abruptly stood up. "I'm just going to say goodbye to Trevor." She took him by the arm and walked him out into the hallway. "Maybe I wasn't supposed to notice," she said, "but I see the medal you're wearing. It makes me happy. We can go to church together sometime, now that you're here. It doesn't have to be on Sunday."

Trevor touched the St. Benedict medal, held it between his fingers. It would be impossible to explain why he was wearing it, that he hadn't actually found any religion. He wasn't sure how to explain it to himself.

"Sure, Mom, I'd like that," he replied. "There's bound to be one a few blocks from here. Let's go tomorrow, while he's having a nap." She gave his hand another squeeze, then slipped back into the room to wait for the doctor.

Good protection, Trevor thought as he walked to the elevator. He pushed the button and the doors opened instantly. He thought again about big loser Lucky who had loved him so much, so selflessly, clumsily, without hesitation, and he couldn't help himself, couldn't stop himself, he felt his face crumple and he started to cry, great convulsive sobs that felt like he'd saved them up for years. He cried all the way down to the ground floor and right through the lobby, out the glass front doors and into the cab. He couldn't even tell the driver where he wanted to go.

He was awake.

He could smell before he could see, his nose twitching as the scents of the wood returned to him. Yarrow, ox knee, bugbane, cocklebur. He pawed at his eyes, crusted shut, scratched at his itching hindquarters. The flies had made a feast of him. Filthy with shit and piss, his muscles stiff and sore, his insides aching. He peeled one eye open. Sunlight seared his vision, blinding him. He squeezed it shut again.

So many dreams. They faded upon waking but left a bitter edge as they receded. Dreams of his time in the North Country, of his life at the

Benison. Dreams of the clearing at the edge of Molly Wood's Bush—a refuge, a playpen, then a trap, then a tomb. Dreams of hunger and lust and destruction and loss.

One such dream: He was being chased, hunted, hounds in pursuit, shots fired. He knew, if they caught him, they would torture him for their pleasure; he had seen what they did to the cunningfolk, and he had narrowly escaped their torments himself. Infernal devices, designed to be pushed deep into the mouth and arse, encasing the cock and balls, splitting and tearing the flesh, disfiguring it, destroying it. He leapt over roots, ducked under branches, first boy then beast then boy to confuse the hounds, but they had his scent and would not let him go. His own snout caught a whiff of rotten leaves, the soft rush of water—a gently murmuring stream, just wide enough and deep enough to cover his tracks. He ran into the middle of it, and then down the length of it, until he felt the pull of a nearby sidh mound, a gateway to the realm. Escape. He caught sight of the cleft in the rock on its face, burst out of the water and raced towards it, slipped through the crack just as a bullet pierced his shoulder. Tumbling forward, bone shattered, blood coursing, down he fell through the passage and onto a hillock cushioned with green grasses and dappled patches of moss. Injured, hungry, filthy, but safe.

Then another: He and young Eli, Master Wood's boot boy, crouched on the cellar stairs of Wood House, listening to the housemaids gossip about how one of the master's rivals, a merchant named Pettibone, had been found near the water south of Corktown, torn apart by what looked to be a pack of dogs. "That was you, weren't it," Eli whispered, astonished, and Nicholas took the boy's pointing finger into his mouth and tickled it with his tongue until he giggled, causing one of the women to thump the door, shouting, "Who's down there?"

And then another from years before: Curled in Tommy's arms in the Benison, late at night, rain pattering at the windows, the whole house silent save for the wind's faint keening as it winnowed its way under the sash. Turning his head up to kiss Tommy's cheek, his lips, reaching around to pull him in closer, hand on his back, something soft and wet and ragged, blood, flesh, decay, the hair and scalp sliding beneath his fingers. Pulling back his hand, recoiling at the sight, the stench, feeling and knowing that Tommy's arms were grey and mouldering, that his sockets were seething with maggots, his eyes turned to slop, his face tattered, his shapely skull exposed. The skeletal fingers suddenly tightened, drew him in, his corpse-cock hard against him—

He sprang awake, teeth bared, eyes wide, his pulse pounding in his ears. So many dreams, so much pain. His restless sleep had left him famished. He would have to drag himself to the creek, wash himself off, shit, then rest, wake again, feed.

He calmed himself, let his breathing slow. *Salem.* The girl, the dog, the hare. She had come through the dream realm and into the everwood. She had saved his life, a kindness of the utmost rarity. Would she have done so if she had known what she was saving?

High above him, the rustling leaves sounded like fluttering pages, and in his mind he saw the blood-red book, inscribed with charms that bound it to him, filled with the writhing words of the men he had taken and those who had been taken from him. It had brought the girl to him and she had fed him and nursed him; now it was calling to him as would a lover, a mother, a lost and crying child. He would rise and weave his way through the forest, then up and into the city to where the red book led him, to his next companion, to his next feast.

He was alive. Nicholas was alive, and he was hungry.

"Sir, sir." The voice was anxious, insistent.

Trevor lifted his head, opened his eyes into darkness.

"Sir, we are here, you must wake up."

Where am I? What time is it?

He blinked and blinked. He was in the cab. The driver was fully turned around and staring at him, afraid for some reason. Had he said something, done something? He remembered feeling the car turn onto the highway, the smooth, low hum beneath him lulling him to sleep. *How long ago was that?*

"Yes," he said. "Sorry, I'm so sorry." Startled and groggy, he squinted at the meter, handed over the cash from his wallet, and bounced out onto the sidewalk before realizing he didn't know where he was. *Shit.* He went to wave the cab back, but it was already too far away.

He turned around and around to get his bearings, saw the CN Tower in the distance. That meant he was east of downtown and south of . . . practically everything. *How did we end up over here? Did I say Berkeley instead of Beverley?* He assumed he was north of the city's old Distillery District, which was being remade into a fortress of condos, shops, galleries, and high-end cafés, driving out the last of the Gooderham ghosts, but this place was nothing like that place. This was a strange no man's land of car dealerships, gloomy industrial buildings, and factories being gutted and—based on the sales and rental signs—repurposed into chicly barren tech and design offices, garden centres, Pilates studios, and live-in workspaces. Cardboard boxes for large-screen iMacs and fancy Eames desk chairs were bundled and tied beside the recycling bins scattered along the sidewalks.

He stopped and watched, breathless, as a fox scampered across the street a few yards ahead of him and slipped into the gap between two brick buildings. He approached the gap with caution, peered down the length of it. A pair of glowing green eyes at the far end met his gaze, then turned away. The small shadow squeezed through a gap in the links of the wire fence and sped off.

Trevor stepped back from the buildings and realized he was right next to what used to be the Toolbox, the city's original leather and denim bar, before it moved farther east to take over the Simcoe Hotel and then ultimately closed down. He remembered it being a black-painted bunker with caged, frosted windows. Now it was freshly painted the colour of putty, a realtor's sign with a 905 area code fastened to the corner wall. He had fond memories of the bar's cruisy basement, its cheap and cheery Sunday brunch and lively euchre games, its bathtub out back for impromptu water sports. Trevor had only gone twice, as a youngster fresh out of the closet; both times, he'd gotten lucky, the second time with Drew, whom he'd dated for nearly five years. But that was a long time ago, well before Sergio.

Poor Sergio. Why were they still together? Anyone else would have given up on Trevor months ago, maybe years ago. "You could do so much better than me," he had told Sergio at breakfast a few days earlier. This used to be a funny joke with them, where Sergio would answer, "I guess I'm just waiting for someone else to come along." But this time, Sergio had only shrugged and eaten another forkful of eggs on toast.

As Trevor walked past the grey-brick building, its front windows boarded as well as barred, its main door padlocked and chained, he was surprised to hear the insistent thump of a disco beat reaching out from within. He looked up and down the narrow street, around the side of the building. No cars, no signs of life. He peered through a crack at the edge of one of the boards. Maybe it was blocked on the inside of the window as well—all he saw was darkness. But now he could hear melody as well as bass, and he could almost make out some words. It must be coming from the basement. He had fond memories of dancing with Drew there, shirtless and sweaty under the dim red-and-blue lights that swept back and forth across the room, always some cluster of guys in the corner swapping hand jobs and blow jobs. He looked along the side of the building. There was no way in from the front; he would have to shimmy his way down a two-foot gap between the wall and the chain-link fence, all the way to the back of the building.

He pressed his face to the brick, scooted along through overgrown brush, empty spiderwebs, rotten plywood planks, old rusted pipes, and tarpaper shingles. He was about halfway along when his knee tugged on the corner of a corrugated metal sheet, threatening to tear his pants. He stopped to carefully free himself, then saw that the metal sheet was covering a basement window. Even though it had been painted over, he could see circling lights, swaying shadows. Someone was down there, something was happening, and he couldn't help it, he needed to be there, to see and hear for himself. *Maybe it's Drew*, though that was impossible. *Where did that come from?* Drew had run off decades before, just dropped out of sight, had supposedly died in Vancouver or somewhere along the way. Trevor moved the metal sheet aside and continued shuffling down to the rear of the building, cringing every time he raised a cloud of dust.

As he reached the rear of the building, he saw the fence ended in a post and then crossed in front of him to create a dead end. The links were fastened to the bricks with screw eyes that had been pinched shut. He looked around and behind, and saw that he'd passed a battered trio of paint cans. He could stack them one on top of the other and hope that he could vault himself up and over before they pitched and tumbled and he fell along with them.

Why am I doing this? he asked himself as he lifted and shook the cans and stacked them against the twisted wire. *Nobody's in there, the bar's been closed for years, the place is probably condemned.* He looked back at the basement window. Was that even where the dance floor had been? He thought it was closer to the back. *I'm having some kind of flashback. All those years of acid and mushrooms and here's what you get.*

He was just about to turn around and head back when the thunk-thunk-thunk of the bass rose again, teasing at his ears and his mind. He knew what it was: Donna Summer's "I Feel Love."

> *falling free*
> *falling free*
> *falling free*
> *falling free*
> *falling*
> *free*

He could see Drew so clearly, wiping down his burly chest with his balled-up T-shirt, inhaling the musk from it and smiling. Trevor had been so angry with him near the end: fucked up almost all the time, couldn't hold a job, lost his apartment, started stealing from the people he crashed with. It didn't matter what you gave him, what you did for him, it was never enough. But that moment, the lights, the music, the crush of bodies, the aroma of poppers, arms in the air, everyone moving together as one, one life, one mind, one flesh, one heart beating, one pulse pounding, his hand reached out to touch Drew, to touch his chest his neck his cheek his mouth his cock *he's down there I know he is—*

"Hey, you there! What are you doing?"

Trevor spun around to see a skinny South Asian man behind him, late twenties, in acid-washed jeans, a riotous Coogi sweater, and a hunter-green Old Navy bomber jacket.

"I'm from across the street, I keep an eye on this place. Did you, uh, lose something?" He seemed nervous, unsure of what to do, and Trevor suddenly realized how ridiculous he looked, covered in muck and teetering on a wobbly stack of paint cans. He decided to stick as close as he could to the truth without sounding insane.

"I was heading up the street to try to catch a taxi," he explained, "and when I passed by here, I heard someone inside, calling for help. It seemed to be coming from the basement. I thought maybe there was a way in through the back."

The young man warily made his way down the side of the building towards him. "I don't hear anything," he said, then stopped by the basement window. "From here? The voice was down here?" Trevor nodded. He peered down at the painted glass, trying to see inside. "Was it a man or a woman?"

"A woman," Trevor said, thinking it would sound more urgent. "A woman or maybe a child. It was a higher voice."

The young man tried the window. It was locked tight. "I still don't hear anything," he said. "Are you sure it wasn't just some kids playing games?"

"There are no kids around here," Trevor answered. And it was true: aside from the occasional car driving through, he and the young man were alone.

He nodded, then motioned for Trevor to follow. "Come here with me." They manoeuvred their way back between the wall and the fence to the front of the building. He turned and extended his hand. "Rajah."

He shook the young man's hand firmly. "Trevor."

"Trevor, I'm going to go inside and take a look around. You're going to stay here. Understand?"

He nodded. He couldn't stop thinking about Drew, down in the basement, dancing.

"Do you have a cellphone?"

Trevor shook his head.

Rajah looked him up and down, then pulled his red Razr flip phone out of his jacket pocket and handed it to him. "Here, take this."

"Wait," Trevor said, then pointed at the building. "Do you hear that?" The song had started again, same as before, louder if anything.

Rajah stood listening, then a puzzled look came across his face. "What are you hearing?"

"Donna Summer," Trevor answered. "Disco song, from back in the seventies. Why, what do you hear?"

"Nothing. I don't hear anything. No Donna Summer."

Trevor looked at Rajah, unsure if he was telling the truth. He looked as if he had heard something, but maybe something different?

They each listened for a moment more, then Rajah reached over and pushed the phone's power button. A digital clock lit up on the screen. "Give me five minutes. If I don't come back, or if you hear anything else, call the police. Stay outside. Don't come in."

Rajah pulled the ring of keys from the retractable reel on his hip, found one marked with an *X* of red nail polish, unlocked the door, then pulled it open. The music was louder, clearer, more distinct. If it was a hallucination, it scored extra points for accuracy.

Rajah looked back at Trevor, mouthed, "Five minutes," and stepped inside, pulling the door shut behind him.

Trevor held the cellphone in his hand, watching as the numbers changed on the digital clock face. At the three-minute mark, a light sprinkle of icy rain started, and a chilly evening breeze flung the droplets against his skin. Five minutes passed, and the music abruptly increased in volume. Trevor looked up the street, around at the buildings behind him. The area was deserted. There weren't even any cars to flag down.

Seven minutes. Trevor said, "Fuck it," and pulled open the door.

The building was dark, stripped bare to the walls, and strangely silent. It was impossible—the music had been blaring at full volume until just that moment. But now, nothing.

He didn't know what to do. Call out for Rajah? Say nothing and move along quietly? He knew he should go back outside and call the police, but he couldn't leave Rajah alone in there—he had to see what was happening, what had already happened.

Trevor carefully closed the door behind him, let his eyes adjust to the dim light from the caged frosted windows at the back of the space, and slowly made his way to the staircase that led to the basement. As he drew closer, he saw that a cigar-sized metal flashlight lay on the ground ahead of him, its beam slashing across the floor to illuminate a pile of mouse-eaten cardboard boxes, old ledgers, and loose papers along the north wall. He picked it up, shone it over his immediate surround-ings—the empty bar, the washrooms, a few damaged tables and stools pushed off to one side—and then over to the wooden rail at the top of the basement stairs.

He stood at the top and aimed the light at the floor below, and gasped when he saw Drew lying at the bottom, his legs splayed across the last few steps. The same white T-shirt, the same five-button 501s, the same studded black belt with the pewter buckle, the same black leather Reeboks. The same age, impossibly, as when Trevor last saw him.

The flashlight died in his hand, plunging the whole area into blackness. Trevor stepped away from the top stair and shook the flashlight furiously, the batteries rattling inside. It flickered back to life, and he pointed it down at the body below. It wasn't Drew, it was Rajah, in the exact position that Drew had been in. As the beam of light struck his face, he winced, turned away, and coughed, raising a puff of dust off the floor. He opened his eyes and moaned. "Police?"

Trevor vaulted down the stairs, his feet barely making contact. He pulled the fallen man's shoulders up and slid his arm underneath, lifted his upper body off the ground, and helped him stand. Rajah hissed and winced when he put his weight on his right leg. A twisted ankle, a broken bone—it was hard to know while they were down here in the dark. "Raj, come on, we have to get out of here. You're going to have to crawl up the stairs."

Rajah put his hands and knees on the stairs and began a slow climb while Trevor stayed alongside him. Suddenly, the music exploded all around, the old red-and-blue lights swivelled and turned, the creaky old disco ball slowly spangled the stairs and walls and floor.

"We have to go faster," Trevor said into his ear. "We're not alone down here."

"I know, somebody pushed me," Rajah whispered. "You shouldn't have come in. You should have called the police."

"I'm not very good at taking direction," Trevor said.

They reached the top step and he helped Rajah to his feet, guided him as he hopped back across the room towards the building's entrance. Trevor grabbed the handle, pulled hard to open it. Grey cloud-light filled the space around them. Trevor pushed Rajah forward out of the building, turned to close the door—and a hand grabbed him by the shoulder. The stink of death struck him like a punch.

He turned. It was Drew, his face a seething, writhing mass. His eyes were gone, his lips and tongue. Little larvae curled and fell from his mouth, sprayed against Trevor's face as he spoke, or tried to speak.

"Find me," he rasped. "Please find me."

"I can't," Trevor whispered, the urge to vomit aching at the back of his mouth. "I can't, I'm sorry." He pulled himself free, lunged across the threshold, and slammed the door shut behind him.

"Trevor?" He turned to see Rajah looking at him strangely. "Are you okay?"

"Yeah," he answered, shaking off whatever he had just seen. "I'm fine, I'm good." He hurried over, helped him hobble across the road to the building where he worked, sat him down on the short flight of steps that led inside. He dialed 911 and handed Rajah the phone. "I have to go," he said. "Are you going to be okay? Do you want me to stay with you?"

Rajah shook his head. "No, I'll be all right. What were you saying at the door?" The tinny ringing sound from the cellphone tickled the air between them. "I thought I heard you say sorry."

"To you," Trevor lied. "I shouldn't have gone in, I shouldn't have even tried. I should have just called for help."

The cellphone call connected, and a voice at the other end asked the nature of the emergency. Rajah gestured for Trevor to go and then asked for a police car and an ambulance. Trevor left him and started running up to the corner, where the headlights of streetcars, taxis, and suvs were streaking past. A fog was moving in, he could feel it in his bones.

❧

"Hey, sorry I'm late," Julie said as she sat down across from Jake and Denis. She set her Starbucks decaf down on the table next to their Tim Hortons black coffees. "Someone od'd in one of the tents at Moss Park last night, a bunch of us ended up in emerg at St. Mike's."

Julie worked at one of the men's shelters on George Street. She also led a harm reduction working group in the Village, as well as a weekly recovery meeting. A big, burly woman with a bleached-blond brush cut and a plethora of stick-and-poke tattoos, she was tough and funny and not to be messed with.

The two men looked at each other. "Who was it? The person who OD'd—was it Aaron?" Jake asked.

Julie shook her head. "It was a woman, early twenties. There's a lot of shit out there right now. She's doing okay, though. They'll hold her for a little while and then maybe send her to detox." She looked at the two of them. "So, this is Aaron Tate you're talking about, right? You don't know where he is?"

Jake nodded. "Yeah, it's going on two days. We went to his place, it's a mess. It looks like maybe someone broke in. Or, I don't know, maybe it's always a mess."

"You're the boyfriend?"

Jake nodded.

"Two days isn't that long," she observed, sipping from her flat white. She stopped, looked past them, rolled her eyes. Jake turned around to see a shaggy student in a toffee-coloured Tim's uniform heading for their table.

"Ma'am, you can't have that in here," the server said. "No outside beverages or food."

"I'm just here to chat with my friends and then I'll go." She reached into her wallet, pulled out a ten. "Listen, I know you're just doing your job. Take this and bring me an empty cup—is that okay for you? I'd really appreciate it."

The server sighed, took the bill from her, reached around the counter, and grabbed a tall red paper cup. She poured her coffee into it and handed him the Starbucks cup. He held it like it was contaminated and tossed it into the trash.

"Thank you," she called after him, then turned back to Jake and Denis. "Sorry about that."

Denis turned to her. "When was the last time Aaron showed up for a meeting?"

Julie looked out the window at the people passing and waving at each other. A fine light drizzle was starting to fall. "I don't know, maybe a month, maybe more. He could be going somewhere else, though.

Lots of meetings downtown these days." She looked back over at Jake. "Do you think he's using again?"

"Oh, I'm sure he's using," Jake replied. "I just don't know where."

"Did he have any reason to go into hiding? Does he owe somebody money?"

Jake shrugged, looked at Denis. "No idea," Denis said. "Maybe. But I think he would have said something, at least to one of us."

"Does he have any family?" Julie asked. "Would he have gone to see them?"

Denis shook his head. "They don't speak."

"Okay, well. Was he . . . depressed, or anxious, or paranoid?" she asked.

Jake furrowed his brow. "What, like suicidal? No. I mean, I guess anyone can be. But he's never said anything or done anything like that."

Denis leaned in closer. "Listen, I see Aaron four or five times a week. We talk on the phone all the time. He's had his ups and downs like anyone, but he's never said anything about not wanting to be here, not wanting to be alive."

Julie looked at him, then looked at Jake, studying them, considering them. "Okay. Two days isn't long, he may just turn up. But I'll ask around. Someone may have seen him. Here's the thing, though: maybe he wants to disappear. If he owes someone money, or he's feeling threatened, or he wants to be high all the time . . ." She shrugged. "People go missing for all kinds of reasons."

"What about the police?" Denis asked. Jake suppressed a laugh.

"They won't do anything now, it's too soon. They probably won't do much later, either." She reached over, put her hand on his. "I'll see what I can do. If nothing turns up, then we'll figure out what comes next. But— just because you want to find him, it doesn't mean he wants to be found."

"I have a bad feeling about this," Denis said. "I think he wants to be found."

Julie pushed her chair back, the feet scraping the floor. She stood up, zipped up her jacket, snapped a lid onto her cup. "Today is a shit show, but I should be able to tell you something by later tomorrow. Don't go back to his place. Don't talk to anyone else. And don't get your hopes up."

Jake stood as well. "I'll be back in a sec. Julie, thanks for coming. We'll wait for your call." He went to the end of the counter, grabbed the key for the washroom, unlocked it, and slipped inside. He lowered his jeans, sat down on the toilet, relaxed as a burst of urine streamed out of him. He reached into his coat pocket and took out the battered red journal that he had found on Aaron's living room rug. He flipped to the middle of the book, turned a few pages more, and looked down at the six words written there.

Remember me when this you see.

Jake sat staring at them, inscribed in thin, jagged lines that looked almost like claw marks. The words, the letters, they were alive—quivering, trembling, vibrating, electric.

This is his handwriting. These are his words. He wrote this for me, I know he did.

This message is for me.

A knock at the door shocked him back into the moment. "Jake, are you okay?" It was Denis.

He slapped the book shut, stuffed it back in his jacket. "Yeah, I'm fine. Just a sec." He flushed the toilet, washed his hands quickly, pulled open the door.

No one was there. He could see across to where they'd been sitting, then farther out the front window. Denis was pacing outside, smoking and drinking his coffee, steam floating up into his face.

"Are you afraid, Jake? Afraid of being alone?" The voice was right beside his ear, curling into it like a lover's tongue. Denis looked through the glass at him and waved.

I am, he thought. *I am.*

❧

Salem set her mug of lemon mint tea down on the coffee table and turned on the TV, flipped from channel to channel aimlessly. She could hear the click-clack of Samson's nails as he went from room to room to room and back again. "Samson," she called. Samson turned and padded over, placed his head on her leg, then lay down at her feet with his head between his paws. "What is it?" Salem asked. "Do you miss Robin?" She reached down to pat the dog on his head. "That's okay, baby, I miss Robin too. She'll be back tomorrow." *American Idol.* That seemed harmless enough.

Samson abruptly sat up, stood up, looked out towards the front of the house, then began to pace again, from kitchen to living room to dining room and back, panting and whining. *What is this about?* He stopped to let out three sharp barks at the front door. Salem got up, looked out. Nothing. No one. Maybe a neighbour's cat was on the prowl.

"Samson, you're being weird," she said.

The dog cocked his head curiously, then sat and kept his eyes on the door, his panting soft and rhythmic, interrupted from time to time by a rumbling growl.

"Samson, come," Salem commanded, and sat back on the couch. Samson followed and sat on the rug near her feet, then just as quickly stood up again, looked up at the living room window, and again started panting and growling. "What is it? Do you need to go out?" He usually just sat by the door and pointedly pawed at it, eager and impatient. This was anxiety, fear. She decided to pull her coat and shoes on and take him for a walk, not least because she was afraid he might go right there on the floor. Maybe he smelled a skunk? Salem would have to be careful—the last time Samson got doused, it took nearly a week and multiple washings for the smell to fade even a bit.

Salem turned off the TV, peeked into the kitchen to check the oven, stove, and kettle, "Off off off," an old habit dating back to the disaster at Robin's old apartment years before, then pulled down Samson's leash from the hook in the hallway. It was usually a surefire way to get him to race to the door. Instead, he sat by the couch whining and looking from the front window to her and back again.

"Come on, you silly thing. Come on. Walkies." She opened the door and a rush of cold night air filled the front hallway. The dog immediately dropped to the floor, placing his head back down between his paws. "Such a big baby! What's gotten into you?"

Finally, she walked over to the dog, clasped the leash onto his collar, and gave him a tug. Reluctantly, he stood, shook himself all over, and allowed himself to be led through the door and out onto the porch. He sat again and whined some more as Salem locked up behind him. "Five minutes. Come on, just to the park and back." She looked up and down the street, around the yard, and between the houses. The streets were slick with fresh ice and shimmered under the street light. No one else was around. *When did all this happen?*

She carefully made her way down the steps and Samson timidly followed, twice bumping into her and nearly knocking her to the ground. "Samson! What is going on with you? It's just a bit of rain."

They stepped onto the front walk and Salem steadied herself—it really was quite slippery—and then opened the gate and pulled Samson through. This was going to be a long five minutes, she thought to herself. She wondered if a storm was coming. Samson was often spooked by thunder, and could sometimes hear it when it was impossibly far away. She tugged on the leash and started walking towards the park. Samson reluctantly followed, still staying uncomfortably close, whining softly every few steps and occasionally bashing into her legs as if he wanted to walk between instead of beside them.

They reached the corner, and Salem instinctively checked in all directions. Many of the drivers in the neighbourhood were older, impatient, had poor night vision, and tended to speed in bad weather. The area was a maze of one-way streets and dead ends, which only increased their frustration. Oddly, though, she could see no traffic at all. No cabs, no fast-food delivery, not even a bicycle. She and Samson could have been the only ones left alive.

Salem gave Samson another tug to prompt him to cross the street, and the dog unexpectedly pulled back, almost taking her hand off. She turned to scold him, then saw that his teeth were bared and he was growling, his eyes trained somewhere past her, up the block, deep in the darkness. She peered ahead and saw, just for a moment, a shift in the shadows, and then a flash of movement in a shaft of street light. *Some kid*, she sighed. Just some kid, lost and likely strung out, not sure where the shelters were.

But then, she felt a change in the air all around them, a hiss, a crackle, the way the wind turns before a summer storm, and Samson lunged forward, barking and gnashing, leash slapping against the pavement, racing to where the boy had been. *Oh no no.* She yelled out, "Samson! Samson!" as she dashed into the night ahead, eyes wide. "*Samson!*" she yelled again as she ran and ran until she reached the corner of the park and, north of it, the Necropolis, where some of the city's oldest graves were located.

The wrought iron gate into the grounds was open. It should have been locked hours before, but here it was, creaking and swaying, taunting her. She heard a familiar bark, several in rapid succession.

"*Samson!*"

She rushed through the gate and around and down to the far end till she found the dog, cornered and shivering, froth gathering at the corners of his mouth, cowering against a large granite monument commemorating the war dead.

"Samson, come here," she said softly, holding out her hand. "Come on. It's time to go home."

The dog seemed so small and sad and afraid in that moment, she had to remind herself that Samson weighed nearly half as much as she did. She carefully approached and slowly bent down, picked up the end of the leash and wrapped it around her wrist. The grounds were meant for daytime visits and so were shrouded in heavy, dark shadows. No lights along the walk here. She gently led the shivering dog back onto the path leading west towards the cemetery's edge. From there, they'd be able to turn south and back out the gate. She looked around carefully as she walked—it was easy to slip on the fresh ice, and many of the stones in this area were low and uneven, like stumps of teeth, hard to see and easy to trip over. And somewhere out there, or maybe in here, was the boy.

When they reached the northwest corner and started their turn downward, Samson stopped abruptly and again began to growl. Salem turned back to coax him forward, and then saw what he saw: more than a dozen dogs, all shapes and sizes, maybe all the dogs from the nearby houses and yards, on the path behind them and scattered among the markers, standing and watching.

"Samson," she said quietly, pulling gently, moving backwards inch by inch. "Let's go."

One by one, the other dogs began to growl, to gnash and snarl.

Behind them all was another dog, a larger dog, larger than Samson, larger than any she had seen before, too large to be real. Cloaked in darkness, it was a silent black hulk with glittering eyes and teeth the size of a child's fingers, glistening with drool.

"Samson," she said again, this time a little louder.

Samson spun his head around to her and barked sharply and savagely, a warning. Salem jumped back, dropping the leash. Several of the larger dogs saw their chance and leaned in, baring their fangs and slavering with rage. Samson turned to Salem once more, barked another warning, then turned and threw himself forward towards the bigger dogs, ready to strike. The others leapt forward and flew down upon him.

Salem ran.

She ran straight south down the paved path that curved among the tombstones, then veered off towards the iron fence that lined the western edge, jumping and dodging markers and stones, hoping they would slow whatever was chasing her. For even as Samson fought to hold off the larger dogs, the other, smaller ones were nipping at her ankles, tearing at her cuffs, trying to trip her and pull her to the ground. *And where the fuck is that other monstrosity?* It must have been a Dane or a mastiff standing on somebody's vault—she couldn't possibly have seen it correctly.

As she neared the southeast corner of the cemetery, she glanced over towards the gate she'd come through. In the dim light, she could see that it was closed and chained and likely padlocked. Straight ahead at the corner was a large wooden sign that had been mounted on a small rise built up out of rocks. Without thinking, she ran up the rise alongside the sign, planted her palms on the crossbar between the wrought metal staves, and heaved herself upward, caught herself on the spikes at the top, then rolled over, fell over, fell down with a crunch and a twist on the rocky rise outside the fence. Her jacket and pant leg were torn, her forearm possibly fractured. She tried to push herself up, to stand; her ankle was sprained, if not worse. Behind her, the smaller dogs yelped and barked and growled. The bigger ones would leap the fence with ease. She'd have to keep running, or at the very least hobbling, across the black ice ahead.

She ran up a few yards to a parked car, a grey BMW, and threw herself against it, then launched herself back up the sidewalk for a few steps until she reached another car she could cling to and rest on. She made her way back to the house in this way, careening from car to car to fence to car, nearly three blocks, until she shoved open her own front gate, dragged herself up the porch steps, pushed the key into the lock, and flung herself into the front door. She slammed it, locked it tight.

Samson.

What should she do? What would anyone do? Call the police, call animal control, but to say what—that her dog jumped the fence at the cemetery? That a huge dog fight was happening in there? The graveyard's neighbours had likely called a hundred times by now.

She pulled herself up the stairs, checked herself over in the bathroom mirror. Tore her jeans, scraped her leg. Nothing bleeding too badly, but she had given herself a black eye and a bruised cheek, and her swollen ankle and wrist were changing colours like storm clouds.

Samson. Samson had warned her away, had told her to run.

She sat on the floor, lay on the floor, and burst into tears, heaving racking sobs, and she didn't stop until her breathing slowed and her eyelids drooped and she fell into a deep, heavy sleep.

When Salem opened her eyes, the room was pitch-black. She couldn't remember where she was, how she'd gotten there, how long she'd been asleep. She tried to raise herself up and was shocked awake by the stabbing pain in her arm. Then it all came back, all of it, and she placed her other hand on the seat of the toilet to push herself up onto her feet.

She stopped, listened. Footsteps, rustling leaves. Something— someone—was nearby. Not in the house. Near the house. In the yard.

Running her right hand along the wall to steady herself, she felt her way to the stairs and down, turned towards the French doors that led from the dining room to the back of the house. The lamppost across the lane threw a slash of light across the yard, and in it stood the boy. In his arms, he cradled Samson, bloodied and maimed. Salem rubbed at her eyes, tried to make sense of the image. Samson was too big for someone so small to hold, never mind to carry for three long blocks in the cold and the dark. As she stood and stared, the boy approached, knelt down, placed the dog's wounded body on the straw matting outside the doors. Then he backed away slowly, past the patio table and chairs, the storage bins, the lilies and hydrangeas, back to the far wall of the yard, and then, somehow, was gone.

Salem rushed to the doors, opened them, fell to the ground, pressed her face against Samson's neck, wrapped her arms around him. She held him close and then froze, her breath caught in her throat.

He was alive. Samson was alive.

Faces. Screaming.

Flames.

Sergio stirred and stretched, squinted, then became very still. The room was dimly lit, but he could see the wood panelling on the walls, could feel the heavy, moist heat closing in around him. A sauna. He was at the baths, the Club Baths, he remembered now, in the sauna, on a wooden bench. He had fallen asleep on the bench, a dangerous thing. Anything could happen to you while you were passed out at a bathhouse. He had dreamed he was on fire, or in a room that was on fire. *What was that about?* The heat from the sauna, obviously.

He felt an elastic band biting into his wrist and, dangling from it, his room key. That was good, at least. How long had he been out? Why hadn't anyone come to wake him? *This is how people die*, he thought. Heart attack in the sauna, in the hot tub. There must have been a dozen guys in and out of here while he slept. He felt as if someone had been standing over him at one point, watching him sleep. His closeted uncle had died a few weeks before—had it been him? *Santi.* He had been the youngest of his mother's brothers, had lived all his life with his ailing mother and had taken care of her well past the time when he might be expected to marry. She had been very religious, but also very superstitious. Sergio had visited their house only twice, and both times he had found it dark and eerie and sad. After Sergio's grandmother died, Uncle Santi lived on in the house alone. No wife, no lover, no roommate, not even any friends as far as anyone knew. A bathhouse seemed like the right place for him to linger. Spirits were said to remain near the living for forty days before moving on to the next world. It was nonsense, of course, the kind of thing his mother had believed, but it felt like someone had knelt down as he slept, had placed a hand upon him, tenderly, a hand so cold it could have been made of ice.

He thought back over the evening. He had huddled with a few guys upstairs in one of the rooms, smoked up a little, nothing heavy, just a warm-up, did a little good-natured groping, then found his way back downstairs. The bathhouse was in an old brick mansion, the whole place a warren of little hallways and odd-shaped rooms—bedrooms, servants' rooms, linen closets; it was easy to get turned around and wander off in the wrong direction. On his way back to his room, he cruised someone who cruised him back, then followed him into the sauna. He had ridden the guy's cock here on the bench, then had fooled around with someone else while jerking off—handsome men, younger men, a run of good luck. He remembered (did he remember?) he had been walking past an open door on the second floor, a small storage room with a window. He had looked out the window over the whole of the Village—except there had been no buildings, no streets, no cars. No lights. No sounds, except for the soft rustle of leaves as the evening breathed through them. A forest, dense and deserted, the kind you only found up north, far away from the city.

Sergio brought his wrist up to his face, checked his watch: 4 a.m. He had to be at the office for 8:30 and had wanted to leave by midnight. *Shit.*

He sat up. Something was wrong, he knew it immediately. He might even have known it in the back of his mind before he opened his eyes. He sat very still and listened intently, past the insistent dance-pop soundtrack that throbbed like a toothache through the space. He realized that someone was around the corner, near the lockers or just outside, in the hall, someone was breathing shallowly and rapidly, struggling for air. One of his co-workers had a near-fatal asthma attack in the office washroom once. This was the same kind of harsh, wet, struggling sound.

He jumped to his feet, and the rush of blood made the room spin. He reached out to the wall to steady himself, reassured by its solidity. Maybe the sound was just the steam, something clogging the pipes? Who knew how old the plumbing was in this place. He wrapped his towel around his waist, made his way across to the door, stepped into the hallway—long and narrow, lined with doors. The gasping, rattling sound was louder. *Someone is choking.* He turned the corner towards his roomette, and the cold air hit him full force. He held the towel together over his hip. *Why is it so cold? Why is nobody here?* He took the key on the band around his wrist, turned it in the knob, stepped inside, and closed the door behind him.

The sound was louder now, coming from somewhere in the room. He looked at the small, dull single bed in front of him. Empty, unused, his clothes neatly folded on the cheap floral sheets that covered the thin foam mattress. Then he looked down at the floor, in the corner beside the bed, and that's where he saw the body, curled into a ball, the body of a young man, mid-twenties, lightly freckled, naked, a stranger. *How did he get in here?*

His skin was so pale and blue that it was translucent, like those tiny sea creatures whose organs are visible through their flesh. The hair on his head was sandy blond, fine and thin like spun glass. His eyes sunken, his cheeks drawn—anyone could see he was dead, not a ghost but actually dead, and yet he was shuddering and fighting to breathe, the air around him shivering as he shivered. He seemed to be willing himself to live, to be, forcing his lungs to swell, his heart to pump. He opened his eyes—his pale, clouded eyes with their vast black pupils—he opened his eyes and stared at Sergio, his face twisted in terror.

"Who are you?" Sergio asked nervously. "What are you doing here?"

The boy's mouth moved like the mouth of a fish on the deck of a boat, reflexively, meaninglessly, the final spasms of a creature pulled from its natural home into a world of chaos and suffocation.

"Are you choking? Have you swallowed something?" Sergio couldn't tell if the boy could hear him or see him. He wished he knew some first aid. He was about to throw open the door and shout for a doctor, for an ambulance, and then the boy went from gasping to keening, softly at first and then louder, an animal sound. Not dead, maybe, but near death. An overdose? A stroke? He was young, it was true, but such things could happen.

Just then, the young man spoke, his voice rattling thickly. "You can't help me."

Sergio knelt down beside him, felt his clammy forehead, tried to calm him. "What's your name? I'm Sergio."

"Ryan," the young man whispered. "It doesn't matter. You can't help me."

"What do you mean, what's wrong?" Sergio asked. "Why can't I help you?"

The boy pulled away, threw himself back against the wall, arching, twisting, and then hissed out some words that Sergio could barely understand:

"We have a secret, just we three,
The robin, and I, and the sycamore tree;
The bird told the tree, and the tree told me,
And nobody knows it but just us three."

The boy smiled grotesquely, then shot out a hand and grabbed Sergio by the arm, digging his icy fingers into Sergio's flesh, pulling him closer.

"She knows where he is. She knows how to find him." And then, in a sly guttural whisper: "Every lock has a key."

Sergio watched as the boy's skin began to blacken and bubble and crack and peel, a hot orange glow emerging from the flesh underneath like coals in a fire. He thrashed and screamed and flailed and clawed at himself until he burst into a whirl of ash, little flakes fluttering about the room like tiny grey flies.

"Sergio?" Robin said, then again: "Sergio—it's all right, you're in the hospital. You're in the ER."

He looked over towards her voice, frantic, and she was there, beside him. She took his hand. His eyes darted around the room. He tried to lift his head, couldn't. He was in a bed, something clamped to his finger, his arm sore, with a drip line running into it. Everything bright, too bright. Cables and wires were stuck to his chest. Machines beeped around him. He saw other beds, heard other voices. In the centre of the room was a large round workstation, a hub with monitors, phones, doctors, nurses.

"There was . . ." he croaked, then stopped himself, swallowed, tried again. "There was a boy." He stopped, frowned. Was there a boy? Who was the boy? Already, the memory was fading, if it was in fact a memory.

"You were at the baths," Salem said. She and Robin were together, sitting beside him. "Someone said you fell asleep in the sauna then got up and went to your room and collapsed. They found you on the floor, curled up next to your bed." She leaned closer, her voice softer yet somehow more grave than it had been moments before. "You were blue, Sergio. You were blue and you couldn't breathe. You almost didn't make it." She looked into his wide, dark eyes. "Do you remember anything?"

He shook his head.

Robin leaned closer. "You said something about a boy."

He shook his head again. He knew he had said it, but he couldn't remember why. "Where's Trevor?" he whispered.

"I've called him, he's coming. He'll be here soon." She saw his expression and frowned. "What is it? What's wrong?"

"I don't know," he said, terrified of something but unsure of what or why. "I don't know, I don't know." And then all the alarms went off as he started to shake and seize, his head thrown back, his arms flailing, and someone from the centre of the room shouted, *He's crashing, he's crashing.*

He's close now. I feel him all around me.

Ever since my mother first read me to sleep with nursery
rhymes and fairy tales, I have sought to find my place
in them. Was I the farmer's wife being chased by three
blind mice? Was I Little Miss Muffet, running screaming from spiders? Or was I the wicked witch, the dark
fairy, the evil stepmother? Even at that age, I knew that
I wasn't the bland, courageous prince who would chop
through a forest of thorns to rouse his love with a kiss.
From the earliest days of childhood through to my teenage
years, the books I read, the movies I was taken to, the
TV shows I watched--everything told me I was destined to
be a villain or a victim, or possibly both.

For most of its history, horror has been an inherently
conservative genre, as fear is an innately conservative
emotion, and horror has traditionally been employed to
uphold conservative values: the triumph of the virtuous,
the punishment of the wicked, the rejection of the
different, the dissident, the unknown, the preservation
of family, country, and God. As I write in the genre, I
continually have to question whether I am demonizing sides
of myself that I should be embracing and celebrating: my
values, my relationships, my sexuality, my otherness.

For centuries, queerness and horror have been intertwined,
horror relying on queerness for shock and pungency, and
queerness relying on horror for visibility and validation.
The genre we describe as horror today has its roots in

the romance and Gothic genres of the eighteenth century,
which in turn were influenced by the pre-Romantic movement known as the Graveyard Poets, the more gruesome
works of Marlowe, Shakespeare, Webster, and Middleton,
as well as the works of Milton and Dante, which described
in graphic detail the torments of Hell that await those
who had sinned. While the Renaissance and Enlightenment
eras were more liberal in their depictions of queer his-
torical figures, relationships, sexuality, and romance
(though often with tragic ends), such positive portrayals declined as the Church and the State both worked to
criminalize and demonize such behaviour. With the arrival
of Gothic novels, the early Victorian thrillers known
as "sensation novels," pulp novels, and penny dread-
fuls, we stepped into the spotlight in one of the few
great leading roles we were allowed to fully inhabit:
the villain. In such works as Matthew Lewis's *The Monk*,
Sheridan Le Fanu's *Carmilla*, Oscar Wilde's *The Picture
of Dorian Gray*, and Bram Stoker's *Dracula* (who warns his
"brides" as they approach Jonathan Harker, "He belongs
to me!"), queer attractions and subtexts could suddenly
be explored, and queer characters could take a role at
the heart of the story, albeit as predatory unnaturals
with perverse desires, seeking out innocents--including
children and animals--to corrupt and consume. From Henry
James's *The Turn of the Screw* to H.G. Wells's *The Island
of Dr. Moreau*, from Wilkie Collins's *The Woman in White*
to Robert Louis Stevenson's *The Strange Case of Dr.
Jekyll and Mr. Hyde*, chances are that if you read a story
from this period that depicts "a secret side," a "hideous
transformation," a "debilitating disease," a "tainted
bloodline," "wanton decadence," "unbridled hedonism,"

"a duplicitous nature," or a "twilight underworld,"
you are likely confronting a carefully coded example of
queer horror.

Queer writers found we could work within the confines of
this most conservative genre, using metaphor and allusion
to describe meeting places, encounters, relationships,
occupations, and networks through which queer people
could find each other, gather, and form community. At
least for a while, it was better to be seen as a monster than to remain unseen. However, in our zeal to use
the genre to portray some aspect of ourselves, what we
most often revealed--or were required to reveal--was our
self-hatred. For queer readers, hatred, and self-hatred,
were the stinging medicines we were forced to consume if
we were to satisfy our need to see ourselves.

So-called sexual deviance and perversity continued to play
a starring role in horror past the turn of the century
and into the early 1900s, through two world wars and the
deeply conformist 1950s and early '60s. As stage plays,
fiction, cinema, and television became more permissive,
explicit portrayals of lusty lesbian vampires, pansexual
covens, mother-obsessed maniacs, and cross-dressing
cannibals shocked and titillated mainstream audiences
and enraged censors and queer activists alike. The lines
between good and evil began to blur, the anti-hero
became a dominant protagonist, and the prim, prudish,
unfailingly heterosexual heroes were subtly mocked
for their dullness while the outlandish monsters and

murderers were quietly cheered for their rejection of
social norms.

Up until this point, family as a microcosm of society had
been held up as a sanctity, as the source of strength and
safety, and heroes would do anything, including sac-
rifice themselves, to destroy the monster and restore
order. Then we began to see a transition from the common
theme of "destroying the abnormal to preserve family and
society" to the implication that family and society were
themselves the abnormal and would destroy you. This new
wave of horror was the one I grew up with, precociously
reading novels such as Ira Levin's *Rosemary's Baby*,
Thomas Tryon's *The Other*, Stephen King's *Carrie*, William
Peter Blatty's *The Exorcist*, and V.C. Andrews's *Flowers
in the Attic*. In these stories, family and society were
where the monsters were made--through divorce, abuse,
neglect, through isolation and exclusion, and especially
through a disregard for and degradation of the rules of
gender and sexual identity that "good families" obeyed.
This was the new order, and while "good people" and "good
families" could try to combat it, they risked sacrific-
ing themselves for no reason or, worse, becoming monsters
themselves in the process. These narratives unfolded in
stark contrast to those I'd seen in old creature features
on television, where the monster, even if created by our
greed or misadventure, was still an external force we
could fight and destroy. Now we were in the era of Bob
Clark's influential proto-slasher *Black Christmas*, where
the obscenity-spewing woman-hating killer--whose perverse
and monstrous tirades alluded to abuse within his family--
was calling from inside the house.

As LGBTQ communities became more vocal and visible in our
demands for civil rights, portrayals of queer monsters
and villains and grotesques were decried as homophobic
and transphobic. As a queer young man who loved horror,
who, like many, was drawn to darkness, I struggled as I
confronted images of myself and my friends that openly
maligned us, and recoiled with a different kind of fear
as I imagined my parents, my employers and co-workers, my
straight friends and their families, seeing these films
as legitimate depictions of my life, my experience,
and my desires.

In recent years, the queer villain/anti-hero has made an
interesting and largely welcome return within horror, as
we have seen an increase in the psychological complex-
ity of its monsters and the conflicted nature of its
heroes and victims. Michel Faber's cerebral sci-fi horror
novel *Under the Skin* (and its more oblique 2013 film
adaptation with Scarlett Johansson) presents an alien
who performs gender, taking on the image of a vulnerable, feminine woman to attract, ensnare, and harvest
her human male prey; her journey both illuminates and
subverts the trope of "trans woman as male deceiver."
In John Ajvide Lindqvist's novel *Let the Right One In*,
the genitally mutilated child vampire Eli befriends and
imperceptibly grooms the bullied boy Oskar to replace the
aging "father" in Eli's thrall. Oskar and Eli ultimately
escape the town where Eli has been feeding; we understand
that Oskar too will grow older, will become protector
and facilitator and "father," as Eli remains ageless.
And then there is the titular creature of the 2014 film
The Babadook, who was embraced by film-savvy queers as

a darkly dapper symbol of queer resistance--"I'll wager with you, I'll make you a bet: the more you deny, the stronger I get." Once it bursts out of the closet, it refuses to be repressed or restrained. In the end, despite all attempts to exorcise it, it cannot be defeated, nor can it be driven away; it can only be integrated into the family, fed and nurtured, accepted and embraced.

I've had to reckon with my own personal history with queer horror, how it has shaped my view of my community and of myself. So much of it is about the aspects in queer culture that straight people fear, that straight society fears: strength and independence in women; vulnerability and intimacy in men; the upending of gender and family roles; the repudiation of the primacy of reproduction; the hollowness and bankruptcy of the dominant social structures; challenges to the pronounce-ments of the Church. And our intrinsic invisibility, our *insidiousness*--that we could be anyone, anywhere, hiding in plain sight. I have to admit, there is something delicious in that--that we would provoke so much unease, so much discomfort, so much irrational, unfounded terror just by existing.

But what are queer people afraid of, apart from the obvious? I asked myself this as I was writing my first novel, *The Bone Mother*, which included an array of queer and trans people among its many monstrous and human characters. We are afraid of death, of course, of vio-lence and torture and sickness and suffering, of being exposed and humiliated and shunned and persecuted. We are afraid of being erased, or unseen, or forgotten. We are afraid of being alone.

Sometimes being queer is about all those things; they are at the heart of our history and the root of our oppression. Sometimes being queer is about being cast out; sometimes it's about casting ourselves out, walking or running away while we still can. Sometimes being queer is about being the monster, the one who corrupts, the one who devours. Sometimes--after everything and everyone has been stripped from us--sometimes being queer is about being the last one standing.

Have I slipped into their world, or have they slipped into mine? I went back to the alley behind where Trax used to be. I know it's not there, it's not even a bar anymore, but sometimes I still see it and that's when I think he'll come. I sat on a guardrail and watched a young guy drop his pants and get fucked for an hour by these other three guys against the glowing glass-brick wall of the payday loan shop next door. A boy sat down next to me. I thought it was him at first, that he had finally come for me, but when I looked closer, I saw that it was just some kid who was high and horny and had nowhere to go. So I tenderly kissed him good night and whispered--

> *"He is coming for us, I know he is*
> *Monsters go where they can feed*
> *We will see him soon"*

mayl

peop

and

and

ber.

who

if Ry

time,

head a

It

in Victor

ing him—

laxed into

revulsion.

was under

"I ai

audible gr

"Yeah,

tor's hands

room and

each other,

," "Trevor _____ ers?" Victor asked.
old her so _____ police might have called her,
on't just d _____ ng us. It's not that big a city,
behind." _____ they ___, they don't leave their clothes

I yer the _____ d gone missing from the bars and clubs
as, one or _____ years, for as far back as he could remem
e had bee _____ off of serial killers, gangs of thugs, cops
ted to "te _____ gs a lesson." He couldn't help but wonder
ad wa _____ the wrong alley, asked the wrong guy for the
now w s face down in the water somewhere along the shore,
r stepped up behind him, put his arms around him, rested his
st Trevor's neck. "Hey," he said, "it's okay."
omforting, and oddly arousing too. Trevor could feel the bulge
ns pressing against him. Something inside him stirred, sur____
almost never played with the same guy twice—but as he re
r's embrace he glanced over at Ryan's bed and felt a rush of
ad a sudden urge to look beneath it, certain that something
, listening and watching. "He's here," he whispered.
raid of no ghosts," Victor whispered back with an
vor answered. "But I am." He turned and, taking Vic
his own, led him out into the hallway, towards his own
his own bed. As they began to undress, to kiss and touch
was sure he heard Ryan's bedroom door click shut.

"He's here,"

"He's here,"

2016

Imagine that something is attacking your family, your friends, your community. Imagine that something is attacking you. You fight back, of course: you fight to stay alive, to keep the people around you alive, to make a future for yourself, yourselves, and everyone who will come after. You do what you can to save people, to keep people safe. But what if you can't see it, the thing that's attacking you? What if you can't tell who it's hurting, or killing? What if it's invisible, in the air, all around you, on the street, in the club, at the bar, in the restaurant, in your home, in your bed, inside your body, your lungs, your heart, your mouth, your cunt, your cock, your brain, what do you do? Terror and anger can't be sustained, they give way to exhaustion. You feel like you're fighting with every breath but your punches land nowhere. You can't fight the wind. You can't fight the night. You can stand under an umbrella for a little while, but you can't fight the rain. You can't save yourself, or anyone really, from something so overwhelming, so all-encompassing. It's like that joke where you're drowning deep in the ocean and a school of fish swims up and they say, "Dude, calm down, just breathe," and then they swim away. But you don't have a choice, you fight, and the fight becomes the blood running through your veins, it becomes your heartbeat. You hear it in your ears, you feel it in your chest, in the pulse in your wrist, your neck, it's a fraction off from everyone else's, a little too fast, or a little too slow, no one else knows it but you, and that beat is the fight, from when you wake up to when you fall asleep and then all through the night, even when you dream. You're fighting with your heartbeat even when you dream. Those years of silent, unseen fighting change you, invade you, erode you. Ten, twenty, thirty years. Forty, fifty if you're lucky. Sixty, seventy, the fight doesn't end until you do. And then, if you're extremely lucky, there are people who love you who bury you, who see you off, who cry for you, and they too are fighting with their hearts and they come home from your graveside and they dry their tears, they sit down to their meals, they climb into their beds, their arms around each other, and with every beat, their hearts keep fighting in your wake, carrying your fight forward.

That's what it's like. In case you didn't know.

Sergio's phone alarm burbled from under the pillow: 2:45 a.m. He slipped out from under the covers in Salem and Robin's spare bedroom, pulled on his long johns and sweatpants, his green plaid flannel shirt and jean jacket, his once-white Adidas running shoes, and a brightly patterned knitted cap with flaps that he tied down over his ears. He shushed Samson and gave him a reassuring pat on the head, quietly closed the front door behind him, and walked six blocks to Allan Gardens, to the sycamore tree that towered over the deserted snow-covered park. It was the second Saturday in February, blue-grey clouds hanging low in the sky, with a frigid wind that sliced through to the bone. He curled up at the foot of the tree among the tangle of roots that reached outward like ancient gnarled fingers, and he closed his eyes, his chattering teeth calming, his pulse slowing, his body cooling. Trevor's old St. Benedict medal, scuffed and worn after years of sweat and showers and sleep, was nestled against his throat on its fine, thin chain. *Brujería.* A light flurry of flakes began to fall, dancing down through the barren branches onto his sleeping body, draping him in a layer of fine white lace.

Sergio had tried and tried, but after his near death in the Club Baths and then again in the emergency room at St. Mike's, his slow decline had in recent years become steep and sharp. He couldn't hold a thought in his head for more than a few minutes; he sometimes struggled to complete a sentence, even in the most mundane conversation. More often than not, he would stay silent and listen instead. He experienced uncontrollable twitches and tremors. He would get lost in his own neighbourhood, directions and landmarks turning around in his head, so that just stepping out the front door could prompt a panic attack. He was plummeting with no way to stop and nowhere to go but down and down. He really only survived because Robin and Salem had been willing to take him in. At first, he spent his days in their spare bedroom while Salem was at work and Robin was on the road; then, after a few months, he was hired on part-time at a coffee place around the corner. When it was good, it was great, he felt like he belonged and had a tiny purpose in the world, but often it was too much—too many people, too many orders, some of them selfishly complicated, and then he would be angry at the patrons and frustrated with himself, that not even this simple thing could be his. He felt sad that he would never see his co-workers or customers ever again, or Salem or Robin, or Samson, but the sadness faded as a quiet anticipation took over. They would all do better without him. In time, they would forget him, and be happy. Here, in the dark, in the snow, among the sycamore roots, he was like a tiny flame in the frozen darkness, waiting for Nicholas to find him and claim him. *Come for me.*

He had brought his grandfather's iron lockbox, passed to his father and then down to him. Inside it, he had concealed the tattered old red book. He hugged the black box close to his chest, its weight wearying his arms, its iciness cutting through layers of fabric into his flesh. He imagined Trevor's arms gently embracing him, warming him, Trevor's lips on his cheek, on the nape of his neck. *I'm here,* Sergio whispered, *I'm here, I'm waiting for you.* That whole first year when Sergio was ill, they were plunged into survival mode, everything else falling away, with barely a chance to breathe. They were both so tense, so afraid. But once Sergio had been in remission for a few months and was feeling stronger, less exhausted, Trevor surprised him with something that made Sergio's heart ache with the sweetness of it: he asked Sergio out to a movie, their first movie in a theatre, *Cruel Intentions,* at a second-run house in the west end. Then their first concert, Cher. Their first musical, *Cabaret.* Their first trip, Montreal, then Christmas in New York right after 9/11, then London the year after that. Their first pet, their only pet, an untameable tabby named Hector who barely ever came indoors and one day ran off and never returned. Trevor had cried and cried over that cat, more than he did over his own mother's death.

Then Trevor's first crisis, one grey winter morning when he couldn't go into the office, couldn't even leave the apartment. He just lay in bed crying and cowering, saw people standing and watching him even though Sergio told him the room was empty. Then he thought people were coming in at night, moving things around, taking things, leaving notes, watching them sleep, or standing outside the shower curtain, reaching in, touching him, grabbing him, scratching him, gouging him. He couldn't work, couldn't sleep, threw up his meal supplements, threw up his pills, couldn't even keep down water. Then came his first ER visit, his first therapist, first psychiatrist, first overdose, first rehab, first MRI, first CT scan. Then their first breakup, their first reconciliation. And then, a few months after their tenth anniversary, Sergio woke up and Trevor was gone, just gone.

Everyone thought that he'd killed himself, flung himself off a bridge or into the lake, and Sergio let everyone believe that he thought so too. But he knew better. The morning that Trevor disappeared, Sergio found the lockbox sitting on the kitchen counter. Neatly placed on the lid was the St. Benedict medal that Trevor had worn around his neck for years, its fine silver chain pooled around it, and a note scrawled on the back of a flyer for a months-old yard sale: *Don't look for me. You can't help me. I don't want to be found.*

Sergio had not taken Trevor's distress seriously enough, and that had left him vulnerable—not to suicide, but to something else. In these last few months, Sergio had been having the same dreams Trevor once had, had been seeing figures in the darkness, animals staring back at him, he had seen the boy, had heard the boy, had heard something that was not the boy—or was it? How could he be sure? But he did know this: something had come for Trevor, and now it was hidden beyond where the light could reach, it was watching him patiently, waiting for its moment. It could smell him. It could taste him. *Come for me*, Sergio breathed, the fog from his mouth now barely visible. *Come for me. I'm right here. Can't you see me?*

I have your book. I read your book. And your fucking book read me.

The tiny flame inside Sergio shrank smaller and smaller, a faint orange ember, the tiniest pinpoint of light, of heat. And then, suddenly, shockingly, it grew brighter and larger, like the strike of a match, it grew into a raging inferno, a conflagration, and it began to consume him.

Come for me, so I can kill you.

Salem's eyes opened, bleary and stinging with tears. Her arm was around Robin, the back of her head, the nape of her neck, her soft black hair, right in front of her.

"Robin. Robin. We have to get up." She gave Robin's shoulder a gentle shake, wincing, knowing how she disliked being woken for anything short of, well, a fire. She pulled herself up, shoved the covers back, swung her legs off the bed, and switched on the lamp on the nightstand.

Robin groaned, threw her arm over her face. "Jesus, Salem. What are you doing?"

Salem grabbed a green Primark hoodie off the back of the chair in front of the closet, her paint-spattered gardening jeans and wool work socks off the seat. "Come on, get dressed, we have to go down to the park." Samson bounded up the stairs and burst into the room. "Yes, that's right, boy, we're going out."

Robin sighed, pushed herself up from the mattress. "What's going on? It's the middle of the night. Are you waking Sergio too?"

"Sergio's already gone," Salem said. She tossed a heavy cabled pull-over and some fleece-lined jogger pants onto the bed. "Come on, we have to hurry or we'll lose him."

Robin shrugged the sweater down over her vintage Corey Hart T-shirt. "It must be minus-twenty outside." Her eyes narrowed. "How do you know he's at the park?"

"I just know," Salem answered, zipping up the hoodie. "And I think I know why."

I see you, said the voice, the voice beneath and beyond Sergio's place of rest. Blistered hands, charred and smouldering arms, reached up from the deepest part of himself, began to rip and tear at his insides, fuel for the furnace burning within him. They reached up into his chest, clutching at his heart, his lungs, reached up into his throat, his eyes, his brain, pulling everything down into the flames. He tried to scream, but he had no voice no lungs no air, no breath to gasp, no breath to sigh, the claws scoured his insides, pulling him down into himself like an abandoned house, engulfed, walls falling in with a flourish of sparks, roof sinking and splitting, windows bursting from the heat, he collapsed on himself, into himself, twisting and flailing and soundlessly screaming until the sycamore roots opened up for him, welcoming him, pulling him close, and then, behind him, a burst of barking, and a short black snout pushed through the soft shroud of snow, teeth clenched around the back of his collar and yanked him back and out, out into the moonlight, the faraway light of the stars, distant voices shouting his name, growing closer, as his hot, wet tears mingled with the melting snow streaming down his face.

❦

That was the year when Carly Rae Jepsen cut to the feeling; when Beyoncé told the ladies to "get in formation." It was the year when we lost both Prince and Bowie. It was the year of *The Witch*, *The Invitation*, and *Train to Busan*—covens, cults, and zombie tsunamis. It was the year of the Pulse nightclub shooting that took the lives of forty-nine queer, trans, and non-binary people of colour and their allies; the year that more than seventy men were arrested for public indecency in a park along Toronto's western lakeshore; the year that Black Lives Matter disrupted the city's Pride parade to present its list of demands for increased space, representation, and safety at the event. It was the year that the HIV drug Truvada was formally approved for pre-exposure prophylaxis in Canada. It was the year that Donald Trump was elected President of the United States. And it was the year that Sergio Federico Mendez, fifty-two, fell asleep in the snow and, for a moment, disappeared.

It was also the year that I wrote and staged a play titled *The Thimble Factory*, which later became my first novel, *The Bone Mother*. It was the year my eighty-year-old mother was diagnosed with an atypical liver cancer, and when I received a message out of the blue on Facebook from a curious, anxious young woman named Salem Carmichael, who had some questions about the peculiarities of northern English folklore.

❦

Salem quietly closed the door to the spare bedroom and walked down the hall to the kitchen. It was nearly 8 a.m. The early light was filtering in through the curtains, bathing the sage-green room in a rosy glow. Robin was sitting at the kitchen table with a pot of tea, two cups freshly poured. The air was lightly scented with bergamot. At the centre of the table was the elaborately cast metal box.

"Well, he's asleep," Salem said as she dropped down onto her chair.

"That took forever," Robin replied. "We should have dragged him to the hospital."

"No hospital, no doctors. He was very clear about that. Maybe the only thing he was clear about." Salem blew along the surface of the tea, sipped a bit of it. Still too hot. She set the cup back on its saucer. "I gave him something to bring his fever down. No frostbite, at least. So, what's this thing?"

"It's weird, it's a strongbox of some kind, very fancy," Robin answered. "Belonged to his grandfather. Sergio got it when his dad died." She turned the box so that Salem could see the intricate moulding on the top: an animal's growling face, mouth open, teeth bared. "No lock, no hinges. It's like a solid piece of iron. Something's in it, though—it rattles when you shake it."

"No idea why he had it with him?" Salem asked.

Robin shook her head. "Did he say anything to you? Did he tell you what he was trying to do out there?"

"He went to the tree to look for Trevor," Salem answered. "That's what he said. Some guy, some boy, had told him that Trevor would meet him there. Wouldn't say his name, wouldn't say where he'd seen him. But he did say that you knew the boy, that he'd been a guest at a bar. Maybe they stopped in to see you one night?"

"No, Trevor never came to any of my gigs. Crowds, noise, drinking—it wasn't his thing." *A guest at a bar, someone she knew.* She turned the lockbox from side to side, examining it closely. The bottom was as elaborately carved as the lid, with a tree much like the sycamore in the park. At the base of the tree, among the roots, stood a small, delicate bird, a drop of ruby-red enamel on its breast.

Salem reached across the table, placed her hand on Robin's wrist. "What's going on here? How did I know that Sergio was heading to the park, to that tree? It's not like I'm a mind reader. I can't even win five bucks on a stupid scratch ticket."

Robin sighed. "Okay, so. There's something I haven't told anyone, not even you, sorry. Truth is, I didn't think there was much to tell, not for a long time. But now there is, and I think whatever it is, we're both caught up in it, and Sergio is too."

Salem sat staring at her, trying to look supportive but unable to conceal her confusion.

"For a while now—years, I guess—I haven't remembered them until recently, but . . . I've been having these dreams. Fragments of dreams, images, flashes. About something hiding under the ground, in that park, near that tree. Something not human."

Salem's eyes widened. "What do you mean 'not human'? An animal?" *Samson in the woods beside her, panting and whining, the beast at her feet.*

"Some kind of . . . creature?"

"Yeah," Robin answered. "Like that. Anyway, I usually don't remember much, but there was one dream before Trevor vanished. I was in his apartment, standing in his bedroom. I watched him slip out of bed while Sergio was sleeping, I watched him get dressed and leave the house. I knew he was on his way to the park, I knew he was heading for the tree. And then I woke up, and I knew, I just knew he was already gone."

"Gone where, though? Under the tree? Into the ground?"

Robin shrugged. "Gone like Mikey, I guess. And Victor, and Julian. I don't know what the tree has to do with them disappearing, maybe nothing, but that's where we found Sergio."

And Julian's backpack, Salem realized. "Jesus. And you've had dreams like these for years?"

"I think so, yes, on and off," Robin answered. "And I think you're having them too."

The beast under the tree. The monster in the cemetery. The bench in the park. "I don't know—maybe. I remember little things, but from, I don't know, months ago, years ago." Salem shook her head. "Dreams don't mean anything, though, they're just brain garbage. We live together, we have the same worries, the same fears, it's not surprising that we'd have similar dreams."

"I think Sergio's had them too. Maybe Trevor did as well."

Salem sighed. "Robin, I get it, it's been a hard year. You and Paulo, me and my dad. Sergio and, well, everything. But, what, you think we're all having some kind of shared delusion? We're being stalked by something?"

Robin turned the box onto its side and let out a little gasp. Something had moved under her finger—a small, smooth shape on the underside of the box. The enamelled bird. She brought it up to her face, looked at it beneath the tree, looked closer. It was a robin, plump and round, with pointed wings and a bill shaped like a seed. A hairline groove outlined the bird, separating it slightly from its surroundings. She touched it with her fingertip, pressed it gently. The tiny bird sank in with a click. Something on the lid unlatched.

"What are you doing?" Salem asked.

"I—I'm not sure," she answered nervously. She turned the box right-side up, examined the moulded metal. She slipped her fingernail under the wolf's tongue and pulled. The wolf's entire face lifted from the lid with a faint metallic squeal, swinging up on a hidden mechanism. Robin looked at Salem, reached in, and pulled out an old folded sheet of paper covered with fine ink lines and snatches of handwriting. She handed it to Salem, who unfolded it carefully.

"It's a map," she said. A grid of streets, some elevation markings, indications of sewer pipes, water pipes, electrical services. Some calculations of the timber required for the cut and cover. And two long tunnels connected to two underground stations. A title block in the lower left corner said TORONTO SUBWAY—CARLTON AND YONGE STREETS—AUGUST 1950. The page was numbered 152 in the upper right corner. Salem pointed to a spot just north of Carlton, where the tunnels curved away from Yonge towards Church. A bend in the line. An *X* was marked in red ink on one of the tunnel walls.

Robin reached back into the box and pulled out two newspaper clippings, one with *Daily Star, October 1950* written along the side, the other dated *March 1951—Telegram.* She handed one to Salem, then traded with her. Two men who had worked on the subway construction had disappeared about six weeks apart, leaving their wives and children impoverished. A lawyer engaged by the two women was preparing to petition the court to have them declared dead, but there wasn't much hope that he would succeed. Robin reached in again and pulled out a larger newspaper clipping, this one from the *Sunday Sun*, March 1979, titled TUNNEL MONSTER OF CABBAGETOWN? (ALMOST LIKE A MONKEY, it exclaimed. EYES ORANGE, RED.) Apparently, it had been seen emerging from a cave-like passage off Parliament Street, just a few blocks away. The accompanying artist's rendering did indeed look like a large, angry monkey, or a human/animal hybrid. "Probably a hungry raccoon," Salem muttered.

Robin took out another piece of paper, unfolded it. It was a page torn from an old book, the paper musty-smelling and powdery to the touch. She passed it to Salem, who read aloud:

LEGENDS, FOLKLORE AND CURIOSITIES OF THE NORTH COUNTRY

After a time, I awoke to a hideous shrieking sound from the church-yard. I rushed to the window in terror and pulled back the curtain to see a huge shadowy shape skulking among the gravestones. It was a barghest or bier-geist, a phantom known across Yorkshire and other parts of the country, a spectral hound in the shape of a mastiff with great white teeth and giant red eyes. It stalked the rows, casting its baleful eyes left and right, and at every turn it would raise its massive head, part its jaws and screech like a ban-shee. I watched in horror as it made its way to the church-yard gate, fearing it would cross the road and inflict its presence upon us but—bless us all—the moment that it reached the archway, the monstrous devil-dog vanished.

"Barghest," Salem said. "That's what he said."

Robin looked up at her. "Who—Sergio?"

"He said you knew the boy he was going to meet. But maybe I got it wrong—what if the boy wasn't 'a guest in a bar'? What if Sergio meant that he was a barghest, like the thing I just read about? Though I can't see how that makes any sense." She looked up from the yellowed page to see Robin holding a piece of broken metal in her hand, black like the strongbox and flecked with rust. It was flat on the back and the edges were dangerously sharp. It appeared to be a fragment of someone's face—part of an eyebrow and cheek, and the entire left eye, part of a much larger panel, sculpted or moulded. A relief of some kind. "What do you think that's from?"

"Not a clue," she replied.

As Robin placed the metal piece on the kitchen table, something inside the box shifted, rustled, and thudded against the box's inner walls. Salem jumped back, pushed her chair back, scraping its feet against the floor. Robin leaned over towards the stove, stretched out her arm, and pulled one of the oven mitts off the wall. She pulled it onto her hand, then reached into the iron box and pulled out a clear plastic bag, folded and taped shut, and in it the old red notebook—the one that had been in the house on Pembroke the night Julian disappeared, the one that Mikey had been carrying the night he vanished.

"Robin, no." As Salem reached for it, the book twitched in the bag, nearly jumping out of Robin's hand. She leapt to her feet as Robin dropped the bag back into the iron box and slammed the lid on it. "Where did that fucking thing come from? How did it get here?"

"Sergio must have found it," Robin replied. "Maybe he got it from Trevor? We need to talk to him when he wakes up."

Salem shook her head vehemently. "We have to get rid of it," she said. "Set it on fire, drive a stake through it, I don't care. We are not keeping it in the house. That fucking book is cursed."

"What do we have in the freezer?" Robin asked. "Ice, vodka, gin?"

"You are not putting that in the freezer with our food, with my mango coconut ice cream," Salem warned.

The book banged against the inside of the iron box, again and again. Robin put her hand on the box to keep it still. The book seemed to sense her—it began smashing itself up against the lid.

"I have an idea," Robin said.

"A priest?"

She shook her head. "Not yet. But I know somewhere we can put it, at least till we talk to Sergio."

As Robin held a whirring hair dryer against the padlock on one of the backyard storage bins, Salem sat in the blue velvet armchair in Sergio's bedroom, her left leg tucked up under her right thigh, searching and searching the Internet for "barghest monster folklore," "barghest legend England," "barghest boy gay murder," "barghest graveyard," "barghest tree," "barghest notebook journal," "barghest victim vanish." She was still shaken by the reappearance of the notebook after so many years, and was still trying to tell herself that she hadn't seen it move in Robin's hand. Sergio lay on his bed beside her, still asleep—a miracle, given that Samson was outside barking furiously at the strongbox as Robin prepared to shut it away.

As she clicked through the results, she found numerous sites that corroborated what had been written on the yellowed page, plus a few other names the creature was called, depending on where it was thought to reside (*black shuck, guytrash, padfoot, gwyllgi, cwn annwn*), but not much beyond that. She saw some mentions of black dogs and spectral hounds in the U.S. but none so far in Canada, though there was some discussion of the wendigo and the rougarou. She wanted to know about the book. She wanted to know about the boy. She wanted to know about the giant black dog. She wanted to know about the forest she had been drawn to in her dreams, and whether the passage to it could be shut tight and locked forever.

She was reading an apocryphal account of an elderly witch who sent a young writer off to an encounter with a spectral hound at a moonlit crossroads when she heard the storage bin lid slam down and then, a few moments later, the back door open and shut. Samson ran into the house, probably tracking snow everywhere. He was no longer barking, but she could hear his high whine and the click-clack of his nails as he paced a circle through the kitchen to the dining room and back again. She sighed, closed the laptop, tucked it into her backpack, and slipped out of Sergio's room to head downstairs.

"Hey," she said as she reached the landing. "How did it go?"

"It's good," Robin replied. She was still by the back door, taking off her boots. "I melted the ice on the padlock, the key worked fine. The box is now sealed up in the storage bin. There's not much it can do from there." She shook the snow off her pants and coat and out of her hair.

"This is all very fucked up," Salem said. "You realize that, right?"

Two loud thumps from the backyard confirmed that, yes, this was indeed all very fucked up. Robin shrugged, unsure of what to say.

"Okay, well, if we're not calling a priest or anything," Salem sighed, "I'm going to head over to Manic to grab a coffee and send some emails. Jenn's supposed to be there till three and I said I'd come by. Are you okay to watch Sergio for a bit?"

"Yeah, I'll be fine," Robin said. "Pick up a couple of muffins when you're heading back. Nothing too healthy." She gave Salem a peck on the cheek and then made her way into the kitchen while Salem suited up to head outside. Even with the book locked in the box, locked in the storage bin, twenty feet away from the house, she couldn't wait to get away from it.

The streetcar arrived at the stop just as she got there, her first stroke of luck. And when she climbed on and paid her fare, she saw that it was nearly empty—an older woman with blue-white hair at the very front who was telling the driver some long-winded story, and a younger Jamaican man in a fast-food uniform sleeping at the back, snoring softly. *I guess I'm not the only one who had a bad night.* She plunked herself down in the seat just in front of the middle door and pulled out her phone: 10:45 a.m. She opened her messages and texted Jenn: *See you in 20.* Three little flashing dots appeared and then Jenn responded *CYA.*

Salem had seen another wave of change in the gaybourhood over the past few years: bars and clubs bought out and torn down for condos; decades-old bistros and brunch spots replaced with pho, pizza, ramen, burgers, and bubble tea; quirky little shops and cafés springing up, thriving briefly, and then faltering, moving to cheaper digs across town or closing up entirely. Other changes too: fewer queer bars, clubs, and events meant Robin was getting less work locally, plus she was aging out of the larger international gigs that she once scored with relative ease. She would be fine, of course. Already, she was producing a few remixes, mentoring young DJs, guesting on podcasts, teaching master classes online. But the gay village as an entity, as a home for queer people, a place of safety and security, a site for political and social change, for community and celebration—all that seemed to be evaporating before their eyes. Queer people lived and worked and shopped and brunched everywhere now, though perhaps less confidently and securely. Church Street was still the only place where she and Robin would hold hands while they walked, or kiss before heading off in separate directions. And that was starting to change as well.

As the streetcar approached the south end of the Village, she glanced out the window and saw a group of six or seven younger men, bundled in thrifted zebra and leopard plush coats, fur-topped boots, and chunky knitted hoods and scarves and gloves, carrying a large, steaming bucket of wheat paste and a sheaf of posters. Cheap plastic Halloween masks were perched on their heads like arty club-kid fascinators—foxes, rabbits, wolves, and cats. The streetcar stopped at the corner of Church Street just as the light changed, and she watched as they slapped up three large posters in quick succession on the construction hoarding at the corner. The posters were large and white, each with a huge dark drawing of a face: human on the left side with feral black eyes and thick black hair, and then something canine on the right side with thick black fur scribbled in charcoal. Both halves of the face had the same piercing eyes and menacing grin, like a comic book supervillain. Underneath the face, each poster simply said HAVE YOU SEEN HIM in big bold type. No name, no address, no email, no website, no phone number. A new movie or TV series shooting in town? An up-and-coming furry pop performer? A weird guerrilla art piece? She couldn't tell, and that was usually a sign that she was getting old.

She had raised her phone and was about to take a photo for her Instagram when a voice whispered into her left ear. "I'm sorry," he said. "I never thanked you properly for your kindness all those years ago."

Salem froze. She wanted to ring the bell and flee, but she would look insane. "What is this?" she whispered back. "Who are you?"

"You were with me when I was at my weakest," he continued. "You fought your fears to help me. You have my gratitude." She started to turn her head to face him. "No, no need to do that. There's really nothing to see. We will meet again soon enough." She felt the weight of him, the heat of him, vanish from beside her ear.

She looked at her phone, unlocked it, opened her photos. She had surreptitiously taken a selfie while he was talking to her. It was blurry, but the camera had captured her startled expression while, next to it, a faint wisp of blackness smouldered just behind her shoulder. It was shaped very much like a face, and very much like the face on the poster. As she looked at the photo, the phone screen blinked and zapped with a sudden surge of power, and snapped off.

♨

I made two trips to Winnipeg that year, before and after my mother died. In February, she had already been having health issues. Shortly after I arrived, she asked me to join her on an early morning trip to Polo Park, the closest mall to our family home and the most comfortable place for her to shop. She had grown more and more fearful and distrustful in her later life, but as she became ill, it seemed that the few filters she had left just switched off completely. As we navigated through the stores on her list, looking for house slippers and women's razors and digestive aids, ill-tempered remarks that she once kept to herself now burst out of her mouth without the slightest hesitation.

We were in the checkout line at the pharmacy when I felt my phone vibrate. Cellphones mystified my mother and filled her with suspicion, so I tried not to spend too much time on them in front of her. I turned away from her slightly, pulled it out of my pocket, peered at the notification. Someone whose name I didn't recognize was trying to send me a Facebook message: "Hi, sorry, you don't know me, I hope you can help me, have a few questions about your work?" I took a quick peek and saw that we shared a few friends in social services and harm reduction, and a few others who were trans or enby, but much of her profile was hidden. I shrugged, accepted her request, and asked her what was up.

Hi, thanks, I'm Salem. Is this a bad time? I saw on Judy's wall that you're writing something about mythology and folklore.

no it's cool, i'm just out at a mall

i'm adapting a play i wrote into a novel

ghosts and monsters in ukraine and romania

baba yaga, rusalkas, that kind of thing

Oh right, that's the play Judy was in

Sometimes I feel like I'm trapped in a horror story

that's surprisingly common, especially these days

i feel like I'm in one myself

**So do you know anything about a creature
called a barghest? A black shuck?**

barghest

um okay well

it's a devil dog, kind of?

they're big, they're black, they howl

in forests, graveyards, sides of roads, the moors

like the hound of the baskervilles

harbingers of death mostly?

they're not really my thing,
i'm more focused on eastern europe

i think they're british/irish/scottish? welsh?

**I'm not finding much about them,
could they be part of the fairy folk?**

hmm in scotland maybe or wales

faeries are their own thing, humanlike,
not really animals or spectral figures

though the fair folk have their own dog things i think

> phantom dogs and such appear across
> a lot of cultures and belief systems

"Why are you on your phone?" my mother asked accusingly. We were now second in line from the cashier.

"Work," I said bluntly. Then I added, "Oh, I'm having dinner tonight with Ian and Greg."

She made a vaguely disapproving noise, as she did whenever I mentioned a couple whose names were conspicuously of the same gender. The woman ahead of us finished up and left, so my mother stepped forward and I continued typing.

> these things are often local legends,
> they vary from place to place
>
> sometimes demons, sometimes ghosts
>
> existing on two different planes, is what some say
>
> so maybe not faerie themselves but faerie-adjacent?

I felt weird even writing it. I knew there were people who believed in faeries, and some who claimed to have seen them, but to me, it was out of the question. I'd have an easier time believing in Mothman. (Please don't message me about Mothman.)

Are they immortal? Can they be killed?

> barghests? some might be immortal
>
> or in a way already dead, very schrodingers cat

maybe you can drive them away though

or injure or imprison them

they're sometimes tied to an object

a special item that can be used against them

a ring, a book, a charm, a coin, a stone

they can be sent back to where they belong

A book.

What kind of book? What does it look like?

i don't know—a book like any other, i think, handmade probably

a journal of some kind, or a testament, a list of accounts

humans who are favoured or owed

or souls collected

or those who are marked for punishment or revenge

it's a whole thing

there are hundreds of these stories,
i'm just going by what i remember

are you writing something? is this research?
i wish i was more helpful

**What do you mean marked? Do fairies
actually leave marks on people?**

Wounds or scars, things like that?

i know more about witch marks than faerie marks

but yeah

usually they mark you as a threat—to them and their world

but there are marks that show you've been kind to them

and others that mark you as a survivor

a witness

or as someone who may pass safely through their realm

there might be more, i'm not the best guy to ask

"Okay, we're going," my mother said.

I looked up and saw that she was scowling at me. She had her shopping bag and wallet in her hand, and I was holding up the line. I slid the phone back into my pocket and walked with her to the west side of the parking lot where the cabs were waiting. Once we had settled into one and given the address, I pulled the phone back out. Another message was waiting.

"Don't these people let you have a vacation?" she asked.

I made a suitably agonized sound to appease her, and started typing.

**Do you think they're real? Or based
on/derived from something real?**

based on wolves i guess, direwolves,
ice wolves, wild dogs—all extinct now

at least in that part of the world, no wolves in britain now

i don't know about real, i can't really say what's real

i've seen some things

belief is what makes a thing real anyway, not the thing itself

why, is this for a paper or a story?

or has somebody run into one?

I meant it as a joke, but then I started to wonder. A few minutes passed with no response. My mother let out a long-suffering sigh. We were only a few blocks away from the house, so I typed out a few more lines.

hey, try me tonight if you need more help

edmond lowe wrote a compendium of
the realm, very old but worth a look

contemporary of lady wilde, oscar's
mother, she was all about irish folklore

he was northern england—out of print but public domain

i think the Merril has a copy if you're anywhere near there

*https://www.google.ca/maps/place/Toronto
+Public+Library+-+Lillian+H.+Smith+Branch/*

i hope you have a better ending ahead
than the one i would write for you

As I finished sending the last message, my battery had dropped to nearly zero, so I decided to shut the phone off until I got to the restaurant. I asked the driver to wait for me while I helped my mother through the front door, then hurried back out to discover that he had left without even getting paid. Winnipeg can be strange sometimes. Rather than go back inside and call another cab, I thought I'd walk as far as I could and see if I could flag one. Of course, the first cab I saw was just five minutes away from the restaurant, so I decided to finish walking the rest of the way and reconcile myself to being late. Luckily, when I stepped in the door of the restaurant, Ian and Greg were standing there waiting for our table. I forgot about Salem and her questions until I was back in my hotel room, exhausted and not entirely sober.

The phone, unsurprisingly, was dead. I plugged it into the socket at the base of the bedside lamp, then took my evening medication and ran a quick shower. Something was going on with my back. Whether from stress or an allergy or some kind of reaction, it felt hot and itchy and sore. It was all I could do not to reach behind and scratch my skin off. I decided I was breaking out—either the dry air or the hotel sheets or some ingrown hairs—and that I would need to wear a T-shirt to bed.

Once I was out of the bathroom, I looked at my phone and found the conversation had been erased. *Odd.* I wasn't blocked, I could still see Salem's profile. I sent her a friend request, to see what would happen. I'm not sure why, I didn't have much more to say. Even if such things existed, what could you do, what could anyone do? You see the creature, you give it chase, you uncover its lair. You raise a party, you bait it, you hunt it, you corner it, you raise your torches and your pitchforks, and, if you're smart and if you're lucky, you trap it, you wound it, maybe even finish it. From a check to a view, from a view to a kill. This is an old story, we tell this story over and over, we've done so for hundreds, thousands of years.

But here's the thing: there's always another monster.

As Salem and I were messaging each other on Facebook, Robin was settling into the chair next to Sergio. Samson had cautiously climbed the stairs with her and now was curled up at her feet. Sergio was still asleep, his back turned to her, his breath rising and falling slowly, rhythmically. Trevor's St. Benedict medal was curled up on the small red lacquered table beside the bed. She picked it up, wrapped the chain around her fingers, and let the medal rest on her palm. She felt the urge to touch Sergio, to wake him, but thought better of it. It was good that he was resting. She flashed on the moment when the tattered red book seemed to jump to life in her hands. Even just thinking about it disoriented her, nauseated her. Once, in Los Angeles, she was at an ATM and, just before a minor earthquake, she had felt a wave of vertigo wash over her as the machine cancelled the transaction and spat back her card. This felt the same somehow. Rules she'd always known and lived by seemed to be falling away one by one.

Samson whined softly, sat up, stood up, trotted back downstairs, where he resumed his pacing. In the distance, Robin could hear a tap-tap-tap-tap. It was the book trying to free itself from the iron box. An aching, hypnotic rhythm, she could organize a set around it. She tried to stop herself, she couldn't help herself, *just for a moment*, she said to herself, she let her head fall to the side, she closed her eyes *just for a moment*, and the floor opened up in front of her.

Down she fell, down through the living room and the basement and down, down through the silt and soil and clay and sand and rock, down into the underground burrow that Nicholas made his home. The candles scattered around the floor threw flickering firelight on the earthen walls encrusted with the bones of hundreds of men, arranged in macabre murals, grotesque and obscene. Spidery figures coupling, toothless skulls in their crotches and at the ends of their limbs. In the centre was the tree, its trunk immense, its branches reaching out in all directions. And, above, twirling birds and bats cobbled out of fingers and toes.

Nicholas sat on the floor, cross-legged, a bloodied sheet of cotton wrapped around him like a blanket. "Welcome to my lovely home," he said. "I'd stand and greet you properly, but I'm afraid I'm a bit under the weather at the moment." He looked as youthful as ever, but he was pale and drawn, his face slack and sallow. Not the same boy she had seen on Church Street all those years ago.

"I know all about you now," Robin stated. "What you are, and what you want."

He looked up at her and smiled, a blood-slicked canine grin. "And I know about you. We have an unusual bond, you and I." His tongue darted out to catch a ruby droplet at the corner of his mouth.

"You took Trevor, didn't you? And now you want Sergio?"

"All these names," Nicholas replied. "Do you name all your meals? Every cow, every chicken? I find it ruins the appetite. But yes, I extended an invitation to your friend Trevor. He was more than happy to accept."

"Is he still here? I want to see him."

"Some bits of gristle here and there, not much to look at. These bones, or maybe those. I can't really be sure." He gestured to the right and then to the left, and she caught sight of his stiff and mottled right hand.

"You're hurt," she said. "Looks like a burn or a rash."

"It's healing, but slowly." He pulled the sheet back and showed her his hand, his arm. "Something I ate disagreed with me. I won't let it happen again." He looked down at her clenched fist, the fine, thin chain wound around her fingers. She was still clutching the silver medal. She opened her hand for him to see.

"This belonged to Trevor. Would you like to see it?" she asked.

He shrank back from her, put up a hand. "Thank you," he replied, shaking his head. "I know these trinkets all too well. Besides, it is best that you wear it. The medal itself is meaningless, but the silver will be your safeguard. You will come to no harm from me, nor from any creature in the everwood. And it will ensure your return to your own kind, if that is what you wish."

"It is," Robin answered as she fastened the chain around her neck. "I have a wife, I have friends and family. I would be missed. And that would be dangerous for you."

"Your people cannot catch what they do not believe in, they cannot touch what they cannot see." Nicholas placed his hand on her bare ankle, caressed it gently. "Now, you might stand a chance, if you knew me better. Perhaps you'd like to join me here. Never to age, never to die. Would you try to kill me, I wonder. You wouldn't be the first."

She pulled her foot back beyond his reach. "If Trevor had worn this, would he still be alive?"

"Pretty Robin Redbreast," Nicholas sighed. "Don't you see? He left the chain behind so that he could be with me. It seems I've developed a bit of a following." One of the candles snapped and sputtered, startling her. "Oh, do stop looming over me and seat yourself." He reached behind and picked up an embroidered pillow, once intricate and sumptuous, now mean and threadbare. He tossed it on the ground in front of her. "We have a few moments. I'll tell you what you want to know."

As she seated herself, Nicholas looked up at the giant bone tree, his eyes glinting at the corners. "It was in the final year of my servitude. Master Wood had spoken of taking us back to his home across the water, Eli the boot boy and I. We were intimates, and had been so with Wood before he departed. But the master became ill during his last visit, and he died before he could retrieve us. When word came to us of his death, the servants and patrons and neighbours made it known that we were unwelcome—that if we did not leave at once, we would be turned over to the constabulary, charged and imprisoned, or worse. There were mutterings of witchcraft, of corruption and unnatural acts. I knew too well where that would lead. We departed to Wood's forest to meet an associate of the master's, he was to assist in our escape to Montreal. It was a trap, of course. A dozen other men emerged, they held us and shackled us, used all manner of vile instruments upon us. I could withstand these tortures, but poor Eli was brought to the very brink. Then, through swollen eyes, we watched as they brought forth the pye on the back of a horse cart. In truth, it was no bigger than a housemaid's bed. Plain it was on all its sides but for the front. On its face was forged the figure of a man-beast, the monster they imagined me to be.

"They put hoods made of flour sacks over our heads and forced us into their cold black box, our battered bodies tangled round each other, then sealed it tight and dropped it into a freshly dug pit at the clearing's edge. The iron, it weakened me—I pushed and pulled with all my strength, but I could not escape. And I could do nothing to help poor Eli. Then, all around, I felt the clatter of objects falling upon us, and then a sudden terrible heat, and then came clear their true intentions. They had dropped their flaming torches into the pit and upon them leaves and branches gathered from the forest floor. Fire for the faggots, faggots for the fire. All I could do was hold him and feel him blister and burn and roast and shrivel in my broken arms.

"After a time, thirty years that felt like centuries, the earth around us heaved and shook and the walls cracked into pieces. I pushed up between the cracks and dug myself free before the box collapsed on itself. I left Eli behind, a mess of charred flesh and ash and shattered bone. I pulled my way up through the dirt and into the open air. The master's forest was all but gone. I surfaced in a modest grove, circled by roads and farms and stately homes. And waiting for me was the book, my precious Book of Shades. As I held it in my hands, I was consumed with rage and sorrow, and a hunger so voracious that I could scarce contain it."

"What a horrible story," Robin replied sadly. "You have lost so much in your life."

"Such was my luck, to have so much to lose, and then to lose it." He looked up at her suddenly, his eyes glistening. "Come to the glade," he said, wiping away a tear with the heel of his ruined hand. "Leave behind this world of horrors."

"Would it stop you from killing?" Robin asked. "From killing people, at least?"

Nicholas smiled and shook his head. "I am afraid not. I would not starve for you, nor you for me." He paused for a moment, theatrically.

"Come, be my guide in the world above, and join me in the hunt. There are many who would fall for you that would never rise for me." The ice-black glint in his eyes enticed her and appalled her.

"I can't," she answered as she rose to her feet. "I'm sorry."

"The loss is yours, my dear," he said darkly. "But your departure is well-timed. Your Sergio has retrieved my book, and soon the book will retrieve him for me." Nicholas lunged forward, grabbed her by the ankles, and pulled them out from under her. She fell backwards onto the ground with a slam.

"Robin? Robin, what's happened? Where's Sergio?"

Robin opened her eyes to see Salem kneeling beside her, terrified.

"Oh god, are you all right?"

Robin looked around the room and realized she was lying on the basement floor. She tried to sit up, failed, eased herself back down. "I don't know," she said. "I was up in his room beside him and—"

"Listen. Robin. He's not upstairs anymore. He's gone." She showed Robin the face of her phone: 6:21 p.m. "Did he hurt you?" she asked. "Should we call a doctor?"

"What do you mean he's gone?" Robin asked.

"It looks like he just grabbed his coat and ran," Salem answered. "I came home, I thought the house was empty, that the two of you had gone somewhere. And then I looked out back. The lock on the storage bin is smashed. He took the box with him."

⚓

I recently revisited Edmond Lowe's book *A Compendium of the Fairy-World* (1838—long out of print and sadly no longer online). It was not quite as I remembered it, but it still had some useful information about faerie portals, faerie marks, the longevity of the fae, and the unusual passage of time in their realm.

While reading it, I was reminded that the fae are considered "liminal beings." They travel between worlds, not only through faerie mounds and rings, but also through other passages where the veil is thin—bridges and tunnels and caves, underground waterways, natural wells, the exposed roots of old trees, and disruptions in the landscape such as mines and digs and excavations. (Allan Gardens has one such waterway passing beneath it, Crookshank Creek, a buried stream that runs beneath the southwest end of the park, under the conservatory alongside the sycamore tree.) It was in this book that I read vivid accounts of people having come across injured or ailing creatures of the fae over the centuries and receiving faerie blessings for sheltering them and helping them heal; that some have claimed to have stumbled upon celebrations and ceremonies, including faerie weddings and funerals; and that many believe the fair folk or little people can live for centuries. It was in this book that I learned of the marks the fae can leave on the skin of human folk, designating them as blessed or cursed, singled out for reward or for abduction into the fairy-world.

One section told of ways to stop, control, and drive away the more troublesome of the fae: wearing talismans or carrying silver charms, flinging down handfuls of salt or sand for them to count grain by grain, or binding or caging them in iron. Yet another section detailed the ways in which the faerie delude and manipulate human folk and even cause them harm: enchanting and seducing them, clouding their minds, stealing their children, luring and trapping them with faerie food and drink, capturing their souls within the pages of enchanted books, and enticing them into portals and passages through which they cannot return.

The book also included descriptions of a selection of creatures of the everwood, and the locations of several well-known faerie forts, wells, stones, mounds, bowers, and holloways in England, Scotland, Ireland, and Wales—including Dunino Den, a famous pre-Christian site in a forest near Anstruther, not far from the Beggar's Benison, with an altar, a grove, a well, and an assortment of carvings associated with the Druids. The book had fewer drawings than I recalled, but among them was a large wolflike creature: a barghest, rumoured to have lived in the forest near Dunino Den. It was said to have terrorized the area until approximately 1808.

One other item of note: if one were to consult the holdings of the Judith Merril Special Collection of Science Fiction, Speculation and Fantasy, one would find that the copy that was donated in 1840 to the York Mechanics' Institute library, later to become the Toronto Public Library, had been given by a local merchant named Alexander Wood.

༄

We have a secret, just we three,
The robin, and I, and the sycamore tree

Robin and Salem sat on the bench near the north end of College station's east platform. It was 1:52 a.m. and the last northbound train was just pulling into the station. The train chimed and the doors slid open. A half-dozen weary shift workers and partygoers staggered out and made their way to the escalator, too tired to take the stairs. The train chimed again, the doors slid shut, and the train sped out of sight down the tunnel.

"What should we do?" Salem asked.

"I don't know," Robin replied. "I was sure he'd be here." She looked over at the web of caution tape and fluorescent pylons a few feet away from where they sat. A stream of dirty, rusty water ran out from behind a cluster of wall tiles and pooled on the floor. On the north wall next to the tunnel entrance, the enamelled metal door concealing the electricals was ajar, held somewhat shut by another length of caution tape tied in an incongruous bow.

"Ladies," an older woman called to them. They turned and saw she was a station officer, uniformed, short butch haircut, round, pink face, also tired, standing by the stairs. "We're closing for the night. Time to go."

"We know, we—were supposed to meet a friend here," Salem replied.

"That was the last train," the officer stated. "Maybe they're waiting upstairs, or at the Starbucks."

Robin couldn't help herself—she started to cry. Trevor was gone, Sergio was gone, she and Salem were trapped in a nightmare, nothing made sense.

"I'm sorry, we just need a few minutes," Salem said to the officer. "We won't be long."

The older woman's expression softened. "Okay, five minutes, but that's it. If I'm not at the booth, I'll be locking the doors. We can get you a cab if you need one." She turned and started up the stairs, then poked her head back around. "Five minutes. Please." She ducked her head back and clop-clopped up the stairs.

"It's okay," Salem said as Robin wiped her eyes on her coat sleeve. "He might be back at the house. If not, we can go looking for him tomorrow."

Robin gasped. A flurry of rats ran out of the tunnel and rushed down the length of the tracks, darting over and under the ties as they made their escape.

"Robin," someone whispered.

She looked towards the tunnel entrance. Sergio was standing there, down between the shining steel rails, shivering.

"Sergio!" Salem hissed. "What are you doing? Get up here, the station is closing!"

"I can't," he said. Tears were streaming down his face. "I've tried and I can't."

Salem moved closer to the edge of the platform. "Look, there are some steps on the side, we can help you over the chain."

Sergio ignored her and started walking down the centre of the tracks. Salem crouched down, her hands reaching for the edge.

"Salem, don't. Don't go down there." A flutter of movement caught Robin's eye. Up near the top of the tunnel, something large and dark was clinging. Black, smoky wisps spun out from it, tickling the air.

Sergio turned, looked up. His eyes widened. "Robin," he said, his voice thin and dry. "Behind the grey door. Throw me the box."

She looked over at the grey enamelled electrical door, the caution tape tying it shut. She vaulted over the construction clutter on the floor, tore the tape off the door, pulled it open. The iron lockbox fell into her hands, the red book thrashing within it. Just as the beast above her leapt out and onto the tracks, she threw the box towards Sergio. It landed between the rails, in front of his feet. He fell on it, and the creature fell on him.

Robin pulled Salem back from the edge as Sergio, clutching tight to the gleaming steel second rail, stretched out his arm, the iron box in his hand, and pressed it against the electrified third rail. A blinding flash and a lightning crack rattled off the walls. The lights flickered and dimmed. Sergio and the creature screamed together as their flesh blackened and bubbled, as their limbs caught fire, as plumes of greasy smoke filled the room.

A rumble grew into a roar and lights tore through the darkness as an out-of-service train charged into and through the station, crushing everything in its path, stopping only after half the cars had entered the northern tunnel. Salem buried her face against Robin's shoulder. Footsteps thudded down the stairs, sirens sang in the distance. Robin forced herself to move one step forward, and then another, slowly and carefully, until she could look down onto the tracks.

Sergio was dead, that much was clear. The iron box was shattered, black shards strewn like shrapnel around his still-smouldering body. There was no sign of any beast, or of the boy named Nicholas.

❦

By mid-October, nine months after the events in the College subway station, my mother's unending indigestion and fatigue were now accompanied by nausea, dizziness, abdominal pain, diarrhea, and loss of appetite. After a fall in her kitchen, she was hospitalized, examined, and eventually told that she had an inoperable tumour on her liver. What's more, the vomiting and diarrhea had left her dehydrated, and she would need to stay until her fluids were back up and the oncologist had briefed her about her options for treatment and care.

Her first stay in the hospital was brief but unpleasant, and she did nothing to make it less so. I remember calling the night nurse soon after she was admitted to find out how she was doing. He quietly asked me if I'd noticed any unusual behaviour from her. When I asked for an example of "unusual," he said that she had told her assigned doctor that she didn't want him near her, that she thought he was a fake. I asked if the doctor was by any chance a person of colour, for example "brown," and the nurse laughed and admitted that, yes, the doctor in question was South Asian. My mother had accused him of being unqualified and told him not to touch her. I advised the nurse that unfortunately this was *not* unusual for her (I believe I referred to her as "an inveterate racist") and emphasized that no one should rearrange schedules or adjust her care staff to accommodate her offensive behaviour. He said she would probably be sent home just after the weekend, and I suggested that would be a relief for everyone concerned.

As I hung up, I saw that I had received a message notification, but it wasn't clear from whom—just a garble of numbers and symbols. *Spam.* Unwisely, I clicked through and found myself looking at a photo of a tattered old book, worn red cover, hints of gilt on the spine. The phone grew impossibly hot, sharply and suddenly, and then shorted out, stinging my fingers. I dropped it onto the kitchen floor, cracking the screen. I quickly turned on the faucet and ran my hand under the water to cool it.

Salem and Robin, meanwhile, had just spent a languorous afternoon in bed drowsing and fucking and cuddling and drowsing some more, luxuriating in each other, and now were up and dressing for dinner. Robin carefully pulled a chili-red T-shirt down over the bandage on her shoulder. "Salem, does this look okay?"

She checked Robin's back, pressed gently on the edges of the bandage. "Yeah, that should be fine." She turned Robin around, gave her a brisk kiss on the lips. "You know what would look good on you?"

Salem reached past her into her side of the closet. "I don't know if it will fit you, but . . ." She flipped from blouse to shirt to blouse then pulled out a pink-and-gold-and-red number, vintage or maybe just old, textured silk, roomy with a bit of a neckline. "Here, try this. If you bleed on it, at least it won't be too obvious. I'll tuck some gauze and tape into my bag."

Once a month, Karyn and Leon held a potluck for friends and room-mates past and present at the house on Pembroke Street, but this one was special: it was the twentieth anniversary of their purchase of the house from their landlady, an older German woman from a few streets over named Elke Nowak. Elke had just turned eighty-eight, was long widowed, and had no family, no children. Karyn had invited her several times to join them, and was startled when this time she agreed to come, and said she'd even bring a vegetable tian that she quite enjoyed making with her mother's old French mandoline.

Jared was back in the city after a few years in Ottawa, and he was bringing his partner Luis, a tiny, burly trans man who was a chef and therefore hated cooking. Jared said he was bringing a salad, but that could mean anything. And Salem was coming with her wife Robin, who was in the music industry and apparently had stories. Something strange, though: Karyn had set out a dozen or so candles around the living and dining rooms, and Leon chased along after her and scooped them back up. Apparently, Robin had some sort of phobia. Good thing the stove was electric.

Elke arrived first, oddly, and nearly forty minutes early. Annoyingly, she also brought a surprise guest—her latest tenant, a Sri Lankan woman named Shivani. She apparently had come to Canada years before to search for her husband, who had travelled here to work and save in order to bring her over but one day just stopped answering her calls and letters. She had never found him and now was in a kind of limbo, neither married nor divorced nor widowed. She was perfectly pleasant, but Karyn wished that Elke had mentioned her guest in advance—there were only so many chairs. The vegetable tian looked lovely, though—little circular slices spiralling around the baking dish, coated with a crust of melted Gruyère. It was going to need a reheat by the time dinner was actually served. And with no one else around, Elke and Shivani had little to do except sit in the kitchen with a bottle of wine between them and watch her prepare the chicken. Karyn tried to engage them, asking about the house, family, travel, the neighbourhood, world events, but every single topic seemed to dry up and drift away. It was odd: Karyn felt like they wanted to talk about *something* but were for some reason afraid to offer up what that *something* was.

Mercifully, the doorbell rang just after six, and Jared and Luis and their suspicious salad arrived, and Salem and Robin were coming up the walk just behind them. Salem and Jared were far more gregarious and inquisitive than Karyn; maybe they could get a proper conversation going.

Jared's salad turned out to be potato, with bacon, onion, and pan-fried kale; it was delicious, as was the tian. But while Salem and Jared and Leon had kept the dinner lively as Karyn ran back and forth to the kitchen, Robin was somewhat shy—so much for the stories—and Elke and Shivani were nearly silent. *Well, you can lead a horse to water,* Karyn sighed to herself, *or in this case, Sauvignon Blanc.* But just as she was about to ask about dessert, Elke cleared her throat. "Shivani has something to show us," she said.

Everyone paused, turned to look at Shivani, who seemed tremendously embarrassed.

"Well," said Elke. "Go on."

Shivani nodded, lifted up the shoulder of her sari, uncovering a small square bandage. She lifted it to reveal what looked like two deep scratches crossing each other, punctuated with tiny droplets of blood. "Can you tell me what this is?" she asked. "Someone here has this too."

Karyn was about to object when Leon, puzzled and unsettled, unbuttoned his shirt to show them the bandage on the left side of his chest. Oddly shaped blots floated in the white of the gauze. Jared looked at Luis, shrugged, then leaned over and lifted the right-leg hem of his jeans. Two scabbed lines crossed on his calf. "I thought it was a reaction, or a rash. Like ringworm," he said. "We have lots of stray cats around." Then Robin looked at Salem, turned around, dropped the shirt off her shoulders, and let Salem pull back the collar of the T-shirt to show the edge of the compress she had taped there.

"How did you know about this?" Leon asked.

"I know it will sound absurd," Shivani replied, lowering her eyes. "After many years, my husband Suda came to me. He was not alive."

"He came to you in a dream?" Salem asked. "Or—as something else?"

"It was not a dream," Shivani replied. "He was on a bench in the park, a few blocks from here. He was pale and cold. Under a great white tree."

Salem reached under the table for Robin's hand and clutched it tightly.

"What did he say to you?" Robin asked.

"He told me to come here with Elke. He said I should come and tell you: the door is still open." She looked around the table. "I am sorry, I do not know what it means, or even why I am here."

A heavy silence fell around the room.

"I think you should tell them some more about your husband," Elke said, looking at Shivani. "And then I should tell them about mine."

Outside the house on Pembroke Street, Ryan's mother Lucille stopped and looked at the address she had written on the back of her bus ticket. The young man, Trevor, had told her the street number, had described the house in detail, and here it was. He had brought some things of Ryan's for her: one of the books from his high school English class, a postcard he'd brought back from New York. *A hole to see the sky through.* She reached into her coat, into her blouse, pressed gently on the gauze covering the *X*-shaped wound above her breast. She gathered up the last of her courage—the day had required so much of it—then used the wrought iron railing to pull herself up the steps and rang the bell beside the door.

❧

A little more than a year has passed since I started writing this. My mother died in the spring of 2017, the day before Mother's Day. I slept through the call telling me to hurry to the hospital. By the time I heard the message and jumped into the cab, she was already dead. My dearest friend Ing, one of the first to read these pages, she too has been diagnosed—an unusual bowel cancer, stage three, inoperable, incurable. Every day we have is a gift.

And the remains of my missing friend were found, and his elderly killer was caught. Eight victims that we know about, very nearly nine. The murderer's face has been everywhere, smiling and summery. Photos with rainbows, photos with waterfalls. He has quietly admitted his guilt, sparing us all a gruelling trial, and has received a single twenty-five-year sentence. He will likely die in prison before he can even request parole. We're told that we should be happy.

On Church Street, Bar 501 is long gone. It was a video store, then a frozen yogurt shop, and now it's an empty grey box with a For Lease sign in the window. I suppose it will become a dispensary. Next door, the martini bar Byzantium was taken over by Glad Day Bookshop, which after many years moved to the heart of the Village and expanded into a restaurant/bar/community hub. The St. Marc Spa is long gone; the AIDS Committee of Toronto is now housed in its building. The Club Baths is now an upscale swingers space called the Oasis Aqualounge. It's quite nice, pretty in fact, nicer than it ever was when it was aimed solely at men. The AIDS Memorial is still in Cawthra Park (now Barbara Hall Park), next to the 519. The Selby Hotel, home of Boots and Bud's, and later reinvented as a Howard Johnson, has been transformed into a forty-nine-storey condo development. No word on the Gooderham ghosts and how they're taking it. And the bone-white sycamore still stands in Allan Gardens, as does the park's conservatory.

I took my phone in to be repaired. Apart from the screen, it was in good working order—no evidence of battery issues or of overheating. I checked my messages, checked my photos. No trace of the conversation I had with Salem, or of the photo of the red book with the worn gilt on its spine. I know what it is, though. I've already seen it once. I expect I will see it again. The door, after all, is still open.

"The day will come when I reach for you," he said. *"And you may yet reach for me."*

I've taken to walking the streets at night—not the wisest choice, I know, for someone my age and build and health. I wake up at two, three, four in the morning, for no particular reason. Bad dreams, perhaps. I pull on pants and a coat over whatever I've slept in, slip on my shoes, and go out into the night. Sometimes I find other men, men who are looking for what I'm looking for. In the parks, down in the ravine, in alleys, places where we think we'll see him, places where he's been seen before. One or another will mark an *X*, with spray paint or tape or those thick graffiti markers, to say that we've been there, that we might be there again. Sometimes we hold each other, touch each other, bring our bodies together, as a kind of invitation. A few months ago, one of us, Alex, disappeared. Last fall, it was Emilio, and then before that, Hakim.

Last night, this morning, I came home to find his footprints in the garden, so I know it won't be long. It could even be tonight. The whistling is on the wind.

They are close now, I feel them. They are just out of sight.

Watching and waiting.

I know they will all be here soon.

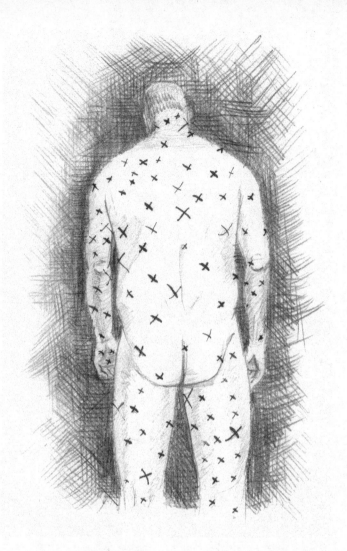

DAVID DEMCHUK has been writing for print, stage, digital, and other media for more than forty years. His debut novel, *The Bone Mother*, was longlisted for the Scotiabank Giller Prize, was shortlisted for the Amazon.ca First Novel Award, the Shirley Jackson Award, and the Toronto Book Award, and received the Sunburst Award for excellence in Canadian speculative fiction. Born and raised in Winnipeg, he lives in Toronto.

Acknowledgments

By now, most readers of acknowledgements know that books are rarely solitary endeavours, and only ever come into existence with the help of many hands. This one is no different.

My greatest thanks to editor and publisher Jordan Ginsberg for all of his intense, insightful work in bringing this book to fruition, and to the entire Strange Light/PRHC team for their invaluable assistance. Jordan was a passionate believer in this book from the start, and showed tremendous care throughout the editorial process. This book would not be what it is without him.

My deep appreciation to Samuel R. Delany, who has encouraged my work as a queer writer for many years, and whose pioneering work in fiction and memoir, across genres, across identities and sexualities, has made so many things possible for the generations of writers he has encouraged and inspired.

And, of course, my love and gratitude to my incredibly supportive, giving, and patient partner, Chris Poirier.

Special thanks to the many people who helped me in my research and development, such as Toronto historian Jamie Bradburn, illustrator Jared

Pechacek, and architectural consultant Christopher Lauzon; Conner Habib, Steve Lucas, Finlay Buchan, Laurie Martin, and Steve Scott; Asif Kamal, Mohini Datta-Ray, and Antoney Baccas; the online queer Toronto chronicles of Denise Benson and Rick Bebôut; and erotic artist and performer Dominic Fournier, who was kind enough to lend his physical presence (with hood by BCALLA).

And thanks as well to the many individuals and organizations that have supported my writing and in particular this project: Brendan Healy and Buddies in Bad Times Theatre; Artscape Gibraltar Point, where my earliest work on this book was conducted; The ArQuives, Glad Day Bookshop, and the Naked Heart Festival; Ann Dion and Diane Frankling Co-operative Homes; Can*Con: The Conference on Canadian Content in Speculative Arts and Literature; Dennis Persowich, Ian King, and Greg Klassen; Brenda Carr and David Currie; Emma Bedard, Kerry Kelly, and Lynn Paul; Derek McCormack, Alan Miller, and Gerald Hannon; and Christopher DiRaddo of Montreal's The Violet Hour and Blue Metropolis.

My early readers Dainty Smith, Anthony Oliveira, Carmilla M. Morrell, Shawn Denton, and Pedro Ivo Lacerda Muniz, whose observations helped guide this book along its winding path.

My dear friend Shelagh Rogers who tried to steer me into fiction many years ago—I'm glad I finally stopped and listened.

My wonderful agent Barbara Berson of the Helen Heller Agency. I am so grateful that we went on this monstrous journey together.

This is, above all, for my beloved friend Ing Wong-Ward: an astute and thoughtful reader, she brought her journalist's eye to this project as well as her open and generous heart. It is a better book in every way because of her, and I a better writer and better person. I miss her every day.

Remember their names: Abdulbasir Faizit, Skandaraj Navaratnam, Majeed Kayhan, Soroush Mahmudi, Dean Lisowick, Selim Esen, Kirushna Kumar Kanagaratnam, Andrew Kinsman. Tess Richey. Alloura Wells.